WICKED OBSESSION

Leaving the house, Anne headed for the pub with wicked thoughts swirling in her young mind. Robin was very good-looking, she reflected, wondering how big his cock was. She'd thought of telling him that he was one of several men that Hayley was seeing, but she didn't want to cause trouble before she'd had the chance to get Robin alone in the woods. They'd go for a walk, she decided as she reached the pub and ordered a drink. They'd walk through the park to the woods, chatting about Hayley, and then she'd drop her knickers and show him her hairless pussy and—

'Hi, sexy,' Alan whispered in her ear.

'Oh, hi,' Anne breathed, turning and facing him.

'Brian was over the moon after seeing you last night. He's really looking forward to the next time, and so am I.'

'You are naughty,' she whispered, grinning at him. 'But I can't meet you again.'

'Why not?'

'I'm not a slut, Alan. I mean, I love sex but not with two men at the same time.'

'You loved it, you silly girl. Why try to deny it?'

WICKED
OBSESSION

Ray Gordon

This book is a work of fiction.
In real life, make sure you practise safe, sane and consensual sex.

Published by Nexus 2009

2 4 6 8 10 9 7 5 3

First published in Great Britain in 2009 by
Nexus
Virgin Books
Random House, 20 Vauxhall Bridge Road
London SW1V 2SA

www.virginbooks.com
www.rbooks.co.uk

Addresses for companies within The Random House Group Limited can be found at: www.randomhouse.co.uk/offices.htm

The Random House Group Limited Reg. No. 954009

Distributed in the USA by Macmillan, 175 Fifth Avenue, New York, NY 10010, USA

A CIP catalogue record for this book is available from the British Library

ISBN 9780352345080

The Random House Group Limited supports The Forest Stewardship Council [FSC], the leading international forest certification organisation. All our titles that are printed on Greenpeace approved FSC certified paper carry the FSC logo. Our paper procurement policy can be found at www.rbooks.co.uk/environment

Typeset by TW Typesetting, Plymouth, Devon
Printed and bound in Great Britain by CPI Bookmarque, Croydon CR0 4TD

After fifteen years of writing erotic novels,
I'd like to thank all my readers for their support.
I'd also like to thank young women the world
over for their inspiration.
My books wouldn't be possible without them.

Symbols key

 Corporal Punishment

 Female Domination

 Institution

 Medical

 Period Setting

 Restraint/Bondage

 Rubber/Leather

 Spanking

 Transvestism

 Underwear

 Uniforms

One

Anne sat on the end of her bed and gazed at her reflection in the dressing-table mirror. Her hair was auburn, shoulder length, and framed her pretty face beautifully. Her eyes were brown and large and her red lips full and succulent. She was eighteen and exceptionally attractive, but she lacked self-confidence. Standing in front of the mirror, she turned this way and that, admiring the violin curves of her young body. What was wrong? she wondered. She was slim, with small but firm breasts, and her bottom was nicely rounded. There was nothing wrong with her physically. But something was missing.

Hayley, her twenty-two-year-old sister, sparkled with life, she had charisma. That was the missing ingredient, Anne decided. The sparkle, the charisma . . . That was the reason why Hayley had men chasing after her. It wasn't her long blonde hair or her perfect body, it wasn't her fresh face or her enchanting smile, it was her personality. Lifting her T-shirt, Anne scrutinised the firm mounds of her petite breasts. They weren't as large as Hayley's, but she was proud of them. She was especially proud of her nipples. They were elongated and rose alluringly from the dark discs of her areolae, and she loved to show them off through the tight material of her tops. She rarely wore a bra because she loved the way her T-shirts outlined her nipples. Men had always looked at her, admired her young body and her pert breast-buds pressing through the clinging fabric of her tops. But men had never chased after her the way they pursued Hayley.

'Very nice,' Hayley said, giggling as she peered around the door. 'Wow, that skirt is rather short, isn't it?'

Anne lowered her T-shirt and glared at her sister. 'I'm going out with Dave,' she said triumphantly. 'Anyway, what do you want?'

'Mum wants to know whether you'll be here for dinner.'

'I don't know,' Anne sighed. 'I might be, I might not.'

Hayley raised her gaze to the ceiling. 'Is this another one of your moods?'

'I'm not in a mood,' Anne returned irritably. 'I just don't like you walking into my room when I'm getting changed.'

'I didn't walk into your room. The door was open and . . .' Hayley looked down at her feet. 'See, I'm standing on the hall carpet.'

'You know what I mean, Hayley.'

'Will you be here for dinner or not?'

'No, I'm going out.'

Anne closed the door as Hayley went downstairs. She wasn't in a mood, she thought agitatedly as she flopped onto her bed. It was just that Hayley had walked into her room and . . . Hayley had never been moody, she reflected. She'd always been happy and had coped with problems with a smile. She'd done well at school and had gone on to college and then university. She'd landed herself a good job and she had money and a new car. And she looked stunning, no matter what clothes she wore. It wasn't fair, Anne thought. Even her name was nice. Hayley had a nice ring to it – it was feminine, sexy.

'What do you want now?' Anne called as a knock sounded on the door.

'It's me, Dave.'

Anne leaped off her bed and opened the door. 'Dave,' she trilled, grinning at her boyfriend. 'What are you doing here?'

'Your sister told me to come up. I know that we'd arranged to meet later but . . . Well, I couldn't wait to see you.'

'God, I'm not ready or anything.'

'You look great as you are.'

'I have to have a shower and—'

'That's OK, I'll wait here. I'll imagine you naked in the shower, rubbing yourself off and—'

'Dave,' Anne sighed. 'Don't be so rude.'

'I'll bet your sister masturbates,' Dave sniggered. 'I can just imagine her with her knickers down and her fingers . . .'

'Dave, stop it.'

'Sorry, I was only joking.'

'Do you fancy my sister?'

'She's OK.'

'What do you mean by that? You *do* fancy her, don't you?'

'Of course I don't, Anne. I was only joking.'

'She's twenty-two, the same age as you. Do you think I'm too young for you?'

'Anne, will you stop going on about Hayley? I'm going out with *you*, OK?'

'I know,' Anne breathed, forcing a smile.

'I thought we'd go to the pub,' Dave said, sitting on the edge of the bed. 'It's a nice evening so we could sit outside.'

'So you can talk about football with your mates?'

'No, no.'

'All we ever do is go to the pub and see your mates. Can't we go somewhere else for a change?'

'There is nowhere else, Anne.'

Anne felt her stomach sink at the prospect of listening to Dave chatting with his friends. She'd been going out with him for three weeks, but things weren't really working out. He filled a void, she mused, watching him brush his dark hair away from his face. She'd not wanted her emptiness filled by evenings sitting in the pub, but it was better than sitting at home in her room. Dave was OK, she thought as he smiled at her. But they hadn't had sex yet, and Anne had often wondered why he hadn't made a move towards her. He was always making lewd comments, joking about sex, but he hadn't once tried to touch her. Several times she'd wondered whether he really did fancy her. He seemed to like taking her to the pub and was disappointed if she didn't go with him. But their relationship was going nowhere, and he was doing nothing to boost her self-confidence.

'We could go to the cinema,' she suggested eagerly. 'I haven't seen that new film about—'

'You know that I don't like being surrounded by people coughing and spluttering,' Dave whined. 'I can't stand the cinema. We'll go to the pub.'

'Hang on,' Anne whispered, moving to the door. 'Hayley, why are you hiding there?' she said, yanking the door open and staring hard at her sister.

'I'm going to my room,' the girl replied. 'I wasn't hiding.'

'You were listening to us. You're always hiding outside my door.'

'You're becoming neurotic,' Hayley said with a giggle as she went to her own room.

Anne closed her bedroom door, sat at her computer desk and stared at Dave. She was pleased that he'd come round, but she'd rather have met him later as they'd arranged originally. Noticing him gazing at her naked thighs, she wondered whether he'd come round early because he'd decided that they were ready for sex. Three weeks was a long time, she thought, parting her legs and displaying the tight crotch of her white cotton knickers beneath her short skirt. They'd often kissed and cuddled, but nothing more, and she was becoming increasingly frustrated.

Dave gazed at her knickers as she parted her thighs wider, but he didn't make a move. He didn't even come out with a crude comment. Didn't he like her young body? Anne wondered. They were more like brother and sister than boyfriend and girlfriend, she thought dolefully. Maybe he was a virgin and he didn't know what to do. That must be it, she concluded, parting her thighs to the extreme and grinning at him. He lowered his head and looked at his watch, and she knew that he was in a hurry to get to the pub.

'You go on and I'll see you later,' she sighed, giving up all hope of arousing him as she pressed her naked thighs together.

'OK,' he agreed rather too readily, heading for the door. 'I'll see you there.'

Anne sighed as he left the room. She'd only had a couple of boyfriends before Dave, but neither of them had needed coaxing. They'd dived into her knickers on the first date and she'd had to fend them off. Not wanting to come across as a slut, she'd made them wait for a couple of days before she'd opened her legs to them. What was it with Dave? she wondered as Hayley passed her door and bounded down the stairs. Hearing the front door close, she gazed out of her

5

window and noticed Hayley walking up the front path. As she reached the pavement, she seemed to be in a hurry. Her walk became a trot until she'd caught up with Dave and Anne wondered what her sister was up to. Dave turned and said something to her, and Anne reckoned that they were seeing each other behind her back.

Leaving the house, Anne kept her distance as she followed them along the street. Dave wouldn't have come round early if he'd arranged to see Hayley, she reflected. Perhaps Hayley had been listening to their conversation and had thought this was her chance to steal Dave from Anne. They were up to something, Anne was sure as she watched them walk past the pub. Wondering again whether Dave thought that she was too young for him, she hid behind a bush as they walked into the park and sat on a bench. She could see them talking, see Hayley laughing, but she couldn't hear what they were saying. Had Dave been screwing Hayley all along? she mused angrily. Was that why he hadn't wanted sex with her?

Anne wondered about confronting them, but she wasn't in the mood for an argument. Besides, they'd only lie their way out of trouble. Walking back to the pub, she felt her stomach churning. Hayley was a bitch, she thought as she walked up to the bar and ordered a large vodka and tonic. And Dave was a bastard. He must have thought that Hayley was more fun to be with, Anne reflected. She had a new car and money . . . And her tits were bigger. Was that what Dave liked? Big tits? How could her sister steal her boyfriend? Anne mused angrily.

Taking her drink to a table, she slumped down as one of Dave's friends noticed her and smiled. He was in his early fifties and more of a hanger-on than an actual part of Dave's group, but he'd always seemed nice enough. Grabbing his beer from the bar, he walked over to her table and asked her where Dave was. This was all she needed, Anne thought, shrugging her shoulders as he sat down opposite her. Again asking her about Dave, he lowered his gaze to her ripe nipples where they were clearly defined by the tight material of her T-shirt.

'He's out with some other girl, I reckon,' she finally muttered.

'What?' the man said. 'You mean you two have split up?'

'I mean he's screwing someone else behind my back.'

He looked genuinely surprised. 'Blimey, that's not like Dave,' he breathed.

'You obviously don't know him, Alan.'

'Who is the girl? Anyone I know?'

'She's my sister.'

'Your sister? Wow, I can't believe it.' Again, Alan looked down at her nipples and smiled. 'So, are you . . . I mean, now that you're not with Dave . . .'

'Are you asking me out?' Anne interrupted him. Deciding that she needed some excitement, she licked her succulent lips. 'Are you asking me out?' she repeated.

'Yes, but I think I'm a little too old for you,' he returned with a chuckle. 'You wouldn't want to go out with an old guy like me, would you?'

Anne felt defiant in the despair of her betrayal. 'I might,' she breathed, her brown eyes smiling.

'Well, in that case . . .'

'Where are you going to take me?'

'What?'

'You're asking me out and I'm saying yes. So, where are you going to take me?'

'Well, I . . .'

'I want you to take me to the derelict house in the woods. Do you know it?'

'Yes, but . . . That's a strange place to go.'

'It's a lovely evening and I like the woods. I love the smell of the pine trees and the wild flowers.'

'OK, if that's what you want.'

'They say that the house is haunted.'

'Right, let's go ghost hunting.'

Finishing her drink, Anne felt a lot better as she left the pub with Alan. She'd rather hoped that Dave would see her as she grabbed Alan's hand and walked down the lane to the woods, but he was probably too busy screwing Hayley to give Anne a thought. Following a narrow path through the undergrowth, Anne breathed in the scent of the pine trees. She'd always loved the woods, and had often played there and picked wild flowers when she'd been younger. But she'd rarely gone into the derelict house because the ghost stories had worried her. Was it really haunted? she wondered, trying to push thoughts of Dave and Hayley from her mind.

'I haven't been here for years,' Alan said as they reached the house. 'This place must have been derelict for ever. I used to play war games here when I was a kid.'

'What games do you want to play now?' Anne asked him impishly.

He grinned as he looked her up and down. 'Anything. I don't mind.'

'How about role-play?'

'Role-play?'

'Yes. You go into the house and I'll knock on the door pretending to be lost.'

'OK, but . . . Then what happens?'

Anne licked her full lips again and grinned at him. 'You invite me in and take advantage of me,' she breathed huskily.

Alan flashed her a look of puzzlement. 'Take advantage of you?' he murmured.

'Pick me like a wild flower and breathe in my scent.'

'Hang on, I'm not with you.'

'You play the role of a dirty old man and you force me to have sex with you,' she explained.

'Oh, er . . . yes, I see.' He chuckled. 'I won't have to *play* the role of a dirty old man because I *am* one.'

'You're up for it, then?'

'Yes, yes, of course.'

Anne felt her stomach somersault as Alan went into the house. She'd always loved role-playing, but she'd never involved sex in her games. She realised that she was only doing this to get back at Dave but, if Alan acted his part properly, she was going to have some excitement at long last. This was far better than sitting in the pub, she reflected, wondering whether Dave had pumped his sperm into Hayley's pussy and was now waiting for her in the pub. How long had this been going on? How could Hayley betray her little sister like this? Dave was a bastard, Anne thought angrily. He'd had his chance, and he'd blown it.

Her clitoris stirring as she imagined a man in his fifties pulling her knickers down and gazing at her teenage pussy, Anne felt an ache in her lower stomach. She'd masturbated regularly, but she'd longed for the feel of a hard cock stretching her young vagina wide open. Her fingers had brought her amazing orgasms, but they were no substitute for a cock or a lapping tongue. Sex was becoming a distant memory, she mused as she walked up to the house and tapped on the front door. But, hopefully, that was about to change.

'Yes?' Alan said, opening the door.

'I'm lost,' Anne sighed. 'I need to use your phone.'

'You'd better come in,' he said, taking her hand and pulling her into the hallway. 'Come through to the lounge.'

'Do you live here alone?' she asked him, again hoping that he'd play his part properly as they went into the front room.

'Yes, I do.' Alan closed the door and looked her up and down. 'You can use my phone, but I want something in return.'

'I . . . I don't have any money.'

'I don't want money.'

'I don't understand. If you don't want money, what do you want?'

'I want to look at your body,' he breathed.

'No, no . . .'

'Take your knickers off,' he ordered her. 'Take them off, or I'll rip them off.'

Anne concealed a grin as she reached beneath her short skirt and tugged her wet knickers down to her knees. She knew that she should have prolonged the game, but her arousal was rising fast and she didn't want to waste time. As Alan stared at the small stain in the crotch of her knickers, she knew that his arousal would also be running high. He must have thought this was his lucky day, she mused as he licked his lips. Wondering how big his cock was as he told her to lift her skirt up, she thought that he was pretty good-looking for his age. His greying hair swept back, his dark eyes sparkling lustfully, he wasn't at all bad-looking. Gazing at the bulge in his trousers, she knew that he was waiting in anticipation as she lifted her skirt slowly.

Anne had never dreamed of behaving like a slut in the past but, now that her sister and her boyfriend had betrayed her, she'd decided to cast her fate to the wind. Finally pulling her skirt high up over her stomach and displaying her neatly trimmed pubes to Alan's wide eyes, she felt her stomach somersault again. But, not wanting to spoil the game by revealing her arousal, she tugged her skirt down and covered her face with her hands as if she was crying.

'I want to go home now,' she whimpered.

'How can you go home if you're lost?' Alan asked her. Again, he focused on the stain in the crotch of her knickers. 'You're a naughty little girl and I'm going to have to punish you,' he said sternly.

'But, I haven't done anything wrong.'

'I'll be the judge of that. Bend over the back of that chair.'

Stepping out of her knickers and taking her position over the back of an old armchair, Anne suddenly wondered what the hell she was playing at. Alan was in his fifties, older than her father, and she was inviting him to push his cock deep into her teenage vagina. Coming to her senses, she was about to stand upright and put a stop to the game when his hand landed squarely across the firm flesh of her naked buttocks with a loud slap. The second slap was harder but, strangely, Anne found the pain pleasurable. She could feel her clitoris swelling, her juices of lust seeping between the unfurling petals of her inner lips, as Alan repeatedly spanked her naked bottom. This was a new experience, Anne thought as the spanking continued and her ripe clitoris called for attention. A new and very exciting experience.

'You're not lost, are you?' he finally asked her, halting the spanking. 'You came here for sex, didn't you?'

'No, I . . . I'm lost and . . .'

'You came here because you wanted me to open your little cunt and fuck you.'

11

Her stomach fluttering, Anne was loving the role-play game. 'Please, I have to go home now,' she whimpered.

'You're not going anywhere. Not until you've had my hard cock up your tight little girlie cunt. Why aren't you wearing a bra?'

'Because I—'

'Because you like older men looking at your tits?'

'No, please – I have to go home.'

Yanking Anne upright, Alan spun her round and lifted her T-shirt. He liked what he saw, she knew as he gazed longingly at her firm mounds, her erect nipples rising from the darkening discs of her areolae. Reaching out and squeezing each rounded breast in turn, he licked his lips again. Her nipples elongated in the relatively cool air of the house and she hoped that he'd suck on her sensitive milk teats as she jutted her breasts out. Hayley's breasts were bigger, Anne thought, recalling the occasions when her sister had come out of the bathroom and deliberately lowered her towel to show off her mammary globes. Hayley had everything, and now she had Dave.

As Alan lowered his head and sucked a ripe nipple into his mouth, Anne breathed heavily in the grip of her arousal. Her sensitive milk teat painfully hard, she closed her eyes as he licked and sucked and sank his teeth gently into the brown budlet. Why couldn't Dave have done this? she wondered. Were her tits too small for him? Was she too young for him? Wasn't she sexy enough? Alan obviously liked younger girls, she thought happily as he mouthed and suckled like a babe at the breast.

Her nipple slipped out of his mouth as he stood upright and pushed her over the back of the chair, and she knew that he was about to drive his solid cock deep into the neglected sheath of her yearning vagina. He was an old man, she thought as his fingers slipped between the tops of her slender thighs and massaged the swell of her full pussy lips. He was almost old enough to be her grandfather, but that didn't bother her. He had a cock, and that was all that mattered.

Unzipping his trousers and pinning Anne down over the back of the chair, Alan grabbed his solid cock by the root and pressed his purple plum between her parted thighs. Anne could feel the hard shaft of his cock against the swollen lips of her pussy, and she parted her feet wider to allow him access to her dripping vaginal hole.

It had been so long, she reflected dreamily as Alan's bulbous knob nestled between the fleshy cushions of her outer labia. His swollen globe slid into the tight duct of her vagina, the stretching sensations driving her wild, and she let out a rush of breath. This was heaven, Anne mused, her sex sheath opening as the man's cock drove slowly into her young body. His knob finally came to rest against her ripe cervix, her vaginal muscles tightening around his rock-hard shaft, and she gripped the arms of the chair.

'Do it,' she gasped, forgetting about the game as he withdrew slowly. 'Fuck me really hard.'

'I had no idea that you were a horny little slut,' Alan breathed, ramming the entire length of his solid organ deep into Anne's contracting vaginal sheath. 'Why the hell did Dave go off with your sister?'

'He never wanted me,' she replied, wishing that Dave could see her now. 'We've never had sex.'

'The man must be mad.'

Anne tried not to think about Dave as Alan gripped her shapely hips and found his shafting rhythm. Dave had chosen to lie and cheat, and their relationship of only three weeks was over. It was his loss, she thought as she listened to the squelching sounds of her lubricious pussy-milk. She now had a man, a real man who enjoyed sex. Although he was older than her father and she knew that she shouldn't be with him, she didn't care. Alan knew how to please a girl, she thought as her clitoris swelled against the pussy-wet shaft of his thrusting cock. He had experience, and he knew how to fuck a young woman.

This was nothing more than a fuck, Anne knew as Alan increased his shafting rhythm and uttered crude words about her young body. There was no love, no strings. Had she loved Dave? she wondered. She was too young to love anyone, she concluded as her vaginal muscles tightened again around Alan's thrusting cock. As long as Alan was around to satisfy her, she didn't need love. She didn't even know whether or not he was married, but it didn't matter. If he had a wife waiting at home for him, that was his problem.

His sperm jetted from his throbbing knob, lubricating their illicit coupling, and he repeatedly rammed his massive organ deep into her trembling body with a vengeance. Anne's orgasm erupting within the pulsating bulb of her solid clitoris, shaking her young body to the core, she squirmed and cried out in the grip of her illicit ecstasy. It had been so long since she'd enjoyed a solid cock deep inside her pussy, she reflected again in her sexual delirium. It had been too long since her teenage pussy had been pumped full of creamy-fresh spunk. Reaching behind her back, she vowed not to go for so long without sex again as she parted the swollen lips of her vagina and allowed Alan deeper access to her tight sheath. Never again would she go without a hard cock and a good helping of spunk.

'God, you're hot and tight,' he gasped. 'I'd forgotten how tight young girls are.'

'And I'd forgotten what a hard cock feels like,' she cried as her orgasm peaked. 'Talk dirty to me. Treat me like a filthy little whore.'

Anne listened to his crude words as her young body jolted with his penile thrusts. *Dirty little slut, common whore, tight-cunted bitch, filthy tart* . . . Her eyes rolling, she again wondered why Dave hadn't wanted sex with her. She was attractive, she loved sex – Hayley must have been a better fuck, she thought as her climax peaked. Hayley was better at everything. She was also a bitch. But now Anne had a real man to satisfy her. All Hayley had was Dave, and he had no experience, he hadn't got a clue how to pleasure a girl.

'We must do this again sometime,' Anne gasped, her orgasm fading as Alan slowed his shafting rhythm.

He stilled his cock deep within her spasming vagina. 'Really? You mean, you want to be with an old guy like me?' he asked her.

'Don't stop. Fuck me nice and slow.'

His cock slid back and forth within her tight sex sheath, his sperm and her orgasmic milk squelching, and he massaged the tight ring of her anus with his thumb. This was heaven, Anne mused as the last ripples of orgasm pulsed from her clitoris. Had Dave taken her to the woods and fucked her rather than sitting in the pub talking to his mates about football . . . Dave was history, she thought as Alan finally slipped his deflating penis out of her sperm-bubbling vagina and helped her up.

'You really want to see me again?' he asked her incredulously.

'You bet I do,' Anne breathed, leaning on the back of the chair to steady her trembling body. 'And I want you to fuck me senseless again.'

'I would have thought that you'd want a young lad, not an old man like me.'

'I want a cock, Alan,' she returned impishly, grinning at him. 'And your cock is perfect.'

'Thanks for the compliment. Do you usually go with old men?'

'No, I . . . Yes, I've been with a few. Older men are experienced, as you've just proved.'

'I suppose we'll have to keep this secret. I mean, you won't want the lads in the pub knowing about us, will you?'

'I don't give a toss about them. Are you married?'

'Well, yes, I am. Is that a problem?'

'It might be for you, but it doesn't bother me.'

'No, no, it's OK. I mean, I wouldn't want my wife to know about us. I don't suppose you have any photos I could have?'

'Of me?' she breathed, tugging her knickers up her slender legs.

'Yes.'

'Only old ones.'

'Would you let me take some photos?'

'If you want to.'

'That's great. I have a thing about young girls, if you know what I mean?'

'I know exactly what you mean. Shall we go back to the pub? I could do with a drink.'

'Yes, yes, of course.'

Anne rather liked the idea of posing nude for the camera. She also liked the idea of Dave seeing the photographs. Hoping that he was waiting in the pub for her, she became aware of sperm running down her inner thighs as she followed Alan out of the derelict house. She would have liked to have stayed at the house for a while longer and have sex with Alan again, but she wanted Dave to know that he wasn't the only one who'd been fucking that evening. Wondering how good Hayley was, whether Dave had enjoyed fucking her, she knew that she was going to have to watch her back where her big sister was concerned. Hayley was a bitch.

Alan bought Anne a drink and hovered at the bar as Dave asked her where she'd been. She took her drink to a table and was fuming as Dave followed and sat opposite her. His tone was accusing, and she wondered how he had the nerve to question her, seeing as he'd been in the park with her sister. She thought how pathetic Dave was as he whined about the time and asked her again where she'd been. Then he asked her why she'd walked into the pub with Alan, and why Alan had bought her a drink. Anne smiled as sperm oozed from the inflamed sheath of her vagina and filled the crotch of her tight knickers. If only Dave knew, she thought wickedly as she sipped her drink. If only he knew that an old man had just fucked and spunked her senseless.

'Well?' he asked. 'I've been waiting here for ages. Where have you been?'

'Seeing as you went to the park with Hayley, I went to the woods with Alan,' she returned triumphantly.

'The woods?' Dave's eyes widened and then he frowned. 'What did you go there for?'

'I was a wild flower growing beneath the trees and Alan picked me.'

'What?'

'I went to the woods with Alan for the same reason that you went off with my sister.'

'You wanted someone to talk to?'

She frowned. 'What do you mean?'

'I went to the park with Hayley because I needed someone to talk to.'

17

'Talk about what?'

'About us, Anne. I wanted to know how you really felt about me, so I asked Hayley. The thing is . . . Seeing as you're a virgin, I didn't want us to have sex until I was sure that you were ready.'

'A virgin?'

'That's what you told me when we first met.'

'Oh, yes, yes, that's right. But Hayley went running after you. I saw her chasing you down the street.'

'I'd left my jacket over the banister at your house and she—'

'So when you were in the park – you just talked?'

'Yes. We were only there for about ten minutes and then she went to see her boyfriend.'

'I didn't know that she had a boyfriend.'

'It's her first date with him. What did you talk about with Alan?'

'I . . . we just went for a walk. I like the woods and you weren't in the pub, so we went for a walk.'

Anne's stomach sank as Dave talked about his love for her and she caught Alan's eye. He grinned at her, obviously recalling their time in the derelict house, and she felt like a common whore. She should never have jumped to conclusions, she reflected dolefully. But it was too late now. What was done was done, and she couldn't change that. Dave started talking about sex, asking her whether she was ready to give up her virginity, and she cringed.

'Yes, I'm ready,' she replied softly as she noticed Alan whispering to one of Dave's friends. 'Not tonight, though.'

'Oh, right. Tomorrow, maybe?'

'I just want to ask Alan something,' Anne said, leaving the table. 'I'll be back in a minute.'

Joining Alan at the bar, she took him aside and explained the mistake she'd made about Dave and her sister. She then asked him not to tell anyone about their time at the derelict house. He agreed, but said that he wanted to meet her there again the following evening. Anne bit her lip as she noticed Dave watching her. Consumed with guilt and remorse, she smiled at Dave. He'd only wanted to talk to Hayley, she reflected. He'd needed someone to talk to and . . . She'd made a huge mistake, she knew.

'I'll pull your wet knickers down tomorrow evening,' Alan whispered.

'I can't,' she said. 'I made a mistake and—'

'That was no mistake,' he cut in. 'You loved every minute of it, and so did I.'

'Yes, but . . .'

'But what? OK, so you're back with Dave. We can still fuck, can't we?'

'Alan, I . . . I did enjoy it, but I can't see you again. If Dave finds out . . .'

'He won't find out, Anne. Dave will never know. Meet me at the house tomorrow evening at six, OK?'

'Alan, I—'

'I'll pull your wet knickers down and spank your bare bottom if you're late. You like being spanked, don't you?'

'Yes, yes, I did like it. The thing is . . .'

'I'll spank your bare bottom and then give you a good seeing-to. We'll play the game again. I'll be a schoolteacher and you can be a naughty little girl and I'll pull your wet knickers down and—'

'Alan, people might hear you.'

'I want you, Anne. I want to lick your beautiful little pussy and suck your clitoris and drink your girlie milk and—'

'All right,' she conceded as she became aware of her clitoris swelling.

19

'Good girl. Don't worry, this is our secret. The house will be our secret.'

'Yes, yes OK.'

'Are your knickers wet with my spunk?'

'I'd better get back to Dave.'

'All right, I'll see you tomorrow.'

Her stomach churning as she joined Dave at the table, Anne couldn't believe that she'd agreed to meet Alan again. She'd only had a couple of boyfriends before she'd met Dave, but she'd never two-timed them. Cheating slut, she thought as Dave talked about the future. Downing her drink, she asked him to buy her another one. This was a nightmare, she thought as he took her empty glass to the bar. Alan grinned at her again, and her gaze met his. He was old, she mused. But he was an attractive man. And his cock was huge and . . . She felt like a common whore as he winked at her.

She should have known that Hayley would never try to steal her boyfriend, Anne reflected as Alan licked his lips and winked at her again. She'd never really got on with her sister, but she should have known that the girl would never dream of stealing her boyfriend. Noticing Alan talking to Dave, she held her hand to her mouth. What would Dave think of her if he discovered that she'd been fucking a man in his fifties? she wondered anxiously. What if people started talking and word got out?

Anne trembled as Dave retook his seat at the table and talked again about the future. She chatted with him for half an hour, trying to come across as relaxed, but she couldn't stop thinking about Alan. He knew how to please a young girl, she thought, recalling his huge cock shafting her tight pussy, his fresh spunk overflowing and running down her inner thighs. He was good company, he knew how to please a girl . . . But she couldn't see him again, she decided finally. She'd enjoyed her time with him, enjoyed the spanking and fucking, but it had been a mistake and she couldn't see him again.

Finishing her drink and leaving the pub with Dave, Anne felt guilty as they walked to her house. She'd forgotten that she'd told him that she was a virgin. That had been another mistake, she reflected as they reached her house and he kissed her good night. She should never have lied, but she knew that lying would now become the norm. Slipping his hand up her short skirt, Dave massaged the swell of her pussy lips through the tight material of her sperm-soaked knickers. She could feel his hard cock pressing against her young body, and she knew that he wanted her.

'You're very wet,' he breathed. 'Your knickers are absolutely drenched. Are you ready for it now?'

'No, I . . . We can't do it here, not in the street.'

'It's almost dark, so let's go into your back garden. No one will see us.'

'All right,' she whispered, again recalling Alan's rock-hard cock pumping sperm deep inside her tight vagina.

Behind the bushes at the end of the garden, Anne looked up at the house and hoped that Hayley wasn't around. Dave started kissing her, thrusting his hand up her skirt again and tugging her knickers down, and she thought once more about Alan. She'd loved being spanked, she mused as Dave slipped a finger deep into her sperm-bubbling vagina. There was something naughty and exciting about going with an older man, she thought as Dave drove a second finger into the tight sheath of her hot pussy. Especially a married man who was older than her father.

Easing Anne onto the ground, Dave slipped her knickers down over her feet and parted her legs wide.

He whispered in her ear as he took his weight on his arms above her and stabbed between her swollen love lips with his bulbous knob. He told her to relax, reminding her that this was her first time and he wanted it to be good. She said nothing as his cock glided deep into the sperm-wet sheath of her contracting vagina. Looking up at the stars sparkling high above her, all she could think about was Alan, the way he'd spanked her and driven his huge cock into her tight pussy.

Dave pumped his sperm into her young body within less than a minute, and Anne had to fake an orgasm. She writhed and gasped as he drained his swinging balls, but she felt guilty again as his sperm overflowed and ran down between the firm cheeks of her bottom to her anal hole. But her guilt mingled with a feeling of wickedness. Alan was right: they could meet at the house and fuck and Dave would never find out. Alan would pull her knickers down, spank her bare bottom, bite her ripe nipples, drive his cock deep into her yearning cunt and fuck her senseless. But she knew that she shouldn't meet Alan again. It would end in tears, she was sure. And word would get round and she'd be labelled a slut.

'That was amazing,' Dave breathed, sliding his cock out of her spermed vagina and settling beside her on the grass. 'You came, didn't you?'

'Yes, yes, I did come,' she lied, realising that she was a slut. 'It was . . . it was great, Dave.'

'You're a woman now. You're no longer a virgin so—'

'I'd better go into the house,' she cut in, leaping to her feet and pulling her knickers on.

'OK, I'll see you tomorrow.'

'Yes, tomorrow – in the pub. I'll be there at seven.'

'I can come here, to your house.'

'No, no . . . Wait for me in the pub. I have to see a friend first.'

'OK, I'll see you at seven. Are you sure that you're all right, Anne? You seem . . . I don't know. You seem distant, as if your mind is somewhere else.'

'It was my first time, Dave. I suppose I'm feeling a little mixed up.'

'The second time will be even better, I promise you.'

'I'd better go.'

Anne finally slipped in through the kitchen as Dave walked around the side of the house. She bounded up the stairs to her room and closed the door. Two cocks in one evening, she thought dolefully as her knickers filled with a second load of sperm. Once more deciding not to see Alan again, she knew that she was going to have to stick to her decision. Alan was married, he was older than her father . . . She dared not meet him at the house again.

Two

Consumed by guilt, Anne couldn't stop thinking about Alan as she walked along the path into the woods the following evening. She'd worn a short skirt and black knee-length leather boots to turn him on and excite him, but she knew that he needed no encouragement. Hayley had frowned at her as she'd left the house and her mother had asked her why she was dressed like a tart. She *was* a tart, she thought as she reached the derelict house. Cheating on her boyfriend, lying, arranging to meet an old man for crude sex . . . What if Dave wanted sex again later that evening? Would she fuck two different men every evening? She was a tart.

Wandering into the house and gazing at the old armchair, Anne pictured Alan spanking her naked buttocks and driving his solid cock deep into her hot vagina. She knew that he only wanted her young body and that he was using her for sex but that was all she wanted from him. Recalling Dave driving his erect penis deep into her young pussy, she thought it ironic that he'd decided to have sex with her the very night that she'd opened her legs to Alan. She should have dumped Dave, she thought anxiously. Two-timing him was a dreadful thing to do and . . . But no one would know. Dave would never discover the shocking truth.

Walking across the room and staring through the broken window, Anne felt guilty again as she imagined Dave waiting in the pub for her. She'd never dreamed that she'd become a cheating slut, but the prospect of Alan's crude words and his rock-hard cock pumping fresh spunk deep into her tight vagina excited her. She should leave the house and go to the pub, she thought as she noticed Alan emerging from the bushes. She should sort out this mess before someone got hurt. But she couldn't deny herself the pleasure of giving her young body to an experienced man and, for some reason, the idea of cheating on Dave was beginning to excite her.

Her clitoris painfully solid, the crotch of her tight knickers soaking up her creamy juices of arousal, Anne felt her stomach somersault as she heard Alan enter the house. Walking into the room, he dumped a leather bag on the floor and grinned at her. He was becoming more attractive by the day, she thought, returning his grin. His eyes sparkled as he looked her up and down and nodded his head approvingly. Then he licked his lips. This was purely sex, she reminded herself as he brushed his greying hair back and stood in front of her. No love, no strings – just cold, hard sex.

'You look great,' Alan said. 'I love the kinky boots.'

'I thought you'd like them,' Anne whispered huskily, breathing heavily as he squeezed her firm breasts through the tight material of her T-shirt. 'You really are a dirty old man, aren't you?' she added with a giggle.

'A *very* dirty old man,' he returned. 'And you're a naughty little girl.'

'I was naughty last night. I let Dave fuck me.'

'You had two men in one evening? Dirty little girl. Was he good?'

'No, he was dreadful. He came within a few seconds and I had to fake an orgasm.'

'He's young – he has a lot to learn.'

'You're older, and you have a lot to teach me.'

'Yes, indeed. I'll teach you everything I know, Anne. Have you been thinking about me?'

'Yes.'

'About my cock?'

'Yes.'

'Tell me what you've been thinking.'

'About wanking it, sucking it and swallowing your spunk.'

'You're a *very* naughty little girl.'

'What have you been thinking about?'

'About your hard little tits and your tight cunt. And I've been imagining you squatting over my head and opening your cunt lips and pissing over my face.'

'Pissing . . . I don't think I want to get into that sort of thing.'

'Why not? Have you tried water sports?'

'No, I've never even thought about it.'

'Will you do it, just for me?'

'No, Alan. I love sex but . . . I don't want to get into that.'

'Oh well, it was worth asking. Are you meeting Dave later?'

'Yes, in the pub.'

'I thought you said that you'd made a mistake about him and your sister?'

'That's right – I'd got it all wrong. Apparently they were just talking.'

'In that case, why is he in the park with her now?'

'What?' She frowned at him, unsure whether she'd heard him correctly. 'Dave is in the park with Hayley?'

'Yes, I saw them on my way here. And they weren't just talking.'

Anne's stomach churned. 'What were they doing?'

'Kissing, holding each other, fondling ... Then they went into the trees by the railway cutting.'

Anne felt her shoulders slump and her stomach sink as she pictured Dave kissing Hayley. He'd lied his way out of trouble, she reflected, recalling his words. *I went to the park with Hayley because I needed someone to talk to. I wanted to know how you really felt about me, so I asked Hayley.* He'd lied about Hayley so that he could fuck Anne. Lying bastard, Anne thought angrily. Cheating, lying, fucking ... And Hayley was a right bitch. They were probably fucking in the woods, she thought as Alan grinned at her again and licked his lips. Dave would be fucking her, spunking up her tight cunt and ... Anne bit her lip. She was cheating on Dave, she reminded herself. But that was different.

'You OK?' Alan asked her, breaking her reverie.

'Yes, yes, I'm OK,' she replied softly. 'So, what's in the bag?'

'Ah, yes,' he breathed, grabbing the bag and opening it. Showing her a camera, he smiled. 'You said that you'd let me take some photographs of you.'

'Of me, or my cunt?'

'You're a very attractive girl, Anne.'

'That doesn't answer my question. Anyway, you don't have to flatter me. I'm a slut, and you know it.'

'Just because you enjoy sex, it doesn't mean to say that you're a slut.'

'What would you call a teenage girl who fucks married men in their fifties?'

'Yes, I see your point.'

'How about a few pictures of me sucking your cock?' she asked him, dropping to her knees and unzipping his trousers.

Fiddling with the camera as Anne lowered his

27

trousers and grabbed his stiffening penis, Alan grinned. 'Perfect,' he breathed. 'I'll look at the photos and think of fucking your pretty little mouth every time I have a wank.'

'How often do you wank?'

'Every day, and I think of fucking your tight little cunt when I shoot.'

Retracting Alan's fleshy foreskin, Anne sucked his purple knob into her sperm-thirsty mouth and snaked her tongue over its velveteen surface. His hands shook as she committed the illicit act but he managed to focus the camera and take several shots as she slipped his knob out of her wet mouth and ran her tongue up and down his solid shaft. Anne realised that the photographs might be seen by the lads in the pub, but she didn't care. If Hayley acted like a slut, then so would she. And if Dave thought nothing about cheating on her, then she'd show him how far she could go in the name of deceit.

Cupping Alan's heavy balls in the palm of her hand, she took his swollen knob to the back of her throat, sank her teeth gently into his veined shaft and breathed heavily through her nose. It had been months since she'd sucked on a throbbing knob and savoured the taste of fresh sperm, and now she vowed never to go more than a day or so without drinking from a hard cock. Was Dave fucking Hayley's mouth? she wondered angrily as Alan took several more photographs. Was Hayley drinking Dave's spunk?

'I want to give you a facial,' Alan gasped. 'I'll spunk all over your face.'

'Dirty boy,' Anne breathed, slipping his glistening knob out of her mouth and wanking his rock-hard shaft. 'Come on, then – shoot it all over me.'

'Lick it,' he ordered her, trying to steady the camera. 'Here it comes, lick it and—'

Although his hands were shaking as his fresh sperm jetted from his throbbing knob and splattered her pretty face, Alan managed to take several photographs. Anne licked his purple globe, sustaining his orgasm as his cream rained over her nose and eyes. She could have done this with Dave, she thought as she savoured the taste of Alan's spunk. They could have been good together, but he obviously preferred to spunk over Hayley's face and in her mouth.

Finally taking Alan's throbbing knob into her pretty mouth, Anne sucked out the last of his sperm as he gasped and trembled. It had been so long since she'd tasted spunk, she thought for the umpteenth time. Swallowing his male offering, draining his huge balls, she finally slipped his deflating cock out of her mouth and grinned at him. He hadn't lasted very long, she mused, rubbing his knob over her spermed face. But they'd be visiting the house again and she'd have plenty of opportunities to swallow his spunk. As Anne licked her lips, Alan took several more photographs of her sperm-dripping face before dropping his camera on the chair.

'You were great,' he said. 'That was perfect.'

'I love spunk,' Anne breathed, wiping her face with the back of her hand and lapping up his cream. 'I haven't sucked a hard knob and swallowed spunk for months. Does your wife suck your cock?'

'No way. I'm lucky if she lets me fuck her once a month. Your sister . . . Do you think she'd meet me here?'

'What?' Anne glared at him, her stomach sinking as she imagined him with her sister. 'You want to fuck my sister?'

'Yes – why not?'

'Because . . . I can't believe this. What's wrong with me – aren't I good enough for you?'

'Anne, I didn't mean . . . All I thought was that, if your sister fucks, then I'd be happy to oblige. I've seen her with you a couple of times and she looks pretty tasty.'

'She's too busy fucking Dave.' Walking to the window, Anne sighed. 'I'm not good enough for you, am I?' she asked him again.

'Of course you are. You were brilliant.'

'So why do you want to fuck my sister?'

'I just thought that she might be into water sports.'

'Don't I mean anything to you? After all we've done together . . . What has Hayley got that I haven't?'

'Nothing, Anne. It's just that . . . You're going out with Dave and . . . I just thought that your sister might be interested in me.'

'I'll piss on you,' Anne said, slipping her knickers off. 'Where do you want me?'

'Squat over my face,' Alan replied eagerly as he lay on the floor on his back. 'Squat over my face and piss in my mouth.'

Taking her position, Anne parted the fleshy cushions of her outer labia and exposed the open entrance to her tight vagina. She'd never dreamed of committing such a vulgar act before, she reflected as Alan licked the pink funnel of flesh surrounding her gaping sex hole. There again, she'd never dreamed of having sex with a man older than her father. Squeezing her muscles as she looked down at Alan's face, Anne knew that she had to prove herself to be better than Hayley. If Alan wanted water sports, then she'd do it. Whatever he wanted, whatever crude act turned him on, she'd agree. And she'd do it far better than her sister.

His mouth filling with her hot liquid, Alan repeatedly swallowed hard as Anne tightened her muscles and sustained the flow. He was a dirty old man, she thought as he pressed his lips hard against her wet flesh and drank from her young body. Were all old men like this? she wondered, imagining her mother pissing in her father's mouth. Was Hayley into water sports? She'd prove herself better than Hayley, she vowed again as she listened to Alan gulping down her golden liquid. She'd show Hayley that she could have any man eating out of her knickers.

Her golden flow finally stemming, Anne looked up at the cracked ceiling as Alan's tongue slipped deep into the creamy wetness of her contracting vagina. This was real sex, she thought as her clitoris swelled. Reaching down and peeling her outer lips wide apart, she gasped as he slurped and sucked on the inner folds of her vagina. This was sex for the sake of sex, and the notion excited her. Alan knew exactly what to do, she mused as he sucked her erect clitoris into his hot mouth. Her young body shaking uncontrollably, her sex juices flowing over his wet face, she knew that his expert attention would soon take her to her climax.

Anne had been licked many times by her two previous boyfriends, but it had never driven her wild like this. Alan snaked his tongue deftly around the base of her solid clitoris, sucking gently and then licking, until she felt her vaginal muscles contract and the birth of her orgasm stirring deep within her young womb. Stretching her sex lips open to the extreme, forcing her solid clitoris out, she whimpered softly as he bit gently on the sensitive protrusion. Alan was amazing, she thought dreamily as he held her on the verge of her climax. As he teased her, making her wait for the relief she so desperately craved, she lost herself in her sexual frenzy.

When he felt that she was ready, he pressed his mouth against her wet flesh and sucked hard on her aching clitoris, sending her arousal to frightening heights. Letting out a rush of breath as her pleasure finally exploded in the pulsating nub of her erect clitoris, Anne threw her head back and cried out in the grip of an incredibly powerful orgasm. Never had she known anything like it as waves of pure sexual ecstasy crashed throughout her quivering body. Her pulsating clitoris pumping tremors of bliss deep into her contracting womb, her orgasmic milk spewing from her gaping vaginal hole and splattering Alan's face, she cried out again as her pleasure peaked and rocked her young body to the core.

'Keep coming,' Alan breathed through a mouthful of wet vaginal flesh. 'Pump out your cunt juice and keep coming.'

'I am,' Anne gasped, rocking her hips and grinding the sexual centre of her teenage body hard against his mouth. 'Again . . . it's . . . it's coming again.'

Anne had never thought that multiple orgasms were possible, until now. As the first wave of pleasure subsided, a second welled up and crashed through her young body. She couldn't believe the sheer ecstasy her trembling flesh was bringing her as her pleasure repeatedly receded and then built again. Alan was a man of experience, she mused dreamily as he licked and sucked on her pulsating clitoris. But it was also the danger, the notion of lying and cheating, that excited her.

'No more,' she finally managed to gasp as she lolled to one side and lay on the floor beside him.

'You're a dirty little girl,' Alan said, chuckling as he propped himself up on his elbow and gazed at her sex-flushed face. 'I'm going to eat your little pussy every day.'

'Yes, yes,' she murmured, her brown eyes rolling. 'Eat my cunt every day and make me come.'

'Would you like my cock up your bum?'

'Yes . . . no, I . . .'

'Have you never tried anal sex?'

'No, I haven't.' Hauling her young body up as Alan climbed to his feet, Anne wondered what she was getting into. 'I don't want to get into anything like that.'

'That's what you said about pissing, but you loved it.'

'Yes I know, but—'

'It's all right, I won't push you. It's just that I want to teach you everything, Anne. I want to teach you everything I know about sex.'

'And you want to teach my sister?'

'No, of course I don't. I only want you.'

'We'd better go to the pub now,' she breathed as she straightened her clothes.

'To see Dave?'

'No, I . . . I just need a drink.'

She did want to see Dave, Anne thought as she left the house with Alan. But she wasn't sure why. Was it to confront him? she wondered as she followed Alan along the path to the lane. Did she want to boast about her sexual conquest? Watching Alan's leather bag swinging by his side, she recalled the photographs he'd taken. If Dave saw them and he told Hayley . . . but Alan wouldn't jeopardise his relationship with a young girl by showing the pictures around in the pub, she was sure.

'Where the hell have you been?' Dave asked her as Alan went up to the bar.

'I went for a walk,' she replied coldly. 'I was a wild flower and I was plucked from the ground and—'

'A wild flower? Anne, what the hell are you on about?'

'Some people trample on wild flowers, Dave,' she said accusingly.

33

'Trample on . . . Where have you been?'

'More to the point, where the hell have *you* been?'

'I've been here, waiting for you.'

'Before you came here, I meant.'

'I came straight here from home.'

'You were seen in the park, Dave, so don't lie to me.'

'In the park?' he echoed. 'I haven't been anywhere near the park.'

'Don't lie, Dave. You've been to the park with Hayley – you were seen there.'

'Whoever told you that I was in the park with your sister was lying. Anne, what's this all about? I left home at six and came straight here. It's almost eight o'clock. I've been here for the last couple of hours.'

'Have you seen my sister?'

'No, not since yesterday.'

'I'll be back later,' Anne said, heading for the door. 'I have to go and see someone.'

'Anne, wait.'

'I'll be back.'

Walking home briskly, Anne felt confused as never before. Why would Alan lie about seeing Dave and Hayley in the park? she wondered. Or was *Dave* lying? Perhaps Alan had lied to lessen Anne's feelings of guilt? Perhaps he'd lied to make her angry and agree to piss in his mouth? There was only one way to find out, she thought as she opened her front door and went into the lounge. She asked her mother where Hayley was, then followed the woman's gaze down to her legs. Her knees were grubby from kneeling on the floor in the derelict house and her skirt was crumpled. She looked like a common slut, she thought as she lied to her mother about falling over in the lane.

'You'd better sort yourself out,' the woman said. 'You can't walk around like that.'

'Yes, yes, I will. So, where is Hayley?'

'She went out with her new boyfriend.'

'What time did she leave?'

'About six, I think. What's the matter, Anne? What's happened?'

'Nothing's happened. I just wanted to talk to Hayley about something.'

'She was meeting her new boyfriend at seven and—'

'But you said that she left at six.'

'She had to meet someone else first, so she left early.'

'I don't suppose she said who it was?'

'No, she didn't. Are you sure there's nothing wrong?'

'I'm fine, mum, honest.'

'Hayley said that she'd be home around half past eight because she's expecting a phone call about a new job.'

'I didn't know that she was after another job.'

'She's been headhunted,' her mother said proudly. 'It's some high-flying position with an oil company. By the way, she's bringing her boyfriend here to meet us.'

'Really? Well, that will be interesting.'

'Dad's doing something in the shed and I'll bet he's got himself filthy dirty. I just hope that he's going to change before they get here.'

Anne checked the wall clock and smiled. 'I'm looking forward to meeting Hayley's new man,' she said, concealing a grin. 'They might be here at any minute so I'll go and get washed and changed. I want to look my best for her new boyfriend.'

'It's unlike you to take an interest in Hayley's friends.'

'Maybe I've changed,' Anne murmured, leaving the room and bounding up the stairs.

This was her chance for revenge, she thought as she showered and dressed in a short skirt and a tight T-shirt. If Hayley was going to steal her boyfriend, then she'd steal hers. Applying a little make-up and brushing her hair, Anne gazed at her reflection in the dressing-table mirror and smiled. 'An eye for an eye,' she breathed, licking her full lips. 'A cock for a cock?' Should she wear her leather boots? she wondered. There was no need to dress like a slut, she decided. But she would behave like a *slut*.

Anne was in the lounge with her mother when Hayley arrived with a good-looking man. He had brown hair and a suntanned face, and Anne thought he was rather dishy. Dressed in blue jeans and an open-neck shirt, he was in his early twenties and she reckoned that he was Hayley's best catch so far. His name was Rick, and she reckoned that Hayley was very proud of him. He had a cock, Anne mused. And she had an accommodating pussy, so seducing him should be easy enough.

Anne's father was still in the shed, but her mother invited Rick to sit on the sofa and offered him a cup of tea. He was *very* good-looking, Anne thought, grinning at him as he looked her up and down. His eyes focused on her naked thighs and she reckoned that he'd be an easy enough conquest. But she had to get him alone, and she knew that wasn't going to be easy.

Hayley looked down at Anne's short skirt and frowned as their mother left the room to make the tea. Anne grinned at her sister and then sat next to Rick on the sofa to further annoy the other girl. She knew that Hayley was fuming as she started chatting to Rick, but this was payback time and Anne was loving it. Asking him where he worked, and at the

36

same time making sure that her skirt rode up her slender thighs, she turned her back on her sister.

'I work for a computer company,' Rick said, his gaze lowering as Anne parted her thighs slightly. 'I'm an IT consultant.'

'Aren't you going out this evening?' Hayley asked her sister.

'I've already been out,' Anne replied without taking her eyes off Rick. 'Working with computers must be interesting. Mine's been doing strange things – perhaps you could look at it for me?'

'Yes, of course,' Rick said. 'Any time.'

'How about now?'

'Anne, Rick hasn't come here to look at your computer,' Hayley sighed.

'It's not a problem,' Rick said, rising to his feet. 'It may have a virus, so the sooner it's sorted out the better. It won't take a minute to check it over.'

'I'll come with you,' Hayley breathed as the phone rang. 'Damn, that'll be the call I'm expecting.'

Leading Rick up to her bedroom as Hayley answered the phone, Anne hoped that the call would keep her busy for a while. This couldn't have worked out better, she thought, hoping that she could tempt Rick with her teenage body. Showing him into her room and switching her computer on, she perched her rounded buttocks on the edge of her bed as he sat at the desk. He was an attractive man, she mused again as he gazed at the screen. Parting her thighs and displaying the triangular patch of white cotton covering her full sex lips as he turned and looked at her, she watched him closely for his reaction.

'So, what's the problem with it?' Rick asked her, his stare transfixed between her naked thighs.

'It does naughty things,' she replied unconvincingly. 'So, how long have you known Hayley?'

37

'We've only just met. I thought it was too early to meet her family but—'

'I'm glad you did,' Anne cut in, parting her thighs further. 'It's been pretty dull around here lately.'

'Dull? I'd have thought that a pretty girl like you would be out having fun. Don't you have a boyfriend at the moment?'

'No, I'm free and single.' Leaving the bed, she came over and stood next to him. 'So, what do you think?' she asked him, pressing the gentle swell of her lower stomach against his arm. 'Is there anything you can do for me?'

'Yes, there is,' Rick replied, grinning at her. 'But I thought you wanted me to look at your computer?'

'You're a naughty boy.'

'And you're a naughty girl. There's nothing wrong with your computer, is there?'

'There was, but . . . well, it must have fixed itself.' Pressing her young body harder against his arm, Anne grinned. 'You might as well take a look while you're here.'

'What, you mean take a look at the computer?'

'You can look at anything you want to.'

Lifting her skirt and revealing the tight crotch of her knickers, Anne reckoned that Rick was game for anything as he ran his fingers up and down her inner thighs. Pulling her knickers to one side, he stroked the swollen lips of her pussy and then looked up at her as if to gauge her reaction. Her stomach fluttering, her clitoris swelling, Anne let out a rush of breath and licked her red lips, giving him the signal to go further. His finger entered the tight sheath of her wet vagina and he pulled her knickers further aside with his free hand to massage her hot inner flesh.

'You *are* a naughty girl,' he whispered.

'And I get naughtier,' Anne breathed softly. 'Maybe you should spank me.'

'Maybe I should meet you somewhere later.'

'Maybe you should meet me in the park sooner rather than later.'

'I can't rush off,' Rick sighed, gazing at Anne's succulent sex lips squeezing his finger. 'Your mum is making tea and . . .'

'You have tea and chat for a while, and I'll go to the park and wait for you.'

'OK,' he said, slipping his wet finger out of her contracting pussy. 'I'd better say that I've sorted your computer out.'

'And then you can come to the park and sort *me* out.'

'Do you do this with all your sister's boyfriends?'

'Only the good-looking ones. Go back to the lounge and I'll see you later.'

As Rick left the room, Anne realised how easy it was to have any man eating out of her knickers. She felt a little guilty as she trotted down the stairs and told her mother that she was going to see Dave, but she also felt incredibly aroused. An eye for an eye, she thought, leaving the house and heading towards the park. Hayley deserved this, she thought as she walked past the pub. Two can play at stealing boyfriends and if that was the game that Hayley wanted to play then Anne would join in willingly – and win.

Sitting on a bench beneath the evening sun, Anne began to think about her life. She'd always been the underdog, especially where Hayley was concerned, but things were changing. For the first time in years, she felt confident and happy with herself. She was becoming bubbly, and very naughty, and she liked the transformation. She was also a cheating slut, she reminded herself, but that didn't bother her. Her goal was to beat Hayley at her own game, which she seemed to be doing with ease. She might see Dave again, she thought, but only for sex.

Smiling at Rick as he approached, Anne parted her thighs and displayed the wet crotch of her white cotton knickers. 'That was quick,' she said as he sat next to her on the bench. 'You must be keen!'

'It's not every day that an attractive young girl pulls her knickers down and . . . I wasn't going to waste any time.'

'Has Hayley pulled her knickers down for you?'

'Yes, but . . .'

'But what?'

'I feel bad enough sneaking off and meeting you here, let alone talking about her.'

'I want to know, Rick.'

'We've had sex but . . . Let's not talk about it.'

'Wasn't she any good?'

'She can't come,' he finally told her. 'She's never had an orgasm in her life.'

'I have multiple orgasms,' Anne replied triumphantly. She rose from the bench and licked her succulent lips. 'Come into the woods with me and I'll prove it.'

Walking into the woods with Rick in tow, Anne couldn't believe that Hayley was unable to come. She'd always thought that her older sister was perfect in every way, until now. This was an amazing revelation, she thought happily. Hayley, unable to achieve an orgasm? Giggling as she sat on the soft grass in a small clearing, Anne lay on her back and looked up at Rick. His dark eyes stared at her young body and he obviously couldn't believe his luck. Settling beside her and pulling her knickers off, he focused on the most private part of her teenage body.

'You're gorgeous,' Rick said, leaning over and kissing the warm cushions of her fleshy outer lips. Breathing in her female scent, he opened her wet valley and licked her inner folds. 'And you taste wonderful.'

'What does Hayley taste like?' Anne asked him, parting her legs as wide as she could.

'Let's not talk about Hayley,' he sighed. 'I want to concentrate on *you*.'

'And I want *you* to concentrate on my pussy,' she returned huskily.

Rick's tongue entered the hot sheath of Anne's tight vagina and he breathed heavily as he lapped up her creamy sex milk. Anne quivered and writhed on the short grass as she looked up at the trees high above her. Was this where Dave had screwed Hayley? she wondered. Had they walked into the woods and found the small clearing and fucked there? Dave would have fucked Hayley's mouth, she reflected. He'd have spunked down her throat and . . . Hayley was a bitch, Anne mused dreamily as Rick sucked her ripe clitoris into his hot mouth. But the tables had turned.

Her orgasm welled from the depths of her contracting womb and Anne dug her fingernails into the soft grass, arching her back as Rick mouthed and sucked on her solid clitoris. Thinking of the old armchair in the derelict house, she imagined taking Rick there. Perhaps she should turn the house into her sex den, she thought as her clitoris pulsated and erupted in orgasm.

Trembling uncontrollably, she cried out as Rick drove two fingers deep into her contracting vagina and swept his tongue repeatedly over the sensitive tip of her clitoris.

Hayley couldn't do this, Anne thought happily in her rising wickedness as her pleasure rocked her young body to the core. Rick would be pleased with her, she knew as he worked expertly between the splayed lips of her teenage vagina. Was Hayley into water sports? she wondered, imagining squatting over

Rick's face and showering him with her golden rain. Anne knew that she'd do almost anything in the name of lust, especially if it helped to destroy her sister's relationships. A cock for a cock, she mused as Rick massaged the inner flesh of her inflamed vagina and sucked on her pulsating clitoris.

Finally drifting down from her illicit climax, Anne breathed deeply as she listened to the slurping sound of Rick sucking out her orgasmic milk. She couldn't imagine her sister lying on the ground with a man licking and sucking her pussy. Hayley's clothes would get crumpled and her long blonde hair would become dishevelled and she'd hate it. There was no way Hayley would have sex in the woods but ... Had Dave really fucked her beneath the trees? Anne wondered. Or had they found somewhere clean and comfortable?

'You're beautiful,' Rick said, lifting his head at last and gazing at Anne. 'I wish I'd met you before I met your sister.'

'It doesn't make any difference,' Anne countered. 'You can have me whenever you want to.'

'You mean you'll share me with Hayley?'

'Yes – why not? It'll be fun knowing that you've fucked her before you've fucked me.'

'I don't think she'd see it that way. But if you're happy with that ...'

'I won't know whether I'm happy with the arrangement until you've fucked me.'

'You want me to prove myself?'

'Of course.'

Closing her eyes as Rick positioned himself between her splayed legs, Anne let out a sigh as he pressed the bulbous knob of his solid penis into her wet sex valley. As he eased the full length of his penis deep into her hot vagina, she wasn't sure whether he was extremely large or whether she was just very tight. Her sex sheath opened wide to accommodate his solid shaft, his bulbous knob pressed against her creamy-wet cervix, and she thought that she'd split open with the sheer girth of his huge cock.

Withdrawing slowly until the wet petals of her inner lips encompassed his purple knob, Rick slid his cock smoothly back into Anne's squelching vagina. He withdrew again and drove into her, finding his rhythm as she gasped and writhed on the grass beneath him. This was heaven, she thought dreamily, her young body rocking gently with the illicit shafting. She found it exciting to think that this was the very cock that had shafted her sister's pussy. Hayley had taken Dave's cock and now, in retaliation, she was taking Rick's.

'Are you OK?' Rick asked her, his sparkling eyes smiling as he looked down at her pretty face.

'Oh yes,' she breathed softly, returning his smile. 'I've never felt better.'

'I want you to come, Anne.'

'And I want your spunk filling my pussy. I want the spunk that Hayley would have had.'

'It's all yours,' he said, chuckling.

Increasing his vaginal shafting rhythm, Rick locked his lips to Anne's in a passionate kiss. She tasted his tongue, breathing heavily through her nose as she wrapped her legs around his body and pulled him closer. The sensitive tip of her solid clitoris massaged by his pussy-wet shaft, taking her closer to her climax, she again imagined his cock driving deep into Hayley's vagina. How had her sister reacted when he'd pumped his spunk into her? Anne wondered. Had Rick gasped in the grip of his orgasm while Hayley had wondered what an orgasm was like?

'Now,' Rick breathed. 'I'm coming now.'

43

'Yes, yes,' Anne gasped as she neared her own climax. 'Fuck me hard – I'm coming.'

His creamy sperm lubricating her contracting vagina as her orgasm erupted within the pulsating nub of her solid clitoris, he once more locked his lips to hers and kissed her. Writhing on the grass, she listened to the squelching sounds of their shafting as he pummelled her ripe cervix with his throbbing knob and flooded her hot sex sheath with his male cream. Her teenage body jolted with each thrust of his rock-hard cock and Anne dug her fingernails into the soft grass as she cried out in the grip of her amazing pleasure. Again and again, waves of ecstasy crashed through her trembling body, taking her to hitherto unknown heights of sexual bliss.

In a dreamlike state, Anne tossed her head from side to side, her eyes rolling and her nostrils flaring as her orgasm peaked. She'd had Dave, Alan and now Rick, she mused. After months of neglect, her teenage vagina was now back in action. As Rick made his last thrusts and her orgasm began to fade, she gazed up at the trees high above her. It was getting dark, she thought as Rick finally slipped his deflating penis out of her sperm-bubbling pussy. But a new light was now shining upon her young body.

'Are you all right?' Rick asked her.

He sounded genuinely concerned, and Anne liked that. 'Yes,' she murmured. 'I feel great.'

'We'd better make a move before it gets dark.'

'Before the monsters come,' she said, hauling her trembling body upright and grabbing her knickers.

'Monsters?'

'There are monsters that come out after dark. Come on, let's go.'

As she walked across the park, Anne knew that she'd be seeing Rick again. He'd probably still go out

with Hayley and fuck her, but that didn't bother
Anne. If anything, she liked the idea of being the
other woman – the other sister. This was Hayley's
comeuppance, she reflected as they neared her house.
This was revenge for the other girl's wicked betrayal.
Rick stopped and took her in his arms before they
reached the front gate. She'd hoped that Hayley
would see them hand in hand, kissing, loving . . .

'I'm supposed to be seeing Hayley tomorrow,' he
said. 'Do you want me to dump her?'

'No, no,' she breathed. 'I like the idea of you
coming to the house to see her and then sneaking off
to fuck me.'

'Well, if you're sure?'

'I'm very sure. We'll go to the park again tomorrow, after you've been with her.'

'OK.' He kissed her passionately. 'Until tomorrow,
then.'

'Thanks, Rick. You were amazing.'

'And you were the best.'

As she opened her front door and climbed the stairs
to her room, Anne pondered on Rick's words. *You
were the best*. That'll teach Hayley, she thought
happily. Her stomach somersaulting as if she was
going over a bridge in a fast car, she flopped onto her
bed and listened to the music coming from Hayley's
room. Hayley was singing along to the tune. She was
obviously happy, thinking that she'd found the man
of her dreams and that she was in love. Little did she
know that her new boyfriend had just fucked her little
sister beneath the trees. Little did she know that, the
next time Rick fucked her, he'd then sneak off and
fuck and spunk her sister again.

Things had certainly changed, Anne thought as she
slipped her hand between her thighs and felt the

sperm-soaked crotch of her tight knickers. Her clitoris swelled as she massaged her puffy sex lips through the tight material. She was looking forward to Alan's cock the following evening. First Alan, and then Dave . . . She'd fuck Alan and then take Dave to the woods and fuck him, she decided. And then, after Rick had seen Hayley, she'd meet him in the woods and fuck *him*. One-upmanship was exciting, she mused. After years of hearing about Hayley's successes, the tables had turned.

Three

'Where did you go last night?' Hayley asked Anne over breakfast.

'I went out and had some fun,' the girl replied impishly. 'Why?'

'You're not mucking about with Rick, are you?'

'I don't muck about with anyone, Hayley.'

'You know what I mean. He left shortly after you and—'

'Don't you trust him?'

'You're the one I don't trust. Anyway, I'm just warning you to keep away from him.'

'Maybe you should have warned your last boyfriend to keep away from me. Ian was always chasing after me and trying to look up my skirt at my knickers. Did you know that he preferred younger girls? That's probably why he dumped you.'

'Ian and I split up because . . . It's none of your business. You should stop messing about with boys and get down to some serious studying.'

'What, like you did?'

'Anne, if you want to go to university and then get a good job . . . I didn't have a boyfriend until I was twenty.'

'All your boyfriends have dumped you,' Anne sniggered. 'No one's ever dumped *me*.'

'That's because you take your knickers off as soon as—'

'At least I can come.'

Hayley looked shocked. 'What . . . what do you mean by that?' she stammered.

'Nothing.'

'Who have you been talking to?'

'Are you two arguing again?' their mother sighed as she walked into the kitchen. 'Come on, or you'll both be late.'

Hayley glared at Anne. 'I'll talk to you later,' she whispered through gritted teeth.

Anne grinned as Hayley left the table and grabbed her bag. She realised that she shouldn't have said anything because Hayley might put two and two together and blame Rick for blabbing his mouth off. But she wasn't really bothered. If Rick said anything to her, she'd deny all knowledge of talking to Hayley about it. Leaving the house and heading for college, she felt a spring in her step as she walked down the road. The sun was shining, the holidays were only a couple of days away, and she felt better than ever. She now had self-confidence, she mused, jutting her firm breasts out and showing off her pert nipples through her tight T-shirt as a middle-aged man walked past.

'Don't you want to see me any more?' someone called out.

Anne turned and gazed at Dave. 'Of course I do,' she returned. 'What do you mean?'

He frowned. 'I saw you leaving the park with some guy last night,' he said accusingly.

'We'd been talking,' she said, concealing a grin. 'The same way you talk to Hayley in the park.'

'Anne . . . he was holding your hand.'

'I was frightened of the monsters so he picked me like a wild flower and made me feel better.'

'I thought you were coming back to the pub last night. I waited for you and then . . . Anne, if you've found someone else . . . I'd rather you told me.'

'Of course I haven't. I was going to go back to the pub and then I met an old friend and we went to the park for a chat. That's all there was to it. Anyway, I know that you met my sister again.'

'We've been through this before, Anne. I didn't meet your sister, or anyone else.'

'If you want to screw Hayley that's fine by me.'

'What do you mean by that?'

'You screw her, and I'll screw . . . I have to go or I'll be late.'

'OK, well – I'll see you tonight?'

'Yes, but make it early. I'll be in the pub at six.'

'OK, I'll see you there. What's all this about wild flowers?'

'I'll see you later.'

Walking on, Anne wasn't convinced that Dave was telling the truth. But she had Rick and Alan to satisfy her, so she didn't really care whether Dave was screwing her sister or not. She didn't care much for college, either, so she decided to go to the derelict house and do some studying. Making her way to the woods, she followed the narrow path through the trees and breathed in the scent of pine. She felt calm and tranquil away from the noise and bustle of people, and she decided that the house was a great place to catch up on her college work.

Wandering into the front room, she gazed at the old armchair and smiled. If only Hayley knew about her antics, she thought, dumping her bag on the floor. Spanking, spunk swallowing, water sports . . . She'd certainly had a good time with Alan, and there'd be many more sessions of crude sex with him in the derelict house. Sitting in the chair and taking her books from her bag, she wished that she hadn't told Dave that she'd be in the pub at six. It would have been nice to have met Alan for sex and then to meet Rick later in the evening for another good shafting.

By lunchtime Anne had had enough and she dropped her books into her bag. Although she'd got some work done she'd been thinking about Alan and Rick, and the crotch of her tight knickers was wet with her juices of arousal. Although she'd had a couple of boyfriends in the past, she felt as though she'd only just discovered sex. She'd come out of her shell, she thought as she pulled her short skirt up and thrust her hand down the front of her knickers. She was desperate for the relief of a massive orgasm and was about to slip her fingers between her swollen pussy lips and appease her solid clitoris when she heard voices outside the house.

She grabbed her bag and gazed through the broken window. She noticed two teenage girls, one blonde and one brunette, walking towards the house. This is all I need, Anne thought, slipping through the hall and hiding in what had once been the kitchen. The voices grew louder and she spied through the crack in the room's door as she heard the front door open.

'Do you think anyone else comes here?' the blonde said.

'I doubt it,' her dark-haired friend replied. 'We've never seen anyone, have we?'

'They're probably frightened of the ghosts,' the other girl said with a giggle as they climbed the stairs and went into one of the rooms.

Anne kept her distance as she crept up the stairs. Hovering on the landing, she peered around the door and almost gasped out loud as she gazed at the girls entwined in a passionate kiss. Lesbians, she thought, reckoning the girls to be about her own age. Watching as they lay on a mattress and began fondling each other, she was pretty sure that they were from her college. She glanced at her watch and realised that they must be on their lunch break. Did they go to the house for lesbian sex every day? she wondered. How many people used the house for sex?

Anne watched with bated breath as the girls stripped naked. She'd often wondered about lesbian sex but had never dreamed of experimenting sexually herself with another girl. She wasn't even sure what lesbians did. She'd assumed that they licked and fingered each other, but had thought that there must be other acts they indulged in too. Pushing the bedroom door open a little further, she watched as the girls ran their hands over each other's young bodies. Squeezing the firm mounds of each other's breasts, they kissed each other again. Were they in love? Anne wondered. Or were they seeking nothing more than sexual gratification? Most teenage boys hadn't got a clue how to please a girl, she reflected. Maybe the girls had got together because each knew what the other wanted.

Anne gazed wide-eyed as the blonde girl lay on the mattress with her legs parted wide. Was the other girl going to lick her pussy? she wondered as the brunette settled between the blonde's thighs. The girl began kissing her friend's swollen sex lips and then licked the open valley of her young pussy, and Anne felt her own clitoris swell. What did she taste like? Anne wondered, her stomach somersaulting, her clitoris calling for attention, as she watched the blonde writhe on the mattress.

'My clit,' the blonde girl breathed as her lesbian lover sucked and slurped between her slender thighs. 'Suck my clit really hard.'

'Mmm, you taste wonderful,' the other girl said. 'I've been dying to get your clit into my mouth.'

Anne lifted her short skirt up and slipped her hand down the front of her wet knickers as she watched the lesbian sex show. Stifling her gasps of pleasure as she massaged the solid bulb of her sensitive clitoris, she wondered what it would be like to lick another girl's pussy. Although she didn't want to experience lesbian sex, she imagined a girl's tongue snaking around her erect clitoris and delving deep into her hot vaginal hole. Sex without a cock, she thought, again wondering what pussy milk tasted like. Did they use dildos?

The blonde girl squirmed on the mattress and cried out as her orgasm erupted, and Anne began to wonder whether she should experiment sexually with another girl. There'd be no harm in trying, she mused dreamily as she massaged her erect clitoris faster. Her orgasm nearing, she felt her sex juices flooding from her contracting vagina and soaking her knickers. The lubricious milk ran down the smooth flesh of her inner thighs and she trembled uncontrollably as her orgasm erupted within the pulsating bulb of her clitoris.

Her legs sagging beneath her, she leaned against the wall and again stifled her gasps of pleasure as she rode the crest of her orgasm. She needed to feel a wet tongue between her swollen pussy lips, she mused as her hot milk spewed from her vaginal sheath. But she knew that she was going to have to wait until the evening before enjoying Alan's and then Rick's oral attentions. Accidentally falling against the door, she slipped her hand out of her knickers as the door banged against the wall with a dull thud.

'What the hell are you doing?' the dark-haired girl yelled, leaping off the mattress and grabbing Anne's arm.

'I was just—' Anne began as she was dragged into the room.

'Just spying on us?' the blonde cut in.

'What are we going to do with her?' the other girl breathed, forcing Anne onto the mattress.

'We'll have to teach her a lesson.'

'I won't say anything,' Anne said shakily. 'Let me go and—'

'You'll go blabbing your mouth off if we let you go.'

'No, I won't.'

'Help me get her knickers off,' the blonde said. 'We'll teach her a lesson she won't forget.'

Anne struggled to break free as the girls almost tore her knickers off but she was no match for them. On her back with her legs held apart and her sex crack blatantly exposed, she felt acutely embarrassed as the girls commented on her creamy-wet pussy lips. She was going to have to endure lesbian sex, she thought apprehensively as the blonde girl positioned herself between her splayed thighs. She should never have spied on the girls but, as the blonde kissed and licked the swollen lips of her young pussy, she felt a quiver run through her young womb.

The girl licked and slurped between the swollen lips of Anne's pussy, and her struggling became perfunctory as her arousal heightened. Why fight? she thought as her womb contracted. The girls wanted to pleasure her, not harm her, so why fight them? Relaxing as the blonde's tongue lapped at her wet vaginal entrance and repeatedly swept over the sensitive tip of her erect clitoris, she breathed deeply and slowly. She felt calm and tranquil as never before, but she reminded herself that this was simply sex and that she wasn't a lesbian.

'Have you ever had a girl lick you?' the dark-haired lesbian asked her.

'No,' Anne breathed softly as the blonde's wet tongue ran up and down her open valley.

'We'd better initiate you,' the other girl said with a giggle as she knelt astride Anne's face. 'Go on, lick my cunt.'

Anne breathed heavily through her nose as the girl pressed the wet lips of her teenage pussy hard against her mouth. Breathing in the scent of the lesbian's open sex valley, she knew that she had no choice other than to commit the Sapphic sex act. As she tentatively pushed her tongue out and lapped the brunette's hot milk, she thought the taste was quite agreeable. She'd often sucked her fingers after massaging deep inside her vagina and had loved the tangy flavour, but this was another girl's pussy cream and, to her amazement, she was pleasantly surprised by the taste.

She hadn't expected this, Anne reflected as the blonde's tongue entered the creamy-wet sheath of her young vagina. Her clitoris responded to the lesbian licking and she felt her young womb contract and her juices of arousal flow. She realised that she was enjoying the feel of another girl's tongue delving deep into her tightening vagina. Savouring the dark-haired girl's pussy milk, she pushed her tongue into her open sex hole and lapped fervently. Never in a million years would she have thought that she'd be enjoying sex with two girls. But she'd had no choice, she tried to console herself. This was forced sex – she wasn't a lesbian.

As two fingers drove deep into her contracting vagina, Anne arched her back and breathed heavily through her nose. Her clitoris sucked into the blonde's hot mouth, she knew that she'd soon be writhing in the grip of her first lesbian-induced orgasm. Would she meet the girls again? she wondered as she sucked the brunette's clitoris into her hot mouth. Repeatedly sweeping her tongue over the solid protrusion, she knew that she'd meet the girls for lesbian sex again. This was only sex, she thought dreamily. She wasn't a lesbian – was she?

Her orgasm erupting, shaking her young body to the core, Anne sucked and mouthed on the other girl's clitoris and took her to her earth-shuddering climax. Writhing on the mattress, lost in her sexual delirium, she reached up and squeezed the firm mounds of the girl's breasts and pinched her ripe nipples to add to her pleasure. The three-way coupling was driving her wild: her mouth flooded with orgasmic milk as she thought how soft and gentle girls were, compared to men. Alan and Rick had been good, she reflected in the grip of her orgasm. But the feel of another girl's tongue, the loving gentleness of the forbidden act . . . Bisexual. The word played on her mind as she sucked on the brunette's pulsating clitoris.

'Wow, you were good,' the dark-haired girl breathed. 'That was brilliant.'

'Would you like to join us again?' the blonde asked Anne, sitting upright and licking her juice-glossed lips. 'We come here most days in our lunch break.'

Anne propped herself up on her elbows as the brunette sat beside her. 'I don't know,' she breathed, the taste of female sex milk lingering on her tongue. 'I'm not a lesbian.'

'We're not lesbians, either,' the blonde said, with a giggle. 'We both have boyfriends but . . . well, there's nothing like another girl's tongue.'

'We'd better get going,' the other girl said, leaping off the mattress and grabbing her clothes.

Anne wasn't sure what to say as the girls dressed. She clambered to her feet, slipped her knickers up her long legs and waited by the door. Should she meet them again? she wondered. She'd certainly enjoyed her initiation into lesbian sex, but she felt uneasy about her new-found pleasure. Her uncharacteristic emotions worried her as she watched the girls kissing passionately. This wasn't right, she thought as her clitoris swelled. Male and female fit but ... but she couldn't deny the immense pleasure she'd derived from the three-way lesbian coupling.

'Will you be here tomorrow?' the blonde asked her. 'By the way, I'm Dee and this is Angela.'

'I'm Anne,' she breathed. 'Yes, yes – I'll be here tomorrow.'

'That's good. I'll look forward to sucking your little tits.'

'So will I,' Angela chipped in.'

'You mentioned that you had boyfriends,' Anne said. 'Do you share them? I mean ...'

'No, never,' Dee replied. 'We're going to be late. By the way, shave your pussy. See you tomorrow.'

Anne closed her eyes as Dee locked her full lips to hers and kissed her. She could taste her own pussy juice as the girl's tongue slipped into her mouth, and she wondered what she'd got herself into. Then Angela kissed her, and she felt her stomach flutter. A battle between right and wrong raging in her tormented mind, she was pleased when the girls finally left. She grabbed her bag, ambled down the stairs and stepped out into the sunshine. She wasn't sure how she felt as she sat on the grass and recalled the lesbian acts she'd indulged in. These were new and confusing emotions, and Anne found herself lost in her swirling thoughts.

She began to think about her teenage body and how she could not only lure men into having sex with her, but attract other girls too. Hayley wouldn't have indulged in lesbian sex, she thought. She was too refined and perfect to do such naughty things. But was it really that bad to have sex with another girl? After all, it was only fun, and most gratifying. But Anne still found her predicament confusing. What if word got out? she wondered. What would people think of her?

It was her life, she decided. What other people thought didn't matter. As long as she was enjoying her teenage years, then what the hell? Besides, no one would discover the shocking truth. Shocking. Anne mulled over the word and realised that her behaviour *had* been shocking. Her mother would definitely be shocked if she discovered that her young daughter had been entwined in lust with two other girls. But the experience had been immensely exciting, and she knew that she'd meet the girls at the house again for another session of girl-sex.

Sitting with her chin resting on her knees, Anne smiled as blades of grass tickled the smooth flesh either side of her tight knickers. She was becoming more aware of her young body, the pleasures it could give her, and she slipped her wet knickers off and allowed the grass to tease the sensitive lips of her pussy. Her crack opening, she breathed deeply as her inner lips emerged as if seeking the blades of grass. She looked down between her knees at the swell of her outer lips and smiled as she imagined shaving her pussy.

It might be fun to have no pubes, Anne mused as she picked a nearby flower and stroked her unfurling inner lips with the soft petals. Her clitoris swelled, her juices of arousal flowed, and she realised that she'd never given sex so much thought before. But her inner desires had been stirred, woken from the deep, and she knew that she'd never look back. It was as if she'd only just discovered sex, she reflected dreamily as she tickled the sensitive tip of her erect clitoris with the flower.

Hearing voices, Anne grabbed her knickers and bag and dived into the bushes beneath the front room window of the house. Spying from her hide, she frowned as she gazed at Alan and another man walking towards the house. What was Alan up to? she wondered as they stood by the front door. Why take someone else to their secret place? Keeping perfectly still, she listened to their conversation.

'She's eighteen,' Alan said. 'And she's a right little slut. She loves spanking and pissing and—'

'You've already told me all this,' the man cut in with a chuckle. 'What I want to know is, will she let me fuck her?'

'And I've already told you, Brian. I don't know. She has a boyfriend but she's happy to meet me here for sex so she's pretty free with her body. I'll have to play it by ear, mention that I have a friend who might want to join in and see how she reacts. Hopefully, she'll meet me here this evening.'

'Will it be OK if I hide somewhere and watch?'

'Yes, no problem. Come into the house and I'll show you the front room.'

Anne left her hide and slipped away as the men went into the house. Walking along the path through the trees, she couldn't believe that Alan wanted to share her with this man Brian who must have been in his late sixties. More confused than ever, she wondered what to do as she headed home. Two men, she mused, her stomach fluttering, her young womb contracting. Two men, two hard cocks ... Things were going to get out of hand, she knew as she reached her house and closed the front door behind her. Fortunately, no one was home so she dashed up the stairs to her bedroom and dumped her bag on the floor. Lesbian sex, sex with Alan and Rick . . . Things *were* out of hand.

Anne tossed her wet knickers into her wash basket, lifted her short skirt and gazed at her pubic curls. Should she shave? she wondered, recalling the lesbian's words. Her curls would soon grow back, she thought, lowering her skirt and wandering into the bathroom. She grabbed a tube of hair-removing cream from the shelf, knowing that it belonged to Hayley. Her sister wouldn't miss a little bit, she mused, lifting her skirt and massaging the cream into the swell of her outer lips and the gentle rise of her mons.

Anne waited for ten minutes and then wiped the cream away with a damp flannel. The transformation was incredible, she thought as she gazed at her reflection in the mirror. Her outer lips were bald and smooth to the touch and her inner lips protruded alluringly from her naked crack. Running her fingertips over her bald flesh, she wondered what Alan would think of her new look. But if she went to the house to meet him that evening, she knew that the other man would be watching her.

The notion excited her. She lowered her skirt, returned to her room and grabbed a clean pair of knickers from her drawer. She let out a sigh of pleasure as the smooth cotton material glided up her long legs and caressed the hairless lips of her pussy. She felt highly aroused as she walked around her room. Her succulent sex lips tingling, her clitoris swelling, she knew that she had to go to the house and meet Alan. Her clean knickers were already wetting with her juices of arousal as she imagined slipping her clothes off, knowing that an old man was spying. He'd gaze at her naked body, her petite

breasts, her hairless pussy and . . . and he'd want to
fuck her.

Her quest had been to get her own back on Hayley,
Anne reflected as she lay on her bed. But meeting
Alan and his friend for sex had nothing to do with
Hayley and she knew that she was going way off
track. But the excitement, the danger . . . She was
discovering a deeper, darker side to her character. As
she fell into a deep sleep, she knew that she was
discovering sex.

'Oh, you're home,' her mother said as she appeared
in the doorway.

'Yes, I . . . I was just . . .' Anne stammered. 'What
time is it?'

'Getting on for six. How was college?'

'Er . . . fine.'

'Are you all right, Anne? Only you look terribly
guilty.'

'I'm fine, mum, honestly.'

'You were sleeping. I think you need a few early
nights.'

'Yes, you're right. Look, I have to go out. I'm
meeting . . . I have to meet Dave in the pub.'

'Well, don't be too late home.'

'I won't.'

Anne left the house before her mother could
suggest that she should eat something before going to
the pub. She walked briskly down the lane to the
woods. Her thoughts turning to Rick, she knew that
he'd be calling at her house to see Hayley and she
wanted to be there to entice him to the park. Unsure
what to do about Dave as she followed the narrow
path through the trees to the derelict house, she
reckoned that he'd already be waiting in the pub for
her. Opening the door and wandering into the house,
she realised how exciting her life had become. This

was far better than sitting alone in her room or listening to Dave and his friends talking about football, she mused as she wandered into the front room.

Wondering whether Alan's friend was hiding somewhere, Anne grinned as she heard a dull thud in the hall. Her stomach somersaulting, her womb contracting, her excitement turned to apprehension as she realised that she was alone in the house with a stranger. This was crazy, she thought fearfully as she heard someone moving about in the hall. She should at least have made sure that Alan was there before venturing into the house.

'God, you frightened me,' she gasped as Alan walked into the room.

'Sorry, I didn't mean to,' he breathed, looking her young body up and down.

'What were you doing out there? Were you with someone?'

'No, no, I was just . . .' He paused, his dark eyes sparkling lustfully. 'Would you mind if I brought a friend here?' he finally asked her.

'What do you mean, a friend? I thought this was our secret place.'

'Yes, of course it is. I just wondered whether you'd like to have some fun with another man.'

'I don't know,' she murmured. 'How old is he?'

'Age doesn't matter, Anne,' he said with a chuckle.

'No, but—'

'He likes young girls and he's just looking for some fun, the same way you are. You like sexy fun, don't you?'

'Yes, very much. OK, I'll think about it.'

'Good girl. Now, why don't you take your skirt and knickers off and show me your little pussy?'

'I have a surprise for you,' Anne said, giggling as she tugged her short skirt down. 'I hope you like it.'

'I'm sure I will.'

She stepped out of her skirt, pulled the front of her knickers down and displayed the hairless lips of her teenage pussy. His eyes widening, Alan knelt before her for a better look as she slipped her knickers off and stood with her feet wide apart. Anne knew that his friend was lurking somewhere, probably in the hall, feasting his eyes on her hairless crack, and she loved the notion of a voyeur. Her young womb contracting, her stomach fluttering, she leaned back and jutted her hips out to give the men a better view of her bald lips.

'You're wonderful,' Alan breathed, reaching out and running his fingertip up and down her wetting crack. 'God, you look so . . . so incredibly beautiful.'

'I'm glad you like it,' she said, keeping an eye on the door.

'What man wouldn't like it? Are you going to do a little piddle for me?'

'Well, I . . .'

'I want to watch it dribble from your tight crack and run down your legs, Anne.'

'All right,' she conceded, making sure that she was facing the door for her voyeur's benefit. 'I'll try.'

Squeezing her muscles, Anne kept an eye on the door as her golden liquid trickled from her bald sex-slit and ran down her inner thighs. She could see movement through the crack in the door, and she knew that the other man was there as her rain splashed onto the floor between her parted feet. Alan also turned and looked at the door, obviously wondering whether his friend could see the girl's arousing exhibition as he moved to one side. Knowing that she was being watched, Anne breathed deeply as her arousal soared and her golden trickle became a gush. Her legs wet, her feet splashed, she parted her swollen pussy lips and squirted her offering over the floor as the men watched.

Never had she felt so aroused. She realised that her young body was a powerful lure to older men. She really could have any man she wanted, she thought dreamily as her flow stemmed and globules of liquid dripped from the tight crack of her young pussy. Feeling alive with sex, Anne threw back her head and gasped as Alan licked the glistening lips of her pussy. Her clitoris swelling, her milky juices oozing between the wet lips of her pussy, she parted her feet as wide as she could.

'You taste wonderful and you look beautiful,' Alan breathed, lapping up her milky fluid. 'I must take some more photos of you next time we're here.'

'Yes, I'd like that,' Anne replied softly, realising that he would have shown his friend the photos he'd taken of her sucking his cock. 'Have you shown anyone?'

'No, no,' he lied, parting her sex lips and lapping at her hot vaginal entrance. 'They're for my eyes only. Now, how about showing us your tits?'

'Us? But there's only you here.'

'I meant . . . It's an expression, show us your tits.'

As Alan licked and slurped between her parted lips, Anne wondered whether she should invite the other man to join in. Her arousal soaring to frightening heights, she imagined two tongues licking between her thighs, one teasing her anus and the other probing her drenched vagina. The notions thrilled her and she pulled her T-shirt over her head and tossed it onto the old armchair. Her nipples rose in the relatively cool air of the old house and she ran her hands over the firm mounds of her teenage breasts as Alan sucked her solid clitoris into his hot mouth.

Pinching and pulling on her nipples, Anne again imagined the second man kneeling behind her and teasing the sensitive eye of her anus with the tip of his tongue. Although she was now desperate to feel two snaking tongues between her slender thighs, she still wasn't sure about inviting Alan's friend to join in. He was so old, she thought as her juices of lust streamed down her inner thighs in rivers of milk. But did that matter? she wondered in her rising sexual frenzy. A tongue was a tongue ... Even if the owner was another girl?

'You'd better come in,' she called.

'Who are you talking to?' Alan asked her, looking up and frowning.

'Your friend, the man in the hall,' Anne replied. 'He might as well join us.'

'How the hell did you know—'

'Come in,' she called again. 'I need two tongues, so come here.'

The man looked rather sheepish as he wandered into the room and stared into her wide eyes. Anne thought how old he looked as she scrutinised his lined face, and she reckoned that he hadn't seen a naked teenage girl in decades. Feeling a little sorry for him as he gazed longingly at the petite mounds of her young breasts, she realised that she was beginning to understand old men. They looked at teenage girls at every opportunity and imagined their firm bodies, they longed to touch and lick ... But the opportunity never arose. She had what they wanted, she concluded as the man reached out and toyed with the brown protrusion of her erect nipple. And they had experience.

The men said nothing as they ran their hands over her naked body and admired the beauty of her mounds and crevices. Although Anne was becoming

64

used to baring the most intimate parts of her young body, the thrill was always there. Men gazing at the swell of her pussy lips and her tight sex crack, her small breasts and elongated nipples, never failed to send quivers through her womb. The feel of their hands exploring her nakedness, the thought of their wide eyes feasting on her nudity, sent her arousal soaring.

As the old man knelt before her and examined the fleshy swell of her pussy lips, Alan moved behind her and parted the rounded cheeks of her naked buttocks. This was what she'd wanted, Anne thought dreamily as her pussy lips were stretched apart to expose her ripe clitoris and milk-dripping vaginal hole. The tongues teasing her, licking her anus and lapping at the pink funnel of flesh surrounding the wet entrance of her sex sheath . . . she breathed heavily and gazed up at the cracked ceiling. This was heaven, she thought as the men worked between her slender thighs. This was sheer sexual ecstasy.

Her clitoris swelled painfully as she wallowed in the complete and utter degradation of her young body and she let out a gasp of pleasure as she listened to the slurping sounds of crude sex. Hayley hadn't lived, Anne reflected, trying to imagine the girl with two men tonguing her sex holes. Apart from a couple of boyfriends and stealing Dave from her little sister, she hadn't lived and fucked and . . . As fingers slipped deep into her contracting vagina, Anne looked around her as if she'd just woken from a dream. She was supposed to be getting her own back on Hayley, she reminded herself, wondering what on earth she was doing with two old men as a finger drove deep into her tight rectal duct. This wasn't what she'd planned.

'I don't have much time,' she breathed as the finger massaged the hot inner flesh of her rectum. 'I have to get home and—'

'We've barely started,' Alan interrupted her, his face grinning as he looked up at her. 'Give Brian a chance to have some fun.'

'No, I have to go,' Anne murmured.

'Not yet, Anne,' Alan said sternly. 'It's not fair to take us this far and then bugger off.'

He was right, she knew as the men continued to lick the tight holes between her thighs. She should never have got herself into this predicament, she reflected. She'd been with two teenage lesbians, with Rick, with Dave, and now two old men were tonguing between her legs. She should have stuck to her original plan and stolen Hayley's boyfriends rather than become a common whore. But as the men rose to their feet and carried her naked body over to the old armchair she knew that it was too late to turn the clock back.

'I'll do her tight little pussy,' Brian said as Alan pushed Anne down over the back of the chair. 'It's been years since I've had my cock in a dirty slut's tight little cunny.'

'I'll take her mouth,' Alan breathed, moving to the front of the chair and lifting Anne's head up. 'Two cocks, Anne,' he said with a chuckle as he pressed his purple plum against her pursed lips. 'Who's a lucky little slut, then?'

Before she could answer, he'd pushed his swollen knob into her wet mouth. The other old man drove his erect penis deep into the contracting sheath of her teenage vagina and she breathed heavily through her nose, wondering what she'd become. From a relatively innocent eighteen-year-old girl she'd turned into a wanton whore, a filthy slut. She'd enjoyed the sex, the danger and excitement, but this wasn't what she'd planned. This was all Hayley's fault, she thought as the double-ended fucking rocked her young body.

'You're a little beauty,' Brian gasped, repeatedly ramming his bulbous knob against her creamy-wet cervix. 'You're a dream come true.'

'I told you that she was a horny little tart,' Alan said triumphantly. 'You love it, don't you, Anne?'

Moaning through her nose, Anne pondered on his words. *A horny little tart.* Never had she dreamed that she'd become a tart and allow two old men to push their solid cocks into her young body. But what worried her most was that she was enjoying the crude sex acts. Her pussy milk squelching with the crude double shafting as she sucked and mouthed on the swollen knob bloating her pretty mouth, she knew that she could never give up her exciting new way of life.

Brian announced that he was coming as Alan's knob swelled within her gobbling mouth, and Anne felt her clitoris swell and her young womb contract as her own orgasm welled from the depth of her pelvis. This was wrong, she thought, her naked body shaking uncontrollably as her vaginal duct flooded with the old man's creamy sperm. Her mouth overflowing with Alan's spunk, she tried to comprehend her uncharacteristic behaviour but then her orgasm erupted within the pulsating bulb of her clitoris.

'More, more,' she gasped as her young body rocked with the double-ended shafting.

'You'll have plenty more,' Brian breathed as he grabbed her shapely hips and repeatedly drove his throbbing knob deep into her spasming sex sheath.

'You'll be drowning in spunk before we've finished with you,' Alan added.

Her eyes rolling, her breathing fast and shallow, Anne cried out in the grip of her illicit ecstasy as she rode the crest of her incredible climax. The men gasped as they shafted each end of her young body and drained their swinging balls and Anne knew that, in their eyes, she was nothing more than a lump of female meat to be used and abused. But she was coming to accept her new role, and she wondered whether she could make some money from selling her services to sad and lonely old men.

Prostitution. The word battered her tormented mind as her orgasm peaked and rocked her young body to the core. The penises were hard, shafting her pretty mouth and her young vagina, and Anne thought again that she was nothing more than a lump of female meat to be fucked. She hadn't taken money for sex, she reflected. But this was as good as prostitution. A cocktail of her sex milk and sperm streaming down her inner thighs, her mouth overflowing as she did her best to swallow the male cream, she wondered how far she'd go in her debauchery. Would she take a cock into her young pussy as another forced its way deep into her tight rectum? she mused anxiously as her orgasm faded. How far would she go in the name of sexual degradation?

As the men slipped their deflating penises out of her trembling body, Anne hauled her trembling body upright and wiped her sperm-glossed lips with the back of her hand. The men chuckled and talked about her as if she wasn't there, and she knew that she had to put a stop to her debauchery. Grabbing her clothes and dressing, she ignored their crude comments about her sex holes. They wanted to meet her there the following evening, they wanted to use and abuse her for their own sexual satisfaction, but she declined.

'I can't,' she breathed softly as she finished dressing and headed for the door.

'The following day, then?' Alan persisted.

'I have to go,' Anne said, leaving the room and fleeing the house.

Walking home, she knew that she had to give up her whoredom and return to the innocent girl she once was. Hayley was right, she should be studying and thinking of the future rather than playing about with boys. Playing about with dirty old men? It was over, she thought happily as she reached her house. Dave, Rick, Alan, Brian . . . No more, she decided.

Four

Anne didn't go in to college on the last day of term. She was confused, her mind wandering, as she slipped out of her bed and stood naked in front of the full-length mirror. She looked so young without her pubic hair, she observed as she parted her feet wide and gazed at the fleshy swell of her outer lips. She should never have removed her pubes, she reflected. Recalling the old man's penis shafting her teenage vagina, she sighed. The images of her debauched acts with two old men were etched in her memory, never to be forgotten. She grabbed a pair of knickers from her drawer and concealed her hairless pussy with the white cotton material. But out of sight wasn't out of mind.

'I want to talk to you,' Hayley said, bursting into the room.

'I'm dressing,' Anne complained, folding her arms to cover her young breasts.

'I don't care what you're doing. Rick and I have split up.'

'Oh? Why's that?'

'You know damned well why. You're a slut, Anne.'

'Thanks very much.'

'I have a new boyfriend, and I want you to keep away from him.'

70

'That was quick,' Anne said, with a snigger. 'You dump one and then find another within a few hours, and you call *me* a slut?'

'As it happens, I've known Robin for a long time. We've been on and off for several months and I've been—'

'Screwing him behind Rick's back? Wow, you really *are* a slut.'

'Anne, I have *not* been screwing *anyone* behind Rick's back. I'm seeing Robin this evening. He's coming here and I want you to keep out of sight.'

'Why should I hide? I live here too, you know.'

'Do what you like – he wouldn't be interested in you.'

'How do you know that?'

'He's not interested in silly little teenage girls. I have to go to work now, so I'll talk to you later about what you said at breakfast yesterday.'

Anne grinned as Hayley left the room. She dressed in a short skirt and skimpy crop-top and made her plans. Not interested in teenage girls? she mused wickedly. 'We'll soon see about that,' she breathed as she went down to the kitchen for breakfast. With a bald pussy, full sex lips and a very tight vagina, she knew that she could have any man she wanted. And that included her sister's boyfriends.

The day dragged on and Anne spent most of her time in her room watching television. No more college for eight weeks, she mused as she checked her watch after dinner. She was going to have to find something exciting to do during the holiday, she thought. Seducing Robin would be a good place to start, she decided as the doorbell rang. Hayley was in her bedroom getting ready, giving Anne a chance to chat to Robin. Slipping into the lounge and sitting on the sofa as her mother answered the door, she felt her stomach somersault with excitement.

'This is Robin,' her mother said, leading the young man into the room. 'Robin, this is Anne.'

'Pleased to meet you,' Anne said, parting her thighs a little. 'Have a seat. I'm sure mum will make the proverbial cup of tea.'

'I could do with a cup of tea,' Robin breathed. 'Things have been rather hectic today and I haven't had time for anything.'

'You've known Hayley for some time, then?' Anne asked him as her mother left the room.

'Yes, for several months. We were just friends until . . . well, I've just come out of a long-term relationship.'

'Long-term relationships are a waste of time. You're very good-looking. I'm sure that you could have any girl you wanted.'

Robin chuckled, obviously feeling more at ease. 'Well, I don't know about that,' he said.

Anne parted her thighs further as he sat in the armchair opposite her. 'I mean it,' she said, with a giggle. 'I wish I'd met you before Hayley did.'

'Oh, well – I don't know what to say. Where *is* Hayley?'

'She's getting ready upstairs. Are you going anywhere nice?'

'We were going to the cinema to see that new film, but . . . Hayley has to be up early tomorrow morning.'

'*I* wanted to go and see that film,' Anne sighed. 'My boyfriend wouldn't take me so I dumped him.'

'Oh, I see.' Robin brushed his dark hair away from his forehead as he gazed at the swell of Anne's tight knickers. 'You're very pretty – I'm sure you could have anyone you wanted.'

'I know I can,' Anne replied impishly. 'So, where are you going this evening?'

72

'Nowhere exciting. We're only going to the pub at the end of the road.'

Anne looked at the door and then leaned forward on the sofa. 'When you've taken Hayley home,' she whispered, again glancing at the door, 'would you meet me in the pub?'

'Well, I don't know,' he muttered, his dark eyes frowning.

'It's just that I need to talk to you about Hayley.'

'Oh?'

'I can't say anything now. But if you can meet me . . .'

'All right. I will if it's important.'

'Yes, it is. I'll be in the pub with a friend, so if you come back later . . .'

'Yes, yes, of course.'

'What are you up to?' Hayley asked as she breezed into the room and glared at Anne.

'I'm going out,' Anne replied. 'See you, Robin. It was nice meeting you.'

'Yes, and you.'

Leaving the house, Anne headed for the pub with wicked thoughts swirling in her young mind. Robin was very good-looking, she reflected, wondering how big his cock was. She'd thought of telling him that he was one of several men that Hayley was seeing, but she didn't want to cause trouble before she'd had the chance to get Robin alone in the woods. They'd go for a walk, she decided as she reached the pub and ordered a drink. They'd walk through the park to the woods, chatting about Hayley, and then she'd drop her knickers and show him her hairless pussy and—

'Hi, sexy,' Alan whispered in her ear.

'Oh, hi,' she breathed, turning and facing him.

'Brian was over the moon after seeing you last night. He's really looking forward to the next time, and so am I.'

'You are naughty,' Anne whispered, grinning at him. 'But I can't meet you again.'

'Why not?'

'I'm not a slut, Alan. I mean, I love sex, but not with two men at the same time.'

'You loved it, you silly girl. Why try to deny it?'

'Because I don't want to be like that. I don't want to be a common whore.'

'That's a shame because Brian is very well off and he was talking about paying you.'

'Alan . . . I'm not a prostitute.'

'I know that. But you might as well take his money. You love the sex and you'll have some cash, too.'

'Well, I don't know,' Anne murmured, beginning to weaken. 'How much is he willing to pay – did he say?'

'Fifty quid a time. How does that sound?'

'God,' she breathed, her eyes wide as she gazed at him. 'That's a lot of money.'

'You're a lot of girl, Anne. In fact, you could earn yourself a small fortune. I know that you're not a prostitute and you shouldn't think of it that way. Still, Brian is loaded, you love sex, and he's willing to help you out financially. There's nothing wrong with that.'

'No, I suppose not,' she said. 'I'll talk to you later, OK?'

Sitting at her usual table, Anne thought about Alan's proposition. She was short of cash and fifty pounds a time would really help her out. But she knew that, whichever way she looked at it, it *was* prostitution. This was all Hayley's fault, she mused as she sipped her drink. Had Hayley not run after Dave and gone to the park with him . . . There again, she couldn't really blame her sister. Wondering about seducing

Robin, Anne knew that she should put a stop to her games. But she could see the old man if he was willing to pay her.

'Hi,' Rick said as he wandered over to her table. 'I suppose you've heard?'

'Yes, Hayley told me. So, what happened?'

'She guessed that I'd met someone and ... well, that was that. Look, I can't stay. Obviously I won't be going to your house again but I was just wondering whether we could still see each other?'

'Yes, of course,' Anne said, grabbing her handbag and writing down her mobile number. 'There you go. Give me a ring when you're free.'

'That's great. I haven't stopped thinking about you since we ... well, you know.'

'It was amazing, Rick. We'll do it again, give me a call.'

'You bet. OK, must dash – I'm working tonight.'

Anne grinned as he left the pub, but then she frowned. She'd vowed to stop playing her games. Now she'd given Rick her phone number and was planning to take money from Brian in return for obscene sex. She was going to have to decide which way she wanted her life to go. She could either find a decent boyfriend and remain faithful to him, or live a life of exciting and crude sex both with men and young girls.

Recalling her time in the derelict house with the teenage lesbians, Anne began to wish that she'd met them earlier that day. They would have been there in their lunch break, and they'd have enjoyed licking each other's wet pussies and ... Her clitoris stirred at the thought of lesbian sex and she realised again that she was going to have to decide which way she wanted her life to go. There was no harm in a girl licking another girl's pussy, she concluded. It wasn't really lesbianism, it was just sex. Besides, a girl knew how to do it properly. Fingering, licking and sucking . . . The notion excited her and she knew that she had to turn her thoughts to Robin, her latest victim.

Hayley finally wandered into the pub with Robin and managed to flash a smile at Anne, but it was obvious that she didn't want to join her little sister. Anne wasn't bothered. She was looking forward to meeting Robin later and luring him into the woods for sex. Her clitoris swelling at the prospect of crude sex, her tight knickers wetting, she wondered whether he'd like her hairless pussy. Would he lick her tight hole? Would he suck her ripe clitoris into his hot mouth? Robin glanced at her several times, flashing her a smile, and she reckoned that he too was looking forward to their clandestine meeting. But he'd have no idea of her plans of seduction.

Her stomach somersaulted with excitement and she downed several more drinks before Robin finally walked Hayley home. He should only be ten minutes or so, Anne thought as she left the pub. It was better to wait outside, she decided. She didn't want to be seen in the pub with him so she'd wait for him and then suggest that they walk to the park to have a chat. Wondering where Dave was, she moved away from the pub and sat on a low wall. The last thing she needed was Dave turning up and questioning her.

'I thought we were going to meet in the pub?' Robin said as he approached.

'It's a lovely evening,' Anne said softly, slipping off the wall and smiling at him. 'How about walking in the park?'

'OK, if you prefer it.'

'We can't talk in the pub – there are too many people there. Did Hayley say anything about me?'

'She told me to keep away from you,' Robin replied as they walked towards the park. 'I think she's jealous of you.'

'That's good. It was always the other way round – I used to be jealous of her.'

'Don't you two get on?'

'Yes, it's just that . . . oh, I don't know. I suppose we've never got on. We're totally different. She thinks that I should be studying rather than having fun.' Reaching the park, Anne walked with Robin towards the trees. 'Have you ever been into the woods?' she asked him. 'There are some lovely flowers there.'

'No, I haven't,' he said, following her along a narrow path.

As they reached the clearing amongst the bushes, Anne recalled taking Rick there. This was an ideal place to seduce Hayley's boyfriends, she thought as she sat on the grass with her chin resting on her knees. Robin sat opposite her and eyed the bulge of her tight knickers between her slender thighs. Would he succumb to her feminine charms? Could he resist a dirty little teenage slut?

'So, what did you want to talk about?' he asked her. 'Not wild flowers, I'm sure.'

'No, no, not flowers. Have you had sex with Hayley?' Anne asked unashamedly.

'Er . . . well, no, I haven't. That's an odd question. Why do you ask?'

'She's a funny girl and . . . She doesn't like sex. I just wanted to let you know that she's a strange girl.'

'I've known her for some time and she seems normal to me.'

'She will come across as normal, until you make a move. If I were you, I wouldn't even attempt anything sexual with her.'

'Oh, well ... Thanks for the tip. But I don't see how we can have a proper relationship without sex.'

'No one can have a proper relationship with Hayley. She's had several boyfriends and they've all dumped her. It's a shame because she's a lovely girl. As I said, we're totally different. I love sex, I can't get enough of it.'

Robin grinned at her and focused again on her tight knickers bulging between her thighs. Was he tempted? Anne wondered. Or hadn't she made it plain enough that she was offering him her young body? Leaning back on her hands, she stretched her legs out and parted her feet to give him a better look at the snug material swelling to contain her full sex lips. She couldn't have made it more obvious that she wanted sex with him, she thought as Robin checked his watch. He seemed fidgety, moving about on the grass as if he was about to leave, and she wondered whether she'd fail in her quest to seduce him.

'I'd better be going,' he finally said.

'Already?' Anne murmured, frowning at him.

'Anne, I know what you're trying to do. The thing is, I'm in love with Hayley and—'

'I'm not trying to do anything,' she cut in.

'Look, you're a very attractive girl but Hayley is the one for me.'

'I'll be honest with you, Robin,' Anne sighed. 'You're a very nice man and you deserve to know the truth.'

'Oh?'

'Hayley has several men on the go. I'm afraid that you're only one of many.'

'What?' he gasped. 'But I thought—'

'She's seeing some bloke called Rick. Before him there was Ian and then ... This story about her having to get up early tomorrow ... she's with Rick now, that's why she wanted to go home early.'

Robin looked genuinely saddened by Anne's revelation, and she felt a bit guilty. But her guilt was outweighed by her soaring arousal as she parted her legs further and displayed the triangular patch of thin material running between the smooth flesh of her slender thighs. As Robin gazed at her, she vowed to have his cock shafting her teenage pussy before he left, and she was prepared to do anything to achieve her goal. Lifting her buttocks clear of the ground, she slipped her knickers off and lay back on the grass with her legs parted as wide as they'd go.

'Anne,' he breathed, staring at the bald lips of her young pussy, her opening sex crack. 'What the hell are you trying to do to me?'

'I'm trying to seduce you,' she replied unashamedly. 'You might be in love with Hayley, but she won't have sex with you. Why don't you see her – when she's not seeing her other men – but come to me for sex?'

'Are you for real?' Robin asked, with a chuckle. 'You mean that you wouldn't mind me going out with your sister, and then just using you for sex?'

'I wouldn't mind at all. As I said, she's seeing other men so . . . Don't you like my hairless little pussy?'

'God, yes, I love it.'

'Come and take it, then. It's all yours, Robin.'

Settling between her legs, Robin licked Anne's opening sex crack as she looked up at the trees high above her. Another successful conquest, she thought dreamily as he parted her smooth outer lips and lapped at her hot vaginal hole. It was a shame that she'd had to lie about her sister not liking sex and going out with other men, but life wasn't always fair. Besides, she was still sure that Hayley had been screwing Dave so what the hell?

'You're a horny little slut and I'm going to fuck

you senseless,' Robin breathed, much to Anne's surprise.

'Wow, you are a man after all,' she said, giggling as he thrust two fingers deep into the creamy-wet heat of her contracting vagina. 'I thought that you were a prude, like my big sister.'

'If she's a prude, how come she's seeing other men?'

'As I said, she's a strange girl. She'll go out with you, but see other men for sex. She's always done that. She'll hang onto one man, and then fuck others behind his back. You're better off without her.'

'I'd love to fuck you in your house while she's in the next room.'

'I'm sure that I can arrange that. When you're next round and she's getting ready in her room, you can come up to my room and fuck me.'

'I'd love that, like I said. When she kisses me she'll taste your cunt juice on my lips.'

'God, and there I was thinking that you were a prude. Why don't you fuck me now and show me what you can really do to a teenage slut?'

Slipping his wet fingers out of Anne's hot vagina, Robin took his shoes and trousers off and displayed his erect penis to her wide eyes. Gasping as she gazed at the amazing length and sheer girth of his huge member, Anne reckoned that he'd split her open. She held her breath as his knob slipped between the wet petals of her inner lips and he drove his cock slowly into her trembling body. The stretching sensation drove her wild – she dug her fingernails into the soft grass and arched her back as he looked down at her pretty face and smiled.

'Big enough for you?' he asked her proudly.

'God, yes,' she breathed, her eyes rolling. 'It's *too* bloody big. Hayley doesn't know what she's missing.'

'Now that I have you, she never will know what she's missing.'

'Leave her to fuck her other men, Robin. You stay with me and I'll keep you happy.'

Withdrawing for an instant, he rammed his weapon back deep into Anne's spasming vaginal sheath. His swinging balls battering her naked buttocks as he found his shafting rhythm, his bulbous knob pummelling her creamy-wet cervix, Robin knew that she was in her sexual heaven as he gazed into her brown eyes. He was good, Anne thought, her young body gliding across the grass with each penile thrust. Her inner lips rolling back and forth along his veined shaft, her swollen clitoris massaged by the sheer girth of his magnificent cock, she realised that he certainly knew how to please a girl.

Listening to the squelching of her vaginal juices, Anne felt the birth of her orgasm stir within the depths of her contracting womb as Robin stepped up his shafting rhythm. Her lower stomach rising and falling with every thrust of his solid cock, her eyes rolling as she lost herself in her sexual frenzy, she cried out as her orgasm erupted. She could feel Robin's creamy spunk jetting from his throbbing knob and lubricating their illicit coupling. His cream overflowed from her spasming vagina, splattering the smooth flesh of her inner thighs, and she cried out again as her orgasm peaked and rocked her young body to the core.

This was the best sex she'd had so far, Anne thought dreamily as Robin threw his head back and shafted her tight vagina with a vengeance. Alan had been good and Rick was fantastic, but Robin was incredible. His spunk ran down between her firm buttocks, lubricating her tight anus, and she imagined his huge cock fucking her tight rectum. Her arousal soared to frightening heights as she pictured the brown ring of her anus stretched tautly around the base of his solid penis and she knew that she'd become a fully-fledged slut. Morals, self-respect, dignity . . . all had been stripped away and replaced by crude sexual acts – and immense gratification.

She'd been taught right from wrong, Anne reflected as her orgasm began to fade and Robin slowed his shafting rhythm. She'd been taught how to be lady-like and refined but her new-found release, her sluttish behaviour, brought her more pleasure from her teenage body than she'd dreamed possible. Not only had the excitement of screwing around and stealing her sister's boyfriends become an obsession, but it had grown into an addiction. She was hooked on obscene sexual acts and ruining her sister's relationships, and she knew that she could never quell her craving for sexual gratification.

'You were fantastic,' Robin breathed as he withdrew his deflating penis and settled by her side on the grass. 'The best fuck I've ever had.'

'Do you say that to all the girls?' Anne said, with a giggle.

'Yes, but I really mean it this time. So, how did I do? Will you be coming back for more?'

'Oh, yes, definitely. That was the best fuck I've ever had.'

'Do you say that to all the boys?' he quipped.

'Of course I do.'

'How many cocks have you had?'

'I don't know – I've lost count. How come you're going out with Hayley?'

'What do you mean?'

'Well, she's not exactly a nymphomaniac. Judging by the way you fuck, I'd have thought that you'd be screwing a right little slut.'

'I *am* screwing a right little slut,' Robin said, chuckling as he slipped his fingertip into her spermed sex crack and massaged her swelling clitoris. 'And I hope to be screwing her every day. What I don't understand is . . . If Hayley doesn't like sex, why does she cheat on me by seeing other men? I mean, she's either a prude or she's not.'

'I've told you, Robin. She's a funny girl. I don't think she knows *what* she wants. Would you like Hayley to catch us fucking?'

'I don't know,' he sighed. 'I love her but . . .'

'How can you say that you love her when you're fucking her little sister behind her back?'

'Maybe I don't love her – I don't know. She's good company and we've had some fun together. But the things you've told me about her have made me think twice about seeing her again. I wouldn't want to hurt her. I don't think it would be fair to have her catch us fucking.'

'I suppose you're right,' Anne murmured, leaping to her feet. 'I'd better be going before it gets dark and the monsters come and get me.'

'Monsters?' Robin echoed, frowning at her as she pulled her wet knickers up her long legs.

'Do you want to come to the pub for a drink?'

'No, no, I'd better get home.'

As she left the woods with Robin, Anne wondered again where her life was taking her. She was thinking about meeting Alan in the pub, maybe fucking him before going home, but she wasn't sure. The notion excited her, but it also worried her. She couldn't keep offering her teenage body to men, she mused as Robin walked beside her and talked about meeting her the following evening for sex. Her stomach somersaulted as she imagined meeting Alan and his friend in the derelict house and then taking Robin to the woods. She stopped outside the pub and gazed at him.

'Are you sure that you don't want to have a drink with me?' she asked him.

'No, I can't,' he sighed. 'I have stuff to sort out.'

'I'll be at home tomorrow evening,' Anne said. 'When you come round to see Hayley, we'll have a quick fuck.'

'Great,' Robin said eagerly. 'With any luck, she'll be in her room. Look, I really must go.'

'Dirty boy,' Anne breathed. 'OK, I'll see you tomorrow and we'll fuck in my house.'

'Be good,' Robin called, chuckling as he walked away.

Anne wandered into the pub and gazed at the sea of faces as she bought a large vodka and tonic. The pub was busy, for a change, but her table was free. As she sat down she couldn't see Alan or Dave, and she began to wish that she'd gone straight home. Wondering when Rick would phone her, she realised that she was going to have to make a list of the men she was seeing and work out a timetable. Knocking back her drink, thinking again what a slut she was, she was about to leave when Alan's friend Brian walked towards her and grinned.

'Hi,' he said, sitting opposite her. 'Alan said that you use this pub.'

'Shouldn't you be tucked up in your bed, Brian?' she asked him. 'It's getting late.'

'I'd like to be tucked up in bed with *you*,' he quipped.

Anne cocked her head to one side and grinned. 'Are you married?'

'Yes, I am. But my sex life finished years ago. My wife and I have separate beds – it was her idea.'

'I need some excitement, Brian. I'm bored.'

'I thought that your life was exciting enough?'

'It is but . . . I love danger, the thrill and danger of getting caught with my knickers down.'

'I'll pull your knickers down for you,' Brian said, winking at her.

'Let's play a game,' Anne breathed huskily. 'I'll call at your house, pretending to be selling something, and you invite me in.'

'What sort of game is that?'

'Will your wife be in bed?'

'No, not for a long time yet. What are you getting at?'

'You invite me in, and we'll have sex.'

'With my wife watching us? No, I don't think so.'

'No, no. You show me round the house and—'

'We've been thinking about buying new bedroom furniture,' he cut in, obviously up for the game. 'I could say that you've come to measure up and give us a quote.'

'OK, that sounds good.'

'How about tomorrow evening, then?'

'Tonight, Brian,' Anne replied. 'We'll go there now.'

'No, we can't do it tonight.'

'Why not?'

'Because my wife's brother is down from Scotland – he's staying with us.'

'Even better,' she said, leaving the table. 'Come on, let's do it.'

Shaking his head as he followed her out of the pub, Brian repeatedly told her that this wasn't a good idea. But Anne wasn't listening. She was imagining giving the old man a blow job in the marital bedroom while his wife was downstairs chatting with her brother. With any luck, the woman would climb the stairs and catch her husband with his cock embedded deep inside Anne's warm, wet mouth and there'd be a huge row.

When they reached the house, Anne gave Brian his instructions and waited outside as he let himself in and closed the front door. She didn't really look like a salesperson or company representative, she thought, gazing at her short skirt. But if she started talking about bedroom furniture and Brian played his part properly, she'd get away with it. Did she really want to wreck his marriage? she wondered. It would be fun if his wife caught him fucking a teenage girl, but . . . Realising the extent of her wickedness, she wondered how far she'd go in her quest for danger and excitement.

Pondering on the scam, Anne wondered whether she should try it with Alan and his wife. Or her next-door neighbour, she mused in her rising wickedness. He was in his sixties and he'd often gazed longingly at Anne over the garden fence when she'd been sunbathing in her bikini. The danger and excitement sending her arousal sky-high, she decided that she'd given Brian long enough. She walked up the path to the front door and rang the bell.

'Can I help you?' a woman asked, opening the door.

'Bedroom furniture,' Anne said. 'Your husband arranged—'

'Oh dear, he obviously forgot to tell me,' she cut in. 'Please come in.'

'Men are all the same,' Anne said, chuckling as she stepped into the hall. 'My husband forgets everything.'

'Oh, the bedroom furniture,' Brian breathed as he joined his wife. 'Sorry, dear, I forgot all about it.'

'It won't take me long to measure up,' Anne said. 'And then I'll get the quote in the post to you.'

Smiling at Anne, Brian winked. 'Er . . . I'll show you upstairs.'

Following him, Anne felt her stomach somersault as she imagined having sex with the old man in the marital bedroom. Luckily, his wife had gone into the lounge, giving her the opportunity to play her wicked game. She loved playing games, and this was the most dangerous one yet. Her clitoris swelled as she followed Brian into the bedroom and she lifted her short skirt and pulled her knickers down to her knees. He gazed at her bald sex folds and grinned as she parted her succulent lips and exposed the inner wings of her teenage pussy. Wasting no time, Brian pushed the door closed and unzipped his trousers.

'You're a naughty little slut,' he breathed softly. 'Bend over the end of the bed and I'll give you the fucking of your young life.'

'And you're a dirty old man,' Anne replied, leaning over the bed and keeping her skirt up.

Brian's swollen knob slid between the hairless lips of her wet pussy and his rock-hard shaft entered her. He grabbed her shapely hips and drove his organ fully home. Anne gasped in the grip of her arousal and excitement as he began his fucking motions. Imagining his wife walking into the bedroom and witnessing his crude act, she reached behind her slender body and parted the rounded cheeks of her bottom wide. Brian was gazing at her tight anal hole, she knew as his swinging balls battered the hairless mound of her mons. Would he fuck her there? she wondered, picturing his huge knob slipping past her anal ring and driving deep into the dank heat of her bowels. Would he pump his spunk deep into the humid depths of her rectum?

'You really are a filthy slut,' Brian gasped as the squelching sound when his rigid prick plunged into

Anne's vaginal juices mixed with Robin's sperm resounded around the room. 'God, you're so wet.'

'You *make* me wet,' Anne breathed. 'I'll bet you never thought that you'd be fucking a teenage girl in your bedroom.'

'I never thought that I'd be fucking anyone again in my life, let alone a horny little beauty like you.'

'I'll have to come round and measure up for bedroom furniture again. Of course, you'll have to make it worth my while.'

'I wondered when you'd ask for money. How much do you want?'

'What am I worth?'

'Does fifty per fuck suit you?'

'Perfectly. Now, give me your spunk.'

Stifling her gasps of pleasure as her solid clitoris exploded in orgasm, Anne was beyond caring about right and wrong. If the old man wanted to pay her to fuck her and take her to massive orgasms, that was fine by her. The idea of prostituting herself didn't bother her any more. Why shouldn't she earn some cash from her young body? she thought as her orgasm peaked and she cried out in the grip of illicit ecstasy. Whimpering softly, she threw her head back and rocked her hips to meet Brian's penile thrusts. If only his wife would walk in, she imagined wickedly, picturing the woman screaming before she left the house in disgust.

Finally coming down from her powerful orgasm, Anne lay face down on the bed as Brian slipped his cock out of her newly spermed vagina and zipped his trousers. Breathing heavily in the aftermath of her wanton debauchery, she wondered what the hell she'd become as he tossed fifty pounds onto the bed. She was a prostitute, she thought anxiously as she felt his sperm oozing from her inflamed vaginal hole. Robin had flooded her young pussy with spunk, Brian had used her to satisfy his base desires . . . Rick, Dave . . . Who was next in line?

"You'd better get out of here,' Brian said, helping her up. 'I don't want my wife coming up here and finding you sprawled across her bed with my spunk pouring out of your dirty little cunt.'

'OK,' Anne murmured softly, pulling her knickers up and adjusting her skirt.

'Come on, I'll see you out.'

Clutching the cash as she followed Brian down the stairs, Anne pondered on his crude words: *spunk pouring out of your dirty little cunt.* She'd wanted to put an end to her obscene games, but the danger and exhilaration were too much to resist. How many more men would give her money in return for crude sex, she wondered as she said goodbye to Brian and left the house. Even if she did change her ways, she was a fully fledged prostitute now, and nothing would change that. She couldn't turn the clock back.

It was dark but, as Anne neared her house, she could make out Hayley talking to Dave by the front gate. What was she up to? she wondered, creeping along behind a row of parked cars so as not to be seen. Moving closer, Anne heard Hayley asking Dave about Alan. She didn't even know Alan, Anne mused, wondering what the hell was going on.

'He's usually in the pub,' Dave said. 'But he's never mentioned you.'

'As I said, I'm not happy with Robin. I'm sure that he'd arranged to meet someone after he'd walked me home this evening, so I might take Alan up on his offer and go out for a drink with him.'

'He's an old man,' Dave said, chuckling. 'He's old enough to be your grandfather.'

'I must admit that when he came up to me in the street and said that he was a friend of Anne's I thought he was rather old. But older men are more caring. He reckoned that Anne had told him about me. God knows what's she'd said to him but he seemed very keen to get to know me.'

'So are you going to see him?'

'He said that he'd be in the pub tomorrow evening so I might as well go along. How are you getting on with Anne? Is she still suspicious about us?'

'I haven't seen her,' Dave sighed. 'I don't know what she's up to. Anyway, I'd better be going.'

'OK – I'll see you soon.'

Watching as Hayley kissed Dave's cheek, Anne felt her stomach churning. *Is she still suspicious about us?* Her sister's words battering her young mind, she was certain now that the girl had been screwing Dave all along. How could she? she wondered angrily as Dave walked off and Hayley went into the house. And what the hell was Alan up to? He was trying to get into Hayley's knickers, Anne mused as she walked up the path and opened the front door. She crept up the stairs, went into her room and closed the door.

This was war, she thought, tossing the fifty pounds she'd earned onto the bedside table. Flopping onto her bed and gazing up at the ceiling, she made her plans. She'd tell Alan that Hayley was a slut who'd pull her knickers down for any man. If Alan thought that Hayley was into crude sex and then lured her to the derelict house and suggested that she piss on his face . . . Grinning, Anne decided to spy on Hayley and Alan in the derelict house. She could hardly wait to see her big sister's face when Alan dropped his trousers and displayed his erect cock.

Slipping her hand down the front of her spunk-drenched knickers, Anne massaged the solid nub of

90

her sensitive clitoris. She needed sex and orgasms all the time, she thought as her eyes rolled and she arched her back. A blend of girl-juice and sperm oozed from her inflamed vaginal hole as she slipped her free hand beneath her thighs and thrust two fingers deep into her yearning vagina. Fingering her sex duct, massaging her solid clitoris, she gasped and writhed on her bed as she imagined several cocks shafting her tight holes and pumping spunk into her young body.

Her orgasm stirring within the depths of her quivering pelvis, Anne pulled the wet crotch of her knickers to one side and slipped a finger deep into her bottom-hole. The sensations drove her wild as she massaged the hot flesh deep inside her sex-inflamed holes. She cried out as her orgasm finally erupted.

'My cunt,' she breathed, trying to stifle her gasps. 'God, my beautiful cunt.' Forcing another finger deep into her rectal duct, Anne moaned through her nose as her orgasm peaked and rocked her young body to the core. Again and again, waves of pure sexual bliss crashed through her quivering flesh and she knew that she was hooked on crude sex. She'd take Robin up to her room and suck his cock while Hayley was in the next room getting ready to go out with him, she thought.

She'd steal all her sister's boyfriends, fuck them and use them to satisfy her lust for obscene sexual acts. Her orgasm peaked again as she managed to drive a third finger deep into her bloated anal duct, taking her pleasure to hitherto unknown heights. Her mind brimming with images of hard cocks fucking her mouth, her rectum and vagina, she finally began to drift down from her amazing climax and lay convulsing on her bed.

'God,' Anne breathed as her fingers left her sex ducts. 'I've never come so much in all my life.' Her eyes closing as she curled up into a ball, she thought about screwing Robin in her bedroom. She'd also fuck Alan in his house while his wife was downstairs and then she'd meet Rick in the woods and then she'd screw Brian again and . . . Life was good, she mused as she drifted into a deep sleep.

Five

Wearing a very short skirt and a skimpy crop-top, Anne arrived at the pub at six o'clock. Looking around, she noticed Dave chatting with a friend and wondered what time Hayley was due to arrive. She had to talk to Alan before Hayley turned up, she reckoned, formulating her plan. If he asked Hayley to go for a walk and they ended up at the derelict house . . .

'Hello, stranger,' Dave said, joining Anne as she sat at a table. 'Where did you get to last night?'

'I went out,' she replied coldly.

'I thought you were going to meet me.'

'Seeing as you were with Hayley, I didn't bother.'

'I *wasn't* with Hayley,' he replied, frowning at her. 'I bumped into her on my way home, but I—'

'Don't keep lying, Dave,' Anne cut in. 'I know that you two have been fucking behind my back.'

'You've got it all wrong, Anne. Hayley and I—'

'I'm not interested in the sordid details. Anyway, I don't mind if you want to fuck her. By the way, you can tell her that I'm not suspicious any more.'

'What did she say to you?'

'It's what she said to *you* that matters. She asked you whether I was suspicious about you two.'

'No, she didn't mean . . . How *do* you know what she said?'

'I know everything, Dave. So, as I said, don't keep lying to me.'

'This is ridiculous,' he sighed. 'All I did was chat to Hayley on my way home last night. What is this thing that you have about her and me?'

'I don't have a thing any more. As I said, you can fuck her as much as you like.'

'That's the end of us, then?'

'Yes, that's the end of us.'

'OK, if that's what you want. But can we still be friends?'

'Yes, of course. I'll still see you in here and . . . oh, there's Alan. I need to talk to him about something.'

'Anne, are you going out with him?' Dave asked, watching Alan head for the bar.

'Going out with Alan? No, no, I'm not. Look, I'll see you later. I want Alan to sit here so—'

'OK, I know when I'm not wanted,' Dave sighed, leaving his seat and wandering back to his friend.

Anne took a deep breath as Alan turned and smiled at her. Wondering again what time Hayley would turn up, she sipped her drink as Alan walked over to her table and sat opposite her. Maybe Hayley would have a change of mind, she thought as Alan joked about her visit to Brian's house and asked her whether she was enjoying her job as a salesperson. Brian had obviously blabbed his mouth off, she reflected. There again, what old man wouldn't tell his friends if he'd fucked a teenage girl?

'You're seeing my sister tonight, then?' Anne asked, grinning at him.

'Oh, er . . . how do you know about that?' Alan asked her sheepishly.

'I know everything, Alan. So where did you meet her?'

'In here. I've bumped into her a couple of times

and . . . well, I saw her in the street and asked her out for a drink.'

'She's a right little slut so you should be well in there.'

'You told me that she was—'

'I lied. The truth is that Hayley will drop her knickers for any man. You should take her for a walk later. Take her to the derelict house, she'd like that.'

'Really? Well, I was going to get to know her before trying anything but . . . Thanks, Anne, you're an angel.'

'She's into water sports, so you'll get on well with her. Although she does like to play hard to get.'

'Right, I understand. So you reckon that I should take her to the house?'

'Just suggest going for a walk, end up at the house and make out that you want to explore and . . . Once she's inside, drop your trousers and she'll be begging for it.'

'But . . . the thing is . . . will you still meet me at the house? I mean, if you know that I'm screwing your sister . . .'

'Of course I will. I wouldn't want to miss out on your lovely cock. I'll leave you to it. If she walks in and sees me chatting to you she might get the wrong idea.'

'OK, thanks. She's due here about now so I'll go back to the bar.'

'I'll sit round the corner so she doesn't see me. Good luck.'

'I'll let you know how I get on.'

Finding a table around the corner as Alan stood at the bar, Anne knew that Hayley would have a fit if he dropped his trousers and showed her his cock. But her sister deserved to be shocked, she reflected, imagining Alan suggesting that she should piss on his face. Leaving her seat every now and then and peering around the corner, she was beginning to think that Hayley wasn't going to turn up. It was a shame, she thought, again imagining her sister's face when Alan pulled his huge cock out and suggested that she should suck it. This was going to be fun, she was sure. But where was Hayley?

Hayley finally wandered into the pub and joined Alan at the bar. Anne felt alive with excitement. She spied on the unlikely couple, her stomach somersaulting as they chatted and appeared to be getting on well together. But would Hayley agree to go for a walk with Alan? If they did go to the house and Alan dropped his trousers, Hayley was bound to run off. That wouldn't be a problem, Anne thought. If Hayley didn't want Alan's cock, then Anne would go into the house and enjoy it.

Anne downed two more drinks and finally breathed a sigh of relief as Alan and her sister left the pub. Keeping her distance behind them she was sure that they were going to the house as she followed them to the woods. Hayley was wearing a knee-length skirt which would make it easy for Alan to slip his hand between her thighs. The girl would scream and have a fit, Anne thought, giggling softly as she crept through the woods.

'I used to come here when I was a kid,' Hayley said as they approached the house. 'I didn't realise that the place was still standing.'

'Let's take a look inside,' Alan suggested, walking through the front door.

Anne hid in the bushes beneath the front-room window and listened as she heard Alan talking to Hayley. They were in the front room, and Hayley was taking an interest in the house. But the real question was, would she take an interest in Alan's cock? Anne raised her head and peered through the broken window. Watching with bated breath, mentally urging Alan to drop his trousers, she wished that she'd brought her camera with her. To have a photo of Hayley gazing at an old man's erect penis would be amazing, she thought in her wickedness.

'I wonder who lived here?' Hayley wondered, looking around the room. 'It's obviously been empty for decades, but someone must have lived here.'

'It was probably a gamekeeper's cottage,' Alan replied. 'Presumably someone still owns it.'

'I think the woods belong to the Somerset Estate.'

'It's an ideal place for lovers,' Alan said, laughing as he watched Hayley for her reaction. 'It's a great place for screwing.'

'You're right,' Hayley said, much to Anne's surprise. 'Thanks for bringing me here, Alan. Most people I go out with take me to pubs, and I find that so boring.'

'You like a little excitement?'

'Yes, yes, I do. My job is very demanding and I never seem to have any fun. I don't know what it is about the boyfriends I've had but they all seem to be so boring. I'm seeing a chap called Robin, and he's as boring as hell.'

'I could give you some excitement,' Alan said, again watching for her reaction. 'I may be an old man but—'

'What sort of excitement?' Hayley cut in.

'I'll show you.'

Anne reckoned that Hayley was about to scream and flee the house as Alan unzipped his trousers and hauled out his erect cock. Pressing her nose to the window, she frowned as Hayley knelt in front of him and took his solid shaft in her hand. What the hell had come over her sister? Anne wondered as she retracted his fleshy foreskin and gazed longingly at his swollen knob. Taking his purple globe into her mouth, she tugged his trousers down and cupped his full balls in her hand.

Sucking and gobbling on Alan's cock, Hayley was obviously enjoying herself. But Anne was stunned. She couldn't believe that this was her prudish sister sucking an old man's cock. For someone who'd never experienced an orgasm, she seemed to be well into sex. The thought occurred to Anne that Alan might think Hayley was better than her. The way she was gobbling and slurping on his bulbous knob, she was doing a good job. Did she give a better blow job than Anne?

This was a sight that Anne had never thought she'd see. Hayley was moving her head back and forth, repeatedly taking Alan's purple plum to the back of her throat and kneading his heavy balls with her free hand. It was no wonder that Dave had gone to the park with Hayley, Anne reflected angrily. This also explained why Dave had never made a sexual advance towards Anne. All along he'd had Hayley's mouth to fuck, her tight pussy to sink his cock into. Hayley was a bitch, Anne thought, determined more than ever to retaliate.

Fuming as Alan announced that he was coming, Anne wished again that she'd brought her camera with her. Thinking about blackmailing her sister, taking photographs and leaving them around the house for her parents to see, she stared wide-eyed as Hayley slipped Alan's huge knob out of her mouth and allowed his spunk to splatter her face. His male milk rained over her nose and ran down her cheeks as she opened her mouth and sucked again on his orgasming knob.

Anne gazed at the incredible sight as Alan watched Hayley sucking on his solid cock and swallowing his fresh spunk, and she began to wonder whether her big sister had lured not only Dave but her previous boyfriends into the woods for crude sex. It was odd to think that Rick had said that Hayley was no good, she reflected. And why hadn't Robin made a move towards the girl? Hayley was obviously a slut, so why hadn't she pulled Robin's trousers down at the first opportunity?

'I love a good facial,' Hayley said, slipping Alan's cock out of her mouth as his sperm flow finally stemmed.

'Obviously,' Alan gasped. 'That was the best blow job I've ever known.'

'People think that I'm a prude,' she said, with a giggle. 'God knows why.'

'So what are you into? Sexually, I mean.'

'Anything and everything.'

Taking her skirt off, Hayley pulled her knickers down and exposed her neatly trimmed blonde pubes to Alan's lecherous gaze. She had a good figure, Anne thought enviously as her sister slipped her top off and unhooked her bra. Standing naked in front of Alan, Hayley proudly displayed her ample breasts, her elongated nipples, and Anne realised that her wicked plan had backfired on her. Hayley was blonde, extremely attractive with a lovely body and large breasts . . . Nothing had changed, Anne mused dolefully. Hayley was better than her in every way, and nothing would ever change that.

'You're perfect,' Alan breathed as he looked Hayley up and down, heightening Anne's anger. 'I can honestly say that you're the most beautiful girl I've ever laid eyes on.'

'Does that include my sister?' Hayley asked him as he reached out and squeezed the full mounds of her firm breasts.

'It includes everyone. Your sister is good company in the pub, she enjoys a laugh, but you really do outshine her.'

'You're just saying that,' Hayley returned, giggling as he knelt before her and planted a kiss on the swollen lips of her pussy.

'No, no. I mean it, Hayley.'

'Well, you'd better prove it and give me a good licking. I could do with a massive orgasm.'

Anne realised just how wrong she'd been about her sister as Alan repeatedly ran his tongue up and down Hayley's sex crack. *I could do with a massive orgasm.* Rick too had been wrong about the girl, she reflected. Why had he thought that Hayley had never experienced an orgasm? After checking her watch, Anne left her hide and dashed through the woods. She had plenty of time to get her camera, she knew as she headed home. Alan and Hayley were in no rush and would no doubt spend a long time enjoying crude sex in the derelict house.

Avoiding her mother as she crept up the stairs and grabbed her camera from her room, Anne slipped out of the house unseen and sprinted back to the woods. Hayley would be fucking Brian next, she thought angrily as she neared the derelict house. Anne's idea had been to steal Hayley's boyfriends, not share her men with the girl. Settling in the bushes, Anne switched her camera on and peered through the broken window.

Hayley was bent over the back of the old armchair, yelping like a dog as Alan repeatedly spanked the rounded cheeks of her firm bottom. Anne took several photographs and decided to print a few copies and pass them around the pub. That'll teach the bitch to steal my boyfriends, she thought in her wickedness. Realising that half the men in the pub would be chasing after the girl once they'd seen the photos, Anne bit her lip. Then she grinned. Hayley's boss might be interested to discover the shocking truth, she mused. Hayley was doing so well in her job but if her boss saw the photos ... There again, she'd probably landed the top job because she'd dropped her knickers.

'Do my arse,' Hayley cried as Alan drove his erect penis deep into her hot pussy. 'I haven't had a huge cock up my bum for weeks.'

'Anything you say,' Alan breathed, slipping his solid shaft out of the girl's dripping vaginal sheath and stabbing at her tight anus with his bulbous knob. 'Here it comes,' he said, chuckling.

'God, yes,' Hayley breathed, her body visibly shaking as he drove the entire length of his rock-hard member deep into her tight rectal duct.

Anne had always thought that Hayley was refined and ladylike and, again, she couldn't believe that this was her sister with an old man's cock embedded deep in her tight arse. As she took more photographs, Anne thought it was a shame that Hayley wasn't in a relationship with someone she loved and planned to marry. Anne knew that Rick and Robin screwing the likes of her little sister wasn't going to bother Hayley at all.

As he pumped his sperm deep into Hayley's bowels, Alan repeatedly spanked her rounded buttocks while the girl whimpered and writhed over the back of the armchair. Anne watched her sister in disbelief – the sheer satisfaction depicted in her expression, her naked body shaking uncontrollably – as Alan repeatedly rammed his solid cock deep into her rectal duct and drained his swinging balls.

'What are you up to?' someone said as Anne took another photograph.

'Get down,' Anne whispered, turning to find Brian looking down at her.

'What's going on?' he asked, kneeling beside her.

'Alan is in the house, screwing my sister.'

'God,' Brian said softly, peering through the window. 'She's a real beauty.'

'Don't *you* start,' Anne whispered through gritted teeth. 'I've had enough of men chasing after my sister.'

'Why are you taking photographs?'

'It's a long story.'

'I don't understand. You're out here, taking photos, and—'

'Shut up, Brian. They'll hear you if you're not careful.'

'I think I'll go and join them,' he whispered. 'She really is a little beauty.'

Leaving the bushes, Anne walked into the woods and sat on a log. Why the hell did everyone compliment Hayley? she wondered irritably. Her sister had big tits and a lovely body but ... It must be her tits, she concluded as Brian joined her on the log. Men obviously liked big tits. Shaking her head as Brian once more praised Hayley's naked body, Anne knew that she'd never beat her big sister. Hayley was prettier, her tits were bigger, and she was better at sex.

'Are you jealous?' Brian asked her.

'Yes, I am,' Anne admitted. 'She's always been better than me. She did well at school and college and university, she has a well-paid job and a new car and—'

'Hey, hey,' Brian said softly, placing his arm around her shoulders. 'I didn't mean that she's better than you. You're amazing.'

'Yes, and her tits are bigger.'

'I don't like big tits, Anne. Not all men like big tits, believe me. Besides, you're even younger than she is and men love young girls.'

'I know,' Anne sighed. 'It's just that all my life I've had to put up with Hayley doing well at everything. She gets all the praise, she's perfect, she's—'

'Are you going to use the photographs to get your own back in some way?'

'That was the idea, yes.'

'Well, make sure that you blot out Alan's face. You don't want to get him into trouble.' Grinning, Brian pulled her close. 'You'd be better off setting her up in some way.'

'How?'

'I don't know. How about getting men to phone your house? They could ask for Hayley, ask how much she charges for sex.'

'So my mum answers the phone and a man asks her how much Hayley charges for sex?'

'Your mum will answer the phone to several different men every day. They'll think that's she's Hayley and ask how much she charges for a blow-job or anal sex and—'

'Yes, that's a good idea,' Anne cut in. 'The thing is, I don't know any men who would do it.'

'I'll do it. I can put on different voices. I'll ring several times a day and—'

'Yes, do it,' Anne said excitedly. 'I'll give you the phone number.'

Taking a pen and paper from his jacket pocket, Brian chuckled as she wrote her number down. 'Your mum will think that Hayley's on the game,' he said. 'And if you inadvertently leave a photograph somewhere where your mother will find it . . .'

'It will all add up to my big sister working as a prostitute. The trouble is, *I*'m the prostitute.'

'You are silly, Anne. I gave you some money to help you out. OK, so we had sex. But the money was just to help you out.'

'You are nice,' she breathed, smiling at him. 'But I *am* a prostitute – there's no other way to put it.'

'They're leaving the house,' Brian whispered, peering through the bushes.

'They might be going to the pub. Shall we follow them?'

'Yes, I could do with a beer.'

Walking through the woods with Brian, Anne realised that her perspective on her quest to get her own back on Hayley had changed. There was no point in bothering about the girl, she decided. Unless Hayley fell in love and planned to marry, there was no point in trying to destroy her relationships. Knowing Hayley as she now did, Anne reckoned that she wouldn't bat an eyelid if she discovered that her little sister was screwing the same men that she, Hayley, was seeing.

Following the unlikely couple, Anne watched as Alan went into the pub and Hayley walked on. Brian reckoned that Hayley was going home and suggested that they should go and have a drink with Alan, but Anne was more interested in her sister. Hayley was heading away from home, towards the other side of the village, and Anne wanted to know where she was going. Arranging to see Brian in the pub later that evening, she followed Hayley.

Keeping her distance, she slipped behind a parked car as Hayley walked up a path to a small cottage and rang the doorbell. What the hell was Hayley up to? she wondered as a man in his forties opened the door and invited Hayley in. Feeling like a thief in the night, Anne slipped into the front garden and spied through the open window. Hayley was in the lounge, kissing the man and giggling. Was this another one-night stand? Anne mused.

'Sorry I'm late,' Hayley sighed, flopping onto the sofa. 'I was held up at work.'

'No problem,' the man said as he poured two glasses of wine. 'I suppose you didn't have time to talk to your parents?'

'No, I . . . I haven't had a chance.'

'You haven't decided yet, have you?'

'Yes, I have. The thing is . . .'

'Hayley, I rang your office and they said that you'd gone home.'

'All right, I lied. I had to do some thinking, Jack.'

'I just want you to decide one way or the other. I've waited two years for you, Hayley. I'll wait another two years, if that's what it takes.'

'I've decided to marry you.'

Clutching her camera, Anne couldn't believe what her sister was saying. She'd never heard of Jack, and she was sure that Hayley hadn't mentioned him to her parents. Marriage? she wondered, frowning as she tried to get comfortable on the rough ground beneath the window. Realising that Hayley led a very dark and secret life, she wondered what the hell her sister had been doing, fucking an old man when she was thinking about marrying someone else.

'I have to get home,' Hayley said as she finished her wine. 'I'll talk to my parents, if my little sister isn't hanging around.'

'That's great. Will you ring me later and let me know the outcome?'

'Yes, I will.'

'I'm forty-five and you're only twenty-two but—'

'I love you, Jack. That's the most important thing. I'm sure that my parents will understand.'

'I can't believe that, after all this time, we're going to get married,' the man said excitedly.

'I know that I've kept you waiting, Jack. But I've finally made up my mind.'

Creeping around the side of the cottage as the front door opened, Anne gazed at her camera as she formulated her plan. She had the evidence of Hayley's debauchery with Alan, and she was sure that Jack would be very interested to discover the shocking truth about his wife-to-be. Marriage, she mused again, unable to believe that Hayley was a two-timing slut. Waiting until she was sure that Hayley had gone, Anne walked round to the front door and rang the bell. She was going to have to play this by ear, she thought as the front door opened.

'Yes?' Jack said, looking her up and down.

'Sorry to trouble you,' Anne said softly. 'A friend of mine said that Hayley was here.'

'She's just left, I'm afraid. Can I help?'

'It's rather difficult,' Anne sighed. 'May I come in for a minute?'

'Yes, yes, of course.' Leading her into the lounge, Jack waved at the sofa. 'Sit down,' he said before refilling his wine glass. 'Are you a friend of Hayley's?'

'Not exactly. She's a friend of a friend.'

'Oh, right. Would you like a drink?'

'Thanks,' Anne replied, settling on the sofa. 'My friend . . . he's been seeing Hayley for a while and he—'

'Seeing Hayley?' Jack interrupted her, his dark eyes frowning.

'Yes, they've been going out together for a few months.'

'Oh, er . . . I see.' He knocked back his drink and looked shocked. 'Please, do go on.'

'He's been wondering whether she's faithful to him. He saw her come here earlier and . . . well, he asked me to find out what sort of relationship you have with her.'

'My relationship with Hayley is ... We plan to marry.'

'Marry?' Anne echoed, staring wide-eyed at him. 'But I don't understand.'

'Neither do I. Are you sure that you've got the right girl?'

'Hayley, yes. She spent the evening with my friend and then he followed her here.'

'That explains why she's been dithering about marrying me,' Jack sighed, refilling his glass. 'She hasn't wanted me to meet her parents. She's been putting it off and I thought that it was because of the difference in our ages. I had no idea that she was seeing someone else.'

'I'm so sorry,' Anne murmured. 'I would never have come here had I known that ... I don't know what to say.'

'I'm glad you came here. I'm Jack, by the way.'

'I'm Rachael. Well, having put my foot in it, I suppose I'd better be going.'

'No, please stay for a while.' Topping up her glass, Jack smiled at her. 'It's nice to have some company, seeing as I'm now finished with Hayley. To be honest, I never thought that it would work out. I'm far too old for her.'

'You're not old,' Anne said, giggling as she reclined on the sofa and parted her thighs a little. 'Anyway, I prefer older men.'

'Obviously Hayley doesn't. I just don't understand her. We've known each other for two years and things have been fine, apart from her dithering about marrying me. God, this is a shock. I feel ... I really don't know what I feel. Let down, used, cheated . . .'

'You're an attractive man, Jack. I don't understand

why she's seeing another man. I really do find you attractive.'

'Really? Well, er . . . are you seeing anyone at the moment?'

'No, I'm free and single.'

Anne knew that he wanted her young body as he gazed at the tight material of her knickers straining to contain her full sex lips. Was he into oral sex? she wondered excitedly. Would he push his tongue between the hairless lips of her teenage pussy and lap up her hot milk? She didn't feel guilty as she parted her thighs further. Hayley had been screwing Alan in the derelict house, cheating on the man she planned to marry, so she deserved to have him cheat on her.

'What's Hayley like?' she asked Jack as he gazed at the triangular patch of material nestling between her slender thighs.

'I thought that she was a lovely girl,' he sighed. 'She's told me about her amazing salary and we'd worked out that we could afford to buy a nice house and . . .' He held his hand to his head and sighed. 'I'm still in a state of shock. To discover that she's been seeing another man is just incredible.'

'Have you never been suspicious?'

'Well, once or twice I have wondered whether she's been telling the truth. She has to work late most nights and . . . Yes, I have had my suspicions.'

'You need a girl you can rely on,' Anne said, grinning at him. 'You need someone dependable and faithful.'

'The trouble is, I'm not getting any younger. Anyway, I thought that Hayley was faithful to me. I thought that she loved me. I know that she'd been dithering about marrying me but . . . as I said, I thought that was because of our age difference. Had you not come here this evening, I'd have married her and . . . You've saved my life, Rachael.'

'How long have you lived here? I've not seen you around the village.'

'Only for a couple of months. I've been living in London – that's where I met Hayley. I work in London but because I wanted to be nearer to Hayley I rented this place. We've had some great evenings here. Nights of sex and passion and . . . well, it's over now.'

'Perhaps I can make you feel better,' Anne said huskily, rubbing the swell of her tight knickers. 'And perhaps *you* can make *me* feel better.'

Kneeling between her feet, Jack leaned forward and kissed the taut material of her wet panties. Anne breathed heavily, parting her thighs wide, as he licked the small indentations at the tops of her thighs either side of her knickers. Her clitoris swelling, her sex milk flowing, she knew that he was teasing her as his tongue repeatedly swept over the smooth flesh of her inner thighs. Desperate for him to rip her knickers off and tongue her wet hole, she moved forward on the sofa and positioned her rounded buttocks over the edge of the cushion.

'You're gorgeous,' Jack breathed, reaching up and squeezing the firm mounds of Anne's young breasts through her skimpy crop-top. 'You're just what I need.'

'What was Hayley like in bed?' Anne asked him, her voice shaky as he lifted her top clear of her petite breasts and teased her ripe nipples.

'She was always very wet,' Jack said softly, biting her fleshy outer lips through her soaked knickers. 'But that was probably because she'd been fucking another man before seeing me.'

'She's a whore,' Anne gasped, her eyes rolling as Jack pulled her panties to one side and gazed at her bald love lips.

'And you're beautiful. God, there's nothing I love more than a hairless pussy.'

'It's all yours, Jack. You don't need that slut Hayley any more.'

Parting the fleshy swell of Anne's outer labia and exposing her open vaginal entrance, he slipped his tongue into her hot sex hole and lapped up her flowing cream. She writhed on the sofa, gasping as her young womb contracted and her outer lips swelled. Jack was good, she mused dreamily as he licked the creamy-wet walls of her teenage vagina. Deliberately avoiding the solid nub of her expectant clitoris, teasing her and sending her arousal soaring, he took her to hitherto unknown heights of sexual craving.

'God, yes,' she breathed, clutching his head and grinding her open vaginal flesh hard against his mouth. 'My clit . . . lick my clit.'

'Naughty girl,' Jack said through a mouthful of hot vaginal flesh. 'Are you ready to come yet?'

'Yes, yes . . . please, I need to—'

'Not yet, my angel. I want you screaming and begging for an orgasm.'

'No, no, that's not fair. Please . . . oh God, my cunt . . .'

Crying out as Jack worked his tongue expertly around her hot vaginal hole, Anne stretched the puffy lips of her yearning pussy apart as far as she could. Again begging him to lick and suck her clitoris, she arched her back and shook uncontrollably. He ignored her pleas, tonguing her sex sheath and sucking out her hot milk but avoiding the solid bulb of her swollen clitoris. She tried swivelling her hips to align her budlette with his mouth, his tongue, but he moved down her gaping sex valley and continued to lap at the pink funnel of wet flesh surrounding her hot vaginal entrance.

Anne thought that she was flying up to her sexual heaven as her neglected clitoris began to pulsate. She could hear Jack slurping as her hot milk spewed from her open hole and flooded his mouth, and she knew that she'd be visiting him again. Why Hayley had cheated on him, she had no idea. The girl must have been mad, she reflected as she cried out and begged him for her orgasm. He chuckled, deliberately neglecting her solid clitoris as she begged and pleaded again for her desperately needed climax.

Finally conceding, Jack moved up Anne's open sex valley, sucked her swollen clitoris into his hot mouth and repeatedly ran his tongue over its sensitive tip. Anne screamed as her orgasm erupted, shaking her young body to the core. Throwing her head back, she wrapped her legs around Jack's body and forced the pulsating nub of her erect clitoris into his hot mouth. Images of his cock sliding in and out of her tightening vagina looming in her mind, she pictured another hard cock shafting the tight duct of her rectum as she sucked on an orgasming knob.

She was a slut, Anne knew as she rode the crest of her amazing climax. Sex now ruled her life, her very being was centred on her teenage pussy, and she vowed somehow to have three or four men attending her young body and spunking her tight holes. Her orgasm peaked as she imagined two knobs forced into her pretty mouth and pumping fresh spunk down her throat. Her fantasies would soon become real, she decided. She'd find men to use and abuse her teenage body and repeatedly take her to her sexual heaven.

'No more,' Anne finally managed to gasp. 'Please, I can't take any more.'

'Was that a good one?' Jack asked her, his pussy-wet face grinning.

'The best I've ever known,' she replied dreamily.

'God, you really do know how to make a girl happy. I want you to fuck me now, fuck me senseless.'

'It'll be my pleasure,' he said, unbuckling his belt and lowering his trousers. 'I love you talking crude like that. Beg me to fuck you.'

Gazing at his huge cock, his ripe plum, Anne could hardly believe the sheer size of Jack's organ. 'Please fuck me,' she breathed. 'Please fuck my tight little cunt hard.'

His bulbous knob drove deep into her contracting vaginal sheath and pressed hard against her wet cervix. Anne let out a rush of breath. He was so big, she thought happily as he withdrew and rammed his huge member deep into her tight sex duct again. Her half-naked body rocking back and forth like a rag doll as he began his fucking motions, the smooth plateau of her stomach rising and falling with the penile shafting, she whimpered and shook uncontrollably in the grip of her sexual ecstasy.

She really had found her sexual heaven, Anne thought as Jack grabbed her shapely hips and repeatedly rammed his cock into her spasming vagina with a vengeance. Her solid clitoris massaged by his pussy-wet cock, the pink petals of her inner lips rolling back and forth along his veined shaft, she cried out again as he pinched and twisted the ripe protrusions of her brown nipples. Her body alive with sex, her head lolling from side to side, Anne again imagined another cock shafting her tight rectum as a swollen knob pumped spunk into her pretty mouth.

Her crude fantasies sending her arousal to frightening heights, she looked down and watched Jack's huge cock gliding in and out of her stretched vaginal sheath. The sensations were heavenly, Anne thought, imagining his swollen knob driving deep into her contracting duct. Never had she known such sexual

112

ecstasy, and she swore that she'd visit Jack again and again for amazing sessions of crude sex. Her outer lips stretched tautly around his thrusting cock, her sex milk pouring out from her bloated vagina and drenching his swinging balls, she screamed again as her mind-blowing pleasure peaked. This was her first multiple orgasm, she thought dreamily as her vaginal muscles spasmed and her clitoris pumped out its pleasure. The first of many with Jack, she was sure.

Jack increased his shafting rhythm, his face grimacing as his sperm-pump fired and his swollen knob throbbed. The creamy liquid gushed into the contracting sheath of Anne's inflamed pussy, overflowing and running down to the tight ring of her anus as she dug her fingernails into the sofa cushion and arched her back as her orgasm peaked again and shook her young body to its depths. She'd never known that such immense pleasure was derivable from her teenage body. This was like a dream, she thought, her climax again rocking her young body and blowing her mind.

Jack made his final thrusts, his swinging balls drained, as Anne began to drift down from her sexual heaven. Gasping and writhing in the aftermath of her multiple orgasm, she could hear Jack talking but she didn't know what he was saying. Her mind swirling with thoughts of crude sex, her breathing fast and shallow, she lay convulsing on the sofa as he slipped his deflating penis out of her sperm-bubbling vagina and sat back on his heels.

'Are you all right?' he asked her. 'Rachael, are you OK?'

'Rachael?' she breathed. 'Oh, er . . . yes, I think so.'

'I thought you'd passed out.'

'I think I did for a minute. God, that was the best orgasm I've ever had. It was my first multiple orgasm, and I thought that it would never end.'

'Good,' Jack said, grinning proudly.

'Was Hayley better than me?' Anne asked him, hauling herself upright and pressing her sperm-splattered thighs together.

'No way,' he replied. 'She was damn good, but nowhere near as tight as you. You were fantastic, Rachael.'

She giggled. 'Do you like my name?'

'Rachael? Yes, it's lovely.'

'Better than Hayley?'

'Yes, of course it is. What's this thing you have about Hayley? You keep asking questions about her.'

'I'm interested, that's all.' Clambering to her feet and swaying on her sagging legs, Anne pulled her knickers on. 'I'd better go,' she breathed. 'It's getting late.'

'You'll come and see me again?'

'You bet I will.'

'Great. I'm here all day tomorrow, if you're free?'

'OK, I might call round during the day. What are you going to say to Hayley?'

'I'll tell her to bugger off,' Jack replied. 'She's supposed to be phoning me later. When she does, I'll tell her exactly what I think of her.'

'It might be best not to mention me,' Anne said, clutching her camera and moving to the door. 'Just say that you know that she got fucked by another man before she came to see you this evening.'

'What's the camera for? I meant to ask you earlier.'

'Nothing special. I usually carry it around with me in case I see something interesting. OK, I'll see you tomorrow.'

'It was great, Rachael. Thanks.'

'Thank *you*,' Anne said, smiling as he showed her to the front door.

* * *

Staggering down the lane with a deluge of sperm filling the tight crotch of her knickers, Anne felt pleased with herself. That was another of her sister's relationships in ruins, she thought happily. Jack was middle-aged but very nice, she reflected. He didn't deserve a slut like Hayley. A two-timing, filthy, cheating little ... Realising that she was no better than her sister, she bit her lip. She'd lied to Jack about her name, her relationship with Hayley ... But it had been worth it for the fuck of her young life.

Six

Hayley wasn't talking at breakfast. Anne had tried to strike up a conversation several times, but her sister had said nothing. Jack had obviously told her to bugger off, Anne thought happily as her mother said that she was going shopping. As she watched her mother leave, Anne wondered whether to say anything to Hayley about Jack. She wanted to rile the girl, but she finally thought better of it. Checking the time as Hayley grabbed her bag and left, Anne wondered how to spend the day.

Anne thought about going to the derelict house at lunchtime to see whether the young lesbians were there. She felt her womb contract. She'd enjoyed the lesbian sex, but the illicit acts still bothered her. It wasn't right to have sex with other girls, she reflected as the phone rang. Wandering into the lounge and flopping onto the sofa, she again recalled licking another girl's wet pussy. She grabbed the receiver. It had been a wonderful experience but—

'Hello, is anyone there?' a man asked.

'Sorry,' Anne replied. 'I was miles away.'

'May I speak to Hayley, please?'

'Er . . . speaking.'

'Oh, hello. My name's Peter. A friend told me about your export business – he gave me your number.'

'Oh?' Anne murmured, wondering what this was about. 'So how can I help you?'

'I was wondering whether we could meet and discuss a proposition I have?'

'A proposition?'

'I'm planning to expand into the export business and I'm looking for new contacts.'

'Er . . . yes, of course,' Anne replied softly. 'Where did you have in mind?'

'I'm in London, near Waterloo Station.'

'Oh, er . . . I'm in Hazelgrove Village, just outside Cranmoore.'

'I don't know the area but I'll find it. Maybe I could pick you up from there?'

'Yes, yes, that's fine. As you drive through the village you'll see a church – you can't miss it. I'll wait there for you. What time?'

'It shouldn't take me long to drive down. Say ten o'clock?'

'OK, I'll be there.'

As she replaced the receiver, it occurred to Anne that she had no idea where Hayley worked. She went off to London every day, but what did she actually do for a living? She'd mentioned an office, but she'd never really talked about her job. Anne knew that she shouldn't meet this man and possibly ruin a business proposition, but she was intrigued. Hayley wouldn't know, she thought as she cleared the breakfast table and went up to her room. Besides, she had nothing else to do so it would pass the time.

Wearing a short skirt and open-neck blouse, Anne brushed her auburn hair and applied a little make-up. Even though she knew nothing about the export business, she wanted to look the part. This was going to be fun, she thought as she left the house just before ten. Walking to the church, she mused again about meeting the lesbians at the derelict house at lunch-time. There was no harm in a little pussy-licking, she thought excitedly.

'Good morning, Anne,' the vicar said as she reached the church.

'Morning, vicar,' she murmured, walking up to him. 'How are you?'

'I'm fine. You look nice – where are you off to?'

'I'm meeting a friend.'

'Ah, right. Well, I'm going back to the vicarage to write up my sermon. Which reminds me – will I be seeing you in church before long?'

'Er . . . yes, yes, I'll make an effort.'

'How about joining us this Sunday?'

'Well, if I can.'

'Hayley often calls in to see me. I think you should do the same, just for a chat now and then.'

'Hayley visits you? I thought that she was always too busy with her work.'

'She calls in once a week, on Friday evenings. Why don't you come and see me this evening and we'll have a nice chat?'

'Er . . . yes, if I can.'

'Or later today, it it's easier for you?'

'Maybe I will.'

'I'll look forward to it,' the priest said, his face beaming as he headed down the lane.

That was all she needed, Anne thought, imagining him lecturing her about morals and the virtues of celibacy. What the hell did Hayley see him for? Did she confess her sins? She'd be confessing every night of the week if that was the case. There was far more to Hayley than met the eye, and Anne was deter-mined to dig deeper into her sister's life. Watching a car pull up by the church gates, she walked over and leaned through the open window.

'Hayley?' the middle-aged man said.

'Yes,' Anne replied, opening the passenger door and sitting next to him. 'You must be Peter.'

'That's me.' He looked at her naked thighs and chuckled. 'The export business,' he said. 'I like it.'

'Do you?' Frowning, she wondered what he was talking about. 'What do you like about it?'

'It's a good ploy, a good front. As I said, I don't know this area very well. Is there anywhere locally we can go?'

'That depends on what you want,' Anne breathed, realising that this had nothing to do with export.

'My friend said that you charge one hundred for half an hour. I thought a good look at your pussy and—'

'Turn around and drive back down the lane,' she cut in. 'I know just the place.'

Her brown eyes wide as he turned the car round, Anne couldn't believe that her sister was working as a prostitute. So *that* was where she got all her money from, she reflected. Her new car, her clothes . . . It was no wonder that she'd never talked about her work. Gazing at the man, she tried to imagine Hayley opening her legs for him. He wasn't particularly good-looking, but he obviously had money. His car was expensive and he was dressed in a suit and looked liked a successful businessman but . . . Hayley was a right slut, Anne thought, eyeing his wedding ring and imagining his wife waiting at home for him. Hayley was a lying, cheating little whore.

Ordering the man to pull up by the trees, Anne got out of the car and walked into the woods. He followed, making lewd comments about her long legs and rounded bottom as she neared the derelict house. One hundred pounds for half an hour? she mused, wondering whether she should be doing this. That was easy money, but . . . It was all very well thinking that Hayley was a whore, she reflected. But Anne herself was now taking money in return for crude sex and so was as bad as her sister.

'This is the place,' she said, hoping that the front room wasn't in use by Alan or Brian as she led Peter into the house. 'I bring all my local clients here.'

'It's, er . . . very nice,' he breathed. 'You're younger than I'd expected. My friend said that you were in your twenties.'

'I'm eighteen.'

'That's perfect. I like fresh young girls.' After stroking her firm breasts through the loose material of her blouse, Peter passed her the cash and smiled. 'At your age you should be nice and tight for my cock.'

'I'm tight, hot, wet . . . and shaved.'

'Really? That's absolutely perfect. Well, let's take a look at your young body.'

Slipping her blouse over her shoulders, he unhooked her bra and allowed the cups to fall away from her petite breasts. Still unable to believe that her sister worked as a prostitute, Anne looked down as Peter sucked on each ripe nipple in turn. This was how Hayley earned her money, she thought incredulously as he slipped his hand up her short skirt and pressed his fingertips into the warm swell of her tight knickers. And now this was how Hayley's little sister was earning *her* money.

'You'd look good in a school uniform,' Peter breathed as he knelt in front of her and tugged her short skirt down. 'Would you wear one for me the next time we meet?'

'Of course,' Anne replied, picturing her old uniform hanging in her wardrobe.

'White ankle socks and Mary Janes.'

'If that's what you want.'

'That's *exactly* what I want.'

Pulling Anne's tight knickers down to her knees, Peter gazed longingly at the bald lips of her teenage pussy and grinned. He was an old pervert, she thought as he opened her sex crack and gazed at her pinken inner folds. But he'd paid her well and she wasn't complaining. He moved forward and ran his tongue up and down her wet valley, tasting her milk, and she breathed heavily, her naked body trembling as his tongue repeatedly swept over the sensitive tip of her erect clitoris. This was easy money, she thought again, parting her feet wide as she felt Peter's finger drive deep into her contracting vaginal sheath.

'I love teenage cunts,' he said unashamedly. 'And yours is perfect in every way. A beautifully hard clitoris, well-formed inner lips, and your little hole is so wet and tight.'

'I'm glad you like it,' Anne said, trying not to giggle.

'Do you finger your cunt?' Peter asked her. 'Do you finger-fuck your hot young cunt and bring yourself off?'

'At least twice a day,' she replied, knowing that her lies would excite him. 'I can't leave my sweet cunt alone. I'm always fucking it with my fingers and massaging my hard clit.'

'Teenage girls are wonderful. Their cunts are so tight and wet and . . .'

Anne thought about Hayley as Peter sucked her erect clitoris into his hot mouth. The girl was clever, she reflected. Hiding her secret life, making out that she had a well-paid job . . . The more Anne thought about it, the more she realised that Hayley had it made. But why had she said that she'd marry Jack? What was the point in marrying when she was doing

121

very well as a prostitute? Maybe she wanted a cover, Anne thought. Maybe she wanted to hide behind a marriage so that the people in the village would think she was a refined young lady.

'I want to see your piss come out,' the man at Anne's feet said unashamedly. 'Would you do that for me?'

'I'll do anything for you,' she replied, squeezing her muscles. 'But your half-hour will soon be up so make the most of me.'

'I intend to make the most of you,' he said, licking his pussy-wet lips. 'Piss on me, and then I'll fuck you.'

Anne's golden liquid gushed, raining over Peter's face as he licked and sucked between the parted lips of her hairless young pussy – he was obviously happy with her performance. But she couldn't imagine Hayley doing this, drenching some dirty old perv with her steamy hot piss. There again, she didn't know her sister at all. Her new car, her money, her clothes . . . all paid for by prostituting herself. It was amazing to think that she'd fooled everyone. How long had Hayley been on the game? Anne wondered. Her quest to ruin her sister's relationship was futile now, she knew as she listened to the man gulping down her hot salty liquid. There seemed little point in bothering with the girl any longer.

Ordering Anne to kneel on all fours, Peter arranged himself behind her as she took her position on the floor. His knob sliding between the hairless lips of her pussy, his shaft penetrating her tight vagina, he rammed his organ fully home and held her hips tight. Another cock, another fuck, Anne mused as he began his fucking motions. She was used to crude sex with different men and now she knew that her sister was a whore the idea of being paid to open her legs appealed to her.

Wondering whether she could steal her sister's clients, Anne grinned as the man grunted with every thrust of his cock. This was so easy that it was unbelievable, she thought happily. It was no wonder that Hayley had turned to prostitution, although it was still a bit surprising. Anne wondered how she could get a list of Hayley's clients as the man announced that he was coming. Perhaps she had a little red book, she thought as her vaginal canal flooded with fresh sperm.

'Tight-cunted whore,' Peter gasped. 'You're the tightest slut I've fucked in months.'

'Don't stop,' Anne breathed, making out that she was enjoying the crude act. 'I'm coming, coming . . . Keep fucking me and fill my little cunt with your spunk.'

'You're a dirty little schoolgirl, a filthy little virgin slut. You're so young and fresh and tight . . .'

Listening to Peter's obscene words, Anne realised that her arousal was heightening. She hadn't thought that she'd reach her climax but with the sensitive tip of her solid clitoris massaged by his thrusting shaft, she felt the birth of her orgasm stirring deep within her contracting womb. Her sex cream blended with his sperm and flowed down her inner thighs in rivers of milk and she cried out as her pleasure exploded and rocked her young body. Her vaginal muscles spasming, tightening around his thrusting shaft, she reached behind her back, parted the rounded cheeks of her naked bottom and ordered him to push his finger into her arse.

'Filthy slut,' Peter said, ramming a finger deep into her rectal duct and heightening her pleasure. 'Dirty little schoolgirl whore.' Forcing a second finger into her hot duct, he rammed his cock harder into the inflamed sheath of her sperm-brimming vagina. 'Sluts like you need a good arse-fucking every day. They need their dirty little cunts fucking and . . .'

His crude words again sent Anne's arousal to frightening heights as she whimpered and writhed over the back of the chair in the grip of her powerful orgasm. She could feel Peter's sperm flooding her contracting vagina, hear the squelching sounds of the illicit coupling, and she thought of her fantasy of having three cocks spunking her wet holes. His finger twisting and bending deep within her rectal duct, she imagined a huge cock shafting her there. What would it be like to have her wet pussy and her tight rectum fucked at the same time? she wondered in the grip of her debauchery. And another cock pumping sperm down her throat?

'You're good,' Peter gasped, slipping his deflating penis out of Anne's young vagina. His finger leaving her bottom-hole, he helped her up from the chair. 'I'll be seeing you regularly, if that's all right?' he said, grinning at her.

'That's fine by me,' Anne replied, her young body shaking in the aftermath of her massive orgasm. 'It's best not to ring the house, so I'll give you my mobile number. I'm surprised that your friend had my home number.'

'He said that it was OK because of the export thing. He said that it's like a code word.'

'Oh, right,' she said as she dressed. Thinking again that Hayley was a dark horse, she gave him her mobile number. 'Ring me any time.'

Taking a pen and paper from his jacket pocket, Peter wrote the number down. 'I'll be in touch,' he said excitedly. 'Do you want a lift back to the church?'

'No, I think I'll walk. Thanks anyway.'

Kissing her cheek, he smiled. 'Thank you,' he said softly. 'You're wonderful. I'm so pleased that we met.'

As Peter left the house, Anne straightened her clothes and pondered on the money he'd given her. She needn't bother with university, she thought happily. Once she'd built up a list of clients, she'd be self-sufficient and could even get her own flat. Why hadn't Hayley moved into her own place? she wondered. Why stay at home and pretend that she had a well-paid job? Leaving the house and walking down the lane, she turned her thoughts to the vicar.

Why did Hayley visit the vicar every week? Was it part of the façade to conceal the shocking truth about her sordid private life? Passing the pub, Anne decided to call on the vicar. He'd been keen for her to go to the church and chat with him, and she was intrigued. He'd have no idea about Hayley's secret life, she was sure as she neared the church. Maybe they just chatted? she mused. Sunday school used to be fun, she reflected. The vicar was fun at times, laughing and playing around. But why would he see Hayley every Friday evening?

'Anne,' the priest said excitedly as she walked down the aisle. 'I'm so pleased to see you.'

'I only have a few minutes,' she said. 'I thought I'd just call in.'

'I'm glad you did,' he said, taking her hand. 'Come into the office and we'll have a chat.'

'I don't know what we'll chat about,' she replied with a giggle, as he led her into a small office. 'Are you going to lecture me about coming to church every Sunday?'

'No, no, of course not.' The vicar looked her up and down and rubbed his chin. 'You've grown into a very attractive girl,' he murmured pensively. 'Tell me, do you have a boyfriend?'

'No, I don't. I'm not really interested in boys.'

'I suppose you're too busy studying?'

'Yes, something like that.'

'Anne . . . I want you to talk openly to me. Are you a virgin?'

Anne held her hand to her mouth. That was the last question she'd expected from him. 'Well, I . . .' She frowned and hesitated. 'Yes, I am,' she finally lied.

'That's good. It would be a shame to think that boys have sullied your . . . your innocence. I've helped many a young girl to get through her teenage years. There are problems with growing up such as confusing emotions, sex and—'

'I don't think I'm having any problems,' Anne cut in.

'No, no, of course not. But are you prepared for sex? What I mean is, are you prepared for when a boy makes sexual advances towards you? Will you know what to do? How will you react when he touches you?'

'Well, I *suppose* I'm prepared.'

'You'd be surprised by the amount of young girls who find their first sexual experience disturbing. As I said, I've helped many teenage girls. And . . .' The priest hesitated, obviously wondering how to pose the inevitable question. 'I'd like to help you,' he finally added.

'Help me? But how?'

'By chatting, talking openly about your body and masturbation and . . .'

'Oh, I see.' Realising what the vicar was after, Anne decided to play along with him. 'I do masturbate,' she confessed.

'Really? And you enjoy it?'

'Yes, very much. I do it most days.'

He gazed longingly at her naked thighs as she perched her rounded buttocks on his desk. 'Most days?' he echoed, again rubbing his chin as she parted her thighs slightly and exposed the tight crotch of her wet knickers. 'What do you do, exactly?' he asked her, his voice shaky.

'Well, I rub myself.'

'And you use your fingers? Inside, I mean.'

'Yes, but . . .' Anne tried to look sheepish. 'I feel quite embarrassed about talking to you like this.'

'That's understandable, Anne. But do remember that I'm a vicar. I'm used to talking to young girls about masturbation and sex, so there's no need to worry.'

The priest was a sad pervert, she thought as he focused again on the triangular patch of her knickers beneath her short skirt. He was undoubtedly picturing her tight pussy crack, wondering how wet she was, when she had last masturbated and had an orgasm. Did Hayley visit him for sex? she thought. Was he one of her clients? He was a vicar, she reminded herself. He was a man of God and . . . There again, vicars were normal men. This could be fun, Anne thought wickedly, imagining him robbing the collection box to pay her for crude sex once a week.

'You were going to tell me about Hayley's visits,' she said softly, parting her thighs wider.

'Was I?'

'Do you talk about sex to Hayley?'

'Yes, I have done for many years. She still enjoys chatting to me and . . . I'd like to help you, Anne. When Hayley was your age, I helped her a lot.'

'We're chatting now,' Anne said. 'But I can't see that it's helping me with anything.'

'Is there anything about your body that worries you? I mean, are you happy with the way you're developing?'

He wasn't very good at seducing young girls, she thought, wondering what to say to lead him on. 'Well, I think I'm all right. I've never seen another girl's body, so I wouldn't really know.'

'As part of my work, in the name of God, I have examined several young girls. If you'd like me to take a look at your breasts . . .'

'What?' Anne gasped, holding her hand to her mouth to feign shock. 'You want me to take my top off?'

'Yes, if you'd like me to make sure that you're all right. Don't be shy, Anne. I've examined most of the girls in the village, so . . .'

'Well, I'm not sure,' she said, hanging her head as if embarrassed. 'I mean, you're not a doctor. What if someone finds out?'

'Have any of your friends told you that they come to see me?'

'No, no one has.'

'There you are, then. None of the girls tell each other, let alone anyone else. And *I* certainly wouldn't tell anyone.'

'You told me about Hayley.'

'Only because she's your sister. All I've said is that she visits me each week. Look, have a think about it. You don't have to decide now.'

'I suppose it'll be all right,' Anne sighed.

'Remember that I'm a vicar, a man of God.'

Releasing her crop-top and exposing the firm mounds of her petite breasts, she wondered again whether Hayley charged the priest for sex. Perhaps he was genuine and he only wanted to help her. No, he was a pervert, she decided as he gazed longingly at her ripening nipples and licked his lips. His cock would be solid beneath his cassock, she was sure as he reached out and squeezed each firm breast in turn. How was he going to get his hands inside her knickers? Would he suggest that he should check her pussy?

'You're coming on nicely,' he murmured, licking his lips again. 'Why don't you lie back on the desk so I can check you over properly?'

'Like this?' she asked him as she reclined.

'Yes, that's perfect.'

Gazing at Anne's naked thighs, the vicar ran his fingertips over her elongated nipples and kneaded each firm mammary sphere in turn. She was enjoying his intimate attention, but she couldn't believe that he'd done this to most of the girls in the village. Reckoning that he *was* paying Hayley for sex and had thought that he'd try it on with her little sister, she wondered how far he'd go. No normal young girl would strip naked for the perverted priest, she was sure. There again, she knew that she was far from normal. The notion of the vicar interfering with her young body excited her and she parted her legs to tease him.

Saying nothing, the man of God ran his hand up the smooth flesh of Anne's inner thigh. He was desperate to go further, she knew as his fingers moved dangerously close to the crotch of her tight knickers. Watching for her reaction, he pressed his fingertips into the swell of her cotton panties and flashed her a reassuring smile. He was lucky that she didn't flee the church screaming, she reflected. There again, if a girl told her mother and the vicar was confronted as a result he'd only deny it. Playing the role of an innocent little virgin girl, Anne bit her lip and tried to look anxious as he kneaded the swell of her pussy lips through her taut knickers.

'I think I'd better go home now,' she said softly.

'Oh, er . . . are you sure that you won't stay for a while longer?'

'I don't think this is right,' she said. 'No one's ever seen me . . . well, like this.'

'Anne, I've seen dozens of naked girls. You're safe with me, I can assure you.'

'No, I think I'll go now,' she persisted.

'Just allow me to check your breasts again and then you can go.'

Encircling each ripe nipple in turn, the vicar once more squeezed the hard mounds of Anne's teenage breasts. She was enjoying allowing him to examine her breasts. She knew what he was thinking, she knew that he wanted to examine her pussy, and the notion excited her. Running his fingertip over the smooth flesh of her stomach, the priest moved down past her navel to the top of her skirt. He was so close to his goal, she thought. But how was he going to get his hands inside her knickers?

'I'd better go now,' she murmured again.

'I'll just check down there before you leave,' he said, lifting her skirt up over her stomach.

'No, I . . .'

Pulling the front of her knickers down, he grinned. 'I just need to—'

'Vicar,' Anne gasped as he gazed at the hairless lips of her pussy. 'Please, I—'

'Have you shaved?' he asked her, his beady eyes frowning. 'At your age, you should have pubic hairs.'

'Yes, I . . . I use cream.'

'Why?'

'Because . . . because I prefer it like that. I think I'd better go.'

'Does Hayley know about this?'

'No, no one does.'

'I might have to speak to her, Anne. You obviously have problems.'

'No, please don't say anything to her.'

'I think that Hayley needs to have a good talk with you, Anne. Girl to girl about your shaving and—'

'No, you mustn't tell Hayley. She'll tell my mother and . . .'

'I really don't know what to do,' the vicar sighed. 'Look, if you allow me to examine you properly I won't say anything to Hayley.'

'Yes, yes – all right,' Anne murmured, trying again to look anxious.

What would he have done had he not been able to threaten to tell Hayley that Anne had no pubes? she wondered as he pulled her wet knickers down and slipped them off her feet. Would he have ripped her knickers off and forced her to open her legs? His fingers ran over the smooth lips of her bald pussy and he patted her fleshy labia wide to reveal the pink petals of her inner lips. Her clitoris swelling as he examined the most private part of her teenage body, Anne wondered whether to threaten him with exposure.

'I'll ask my friends,' she said, concealing a grin.

'Ask them what?'

'About coming here and taking their knickers off and allowing you to examine them.'

'No, Anne,' the priest replied with a hint of anger in his voice. 'You mustn't do that. This is a private thing between us. Your friends would only deny it, anyway.'

'I'll ask Hayley, then.'

'Look, there's no need to say anything to anyone. All I'm trying to do is help you.'

Deciding to bluff him, Anne grinned. 'Hayley has told me about her visits,' she said. 'You pay her, don't you?'

'I, er . . . of course I don't pay her. Goodness me, why would I give her money?'

'You can pay me. Give me fifty pounds, and you can do what you like to me.'

The man of God looked genuinely stunned as he withdrew his hand and stared at Anne. Had she got it wrong? she wondered anxiously. She was asking the vicar for money in return for sex and . . . If she was wrong, would he tell her mother that she was a prostitute? His eyes darted between her pretty face and the hairless lips of her teenage pussy and he frowned. Perhaps he *was* only trying to help, she thought. Then, opening the desk drawer, he pulled out a wad of notes and smiled at her.

'Fifty,' he said, passing her the money.

'Thank you, vicar,' she breathed with a sigh of relief. 'Now I'm all yours.'

'You're a dirty little girl, Anne,' he said, parting her legs wide and hanging her feet down either side of the desk. 'Taking money in return for sex is a terrible thing for a young girl to do.'

'It's what you want, isn't it?

'Yes, well . . . Open your cunt with your fingers. I'm going to treat you like a dirty little girl should be treated. I'll lick your dirty young cunt out.'

Complying, Anne parted her swollen pussy lips and exposed the wet entrance to her tight vagina as the priest knelt on the floor. Pushing his tongue into her hot hole, the priest lapped up the cocktail of sperm and girl-milk and commented on how wet she was. Anne grinned, saying nothing as he sucked out the products of her coupling with Peter in the derelict house. He *was* a sad pervert, she thought happily, clutching the money as he pushed his tongue deeper into her contracting vagina.

One hundred and fifty pounds in one day, she

mused. And both men were Hayley's clients. How many more could she steal from her sister? Anne wondered as the vicar grabbed a huge church candle from a shelf. Stretching her outer lips apart as far as they would go, he pressed the rounded end of the candle hard against the pink funnel of flesh surrounding her vaginal entrance. She grimaced as her tight hole opened, her knuckles whitening as she clutched the side of the desk.

'I love teenage girls,' the priest said, with a chuckle. 'I love forcing their little cunts open wide and sucking out their sweet sex juices.'

'You're a filthy pervert,' she replied.

'And you're a dirty prostitute,' he countered.

'How many girls do you bring here each week? How many young girls do you violate and—'

'None,' he cut in as he forced the candle deep into her bloated vaginal duct. 'Your sister is the only one. I'd like to have the two of you together. I'd ram my cock into your tight cunt and then into hers and . . .'

His crude words excited her and she gasped as the candle drove fully home. Leaving the waxen phallus in place, the vicar lifted his cassock and exposed the solid shaft of his cock to Anne's wide eyes. He was well endowed, she observed as he retracted his foreskin and ordered her to open her mouth. Parting her red lips, she breathed heavily through her nose as his purple knob slipped into her pretty mouth. This was the same cock that had fucked her sister, she thought as he squeezed the firm mounds of her breasts and pinched her ripe nipples. Which sister did he prefer? she wondered, rolling her tongue around his salty knob.

It occurred to Anne that she could work with her sister. She could share the clients with Hayley and earn a fortune. They could even share a flat, she mused as the perverted vicar rocked his hips and repeatedly rammed his bulbous knob to the back of her throat. But Anne was younger, tighter, fresher . . . She could earn money without her sister's help. Besides, if Hayley was going to marry Jack she'd probably have to give up her secret life. Anne was going to have to decide which way she wanted her life to go, she knew as the vicar gasped and rocked his hips faster.

Grabbing the huge candle, he rammed it repeatedly deep into her painfully stretched sex sheath, battering her young cervix as he chuckled wickedly. As his sperm gushed from his throbbing knob and bathed her snaking tongue he clutched her head, forcing her to drink from his huge cock. Swallowing hard, gulping down his orgasmic cream, she knew that she'd be a regular visitor to the church. Maybe she should turn up on a Friday evening, she mused, imagining spying on Hayley as the girl took the vicar's knob into her mouth.

'Filthy whore,' the priest gasped, finally sliding his deflating cock out of Anne's spermed mouth. 'Dirty little schoolgirl slut.'

'I'm a virgin,' she breathed, licking her cream-glossed lips.

'The candle should have loosened you up,' he said, chuckling as he yanked the wax shaft out of her inflamed vagina with a loud sucking sound. 'Now I'll break you in properly. You want to be fucked, don't you? A little teenage girl like you needs her cunt breaking in and spunking. I'm going to fuck you so hard and fill you so full of spunk that . . .'

Hardly able to believe that he was a vicar as he rambled on, Anne grimaced as he pulled her forward on the desk until her naked buttocks were over the edge. As his huge knob stabbed at her gaping vaginal entrance, she let out a rush of breath when his cock drove deep into her young body. How could he manage another erection so soon? she wondered as he lifted her legs and placed her feet over his shoulders. His shaft sliding in and out of her contracting sex sheath, his swollen knob battering her ripe cervix, he again muttered crude words of sex.

Thinking that she should have charged him double, Anne gripped the sides of the desk as her young body jolted with every thrust of the priest's huge cock. He was good, she thought dreamily as her clitoris swelled against his pussy-wet shaft. He was so good that she reckoned that *she* should pay *him* for sex. But this was business, and she was going to earn a small fortune from her teenage body. Dirty old men would line up to pay her, she knew as her orgasm neared. To get their hands on an attractive teenage slut with a hairless pussy they'd pay almost any price.

The vicar gasped as his face grimaced, and Anne knew that he was about to flood her inflamed vaginal duct with his lubricating sperm. Her own orgasm welling from the depths of her rhythmically contracting womb, she cried out as his sperm gushed and her pleasure exploded within the pulsating bulb of her erect clitoris. His male cream overflowed and ran down to the small hole nestling between her rounded buttocks as she writhed and shook uncontrollably in the grip of her climax while she imagined his purple knob driving deep into her hot bowels.

Her head lolling from side to side, her eyes rolling, Anne whimpered and writhed as her orgasm peaked and shook her teenage body. She was having better sex than she'd ever imagined possible, she reflected in her delirium as the vicar increased his shafting rhythm. She was enjoying different men, huge orgasms, and she was being paid for it. Her pleasure finally subsiding as the vicar's swinging balls drained, she panted for breath after her amazing climax. She'd definitely be calling on the vicar again, she thought dreamily. And taking his money.

'Have you finished with me?' she asked him, propping herself up on her elbows and gazing at the creamy liquid oozing from her gaping hole.

'For the time being,' the priest replied, grinning at her. 'Next time I'll tie you over the altar and fuck your tight little arsehole.'

'Is that what you do to my sister?'

'Hayley doesn't come here,' he said, chuckling softly as she clambered off the desk.

'What? But you said—'

'I lied, just to get your knickers off. I don't have *any* girls calling on me.'

'Well, you have now,' Anne replied, clutching the money and pulling her knickers on. 'I didn't think that young girls would come here and . . . When do you want to see me again?'

'Sunday, after the morning service.'

'OK, I'll be here.'

'It would be nice if you were here for the service. I could look at you from the pulpit and think about fucking your tight little arse over the altar.'

'OK, anything you say. I'll listen to your hypocritical sermon, and then take my knickers off for you.'

'That's my girl. Now get out of here before some old busybody sees you.'

'See you Sunday, then,' Anne said as she left the office.

Walking out of the cold church into the bright sunshine, Anne made her way home with sperm filling the crotch of her tight knickers. She wanted to talk to Hayley, drop a few hints about the girl's secret life, but she knew that she was going to have to be careful. If she said too much Hayley would become suspicious. Life was good, she thought as she opened her front door and bounded up the stairs to her room. She had a good sex life, plenty of money ... Her thoughts turning to Jack, she wondered whether Hayley would marry him. He'd make a good brother-in-law, she mused as she went to the bathroom to take a shower.

'Oh, it's you,' Hayley said as she emerged from her room. 'What are you up to?'

'I'm about to have a shower,' Anne replied, grinning at the girl. 'There was a phone call for you earlier. It was some man about the export business.'

'Export ...' Hayley looked concerned. 'I've had calls like that before,' she murmured pensively. 'I have no idea what they're about.'

'You mean you don't know?' Anne said, frowning at her sister.

'No, no, I don't. I have no idea why these people ring me. They're always men and they want to meet me but ... They obviously have the wrong number.'

'Yes, I suppose so,' Anne said, sure that her sister wasn't lying. 'He mentioned your name, which is strange.'

'They usually ask for Hayley. But some ask for Miss Bradbury. There's obviously a mix-up some-where. If you answer a call like that again, tell them that they've got the wrong number. I've told mum to do the same.'

'Yes, I will.'

Confused, Anne went into the bathroom and locked the door. The vicar had admitted that he'd been lying about Hayley visiting him, she reflected. Perhaps her sister *wasn't* a prostitute, Anne mused as she slipped out of her clothes and stepped into the shower. Hayley would never have given clients her home phone number so . . . Realising that she'd been very wrong, Anne wondered nonetheless why Hayley had behaved like a common slut with Brian in the old house. Washing the sperm from her swollen pussy lips, she turned her thoughts to Jack. Perhaps Hayley *was* going to marry him, but she'd had a final fling with Brian before tying the knot.

This was a mess, Anne thought as she left the shower and went into her bedroom. Closing the door, she thought about the money she'd earned. Did she really want to be a prostitute? she asked herself. In her quest to steal her sister's boyfriends, she'd gone way too far and had become a common whore. Wishing that she'd never gone to see the vicar, she knew that she was going to have to do some serious thinking about her future. Who were the men who rang the house asking for Hayley? Was there a mix-up? Or was Hayley trying to hide the shocking truth about her private life?

Seven

Anne wandered down the lane to the pub at six o'clock. She was still confused, trying to work out what was going on. Where had the men got the home phone number from? Hayley wasn't a common name so was it coincidence or was she really working as a prostitute? Walking up to the bar, Anne ordered a large vodka and tonic and settled at her usual table. There weren't many people in the pub, but she did notice Alan lurking in the corner at the end of the bar.

He was a nice chap, she thought, wondering whether to go to his house and pretend to be a salesperson as she watched him laughing and joking with the barman. Brian had loved the scam but would Alan be up for it? she wondered wickedly. If his wife found out that he'd been screwing a teenage girl in the marital bedroom while she, his missus, had been downstairs, she'd go mad. But it would be fun. Brian had given her fifty pounds for the pleasure. Would Alan pay her? Smiling as he walked towards her, she asked him whether he'd enjoyed himself with Hayley in the derelict house.

'You were right,' he said, sitting opposite her. 'She really is a horny little slut. You should have seen her. She was into everything and—'

'I saw . . .' Anne began, almost dropping herself in it. 'I mean, I went to the old house and saw the front room and thought of you two.'

'I can't thank you enough, Anne. She really is a horny girl.'

'Are you seeing her again?'

'No, I don't think so. She was talking about some chap or other and I got the impression that she's going to marry him.'

'I can't see Hayley getting married,' Anne said, with a giggle. 'Still, you never know. Did she mention other men? I mean, did she say anything about meeting other men for sex?'

'No, she didn't. I got the impression that she was only with me because . . . oh, I don't know. I thought that it was some kind of last fling before she commits herself to marriage. Shame, really. I'd have liked to have seen her again.'

'You've still got me, Alan. Mind you, I might have to charge you fifty pounds.'

'You are a naughty girl. You're also a dirty little girl and I'm glad I met you. You're well worth the money. Tell me, do you do this for a living?'

'Well, I . . . no, not really. It's a long story. I thought that Hayley was on the game so I—'

'She's not on the game,' Alan cut in, chuckling. 'She was telling me that I was her first real sexual encounter. She's had boyfriends, of course. But she was saying that none of them have turned her on. She reckons that I'm the first man she's had an orgasm with.'

'Ah, that explains it,' Anne murmured. 'I'm discovering quite a lot about my big sister. I'm also discovering a lot about myself. It will be strange if she marries and moves out of the house.'

'You're not going to get married yourself, then?'

'No, no way. I have fantasies to live out and . . .'

'Tell me about them.'

'Well, my main one is being with three men. Three cocks . . . you get the idea?'

'Yes, I do. You really *are* a naughty little girl, aren't you?'

'I try to be.'

'I have a couple of friends who would be interested. Are you up for it?'

'Yes, definitely.'

'I'll contact them and suggest it.'

'Fifty pounds each?' Anne said, grinning at him. 'A young girl has to survive, Alan.'

'No problem. I'll let you know when I've spoken to them, probably tomorrow.'

'OK, that's great.'

'Oh, there goes your sister,' Alan said, looking through the window.

'I wonder where she's off to,' Anne murmured, watching the girl head down the lane. 'I'll be back in a while. I just want to . . .'

'Follow her?'

'Yes, I'll be back soon.'

Leaving the pub, Anne knew that Hayley was going to see Jack. She was probably going to try to put things right with him, she thought, watching the girl ring his front doorbell. Wishing that she hadn't told Jack a string of lies about her sister, she hid in the bushes beneath the lounge window as Jack invited Hayley in. She could hear them talking as they went into the lounge. They were arguing, and she reckoned that the relationship was over.

'I told you on the phone,' Jack said. 'I'm not going with a two-timing slut like you.'

'Jack, listen to me,' Hayley sighed. 'It was a one-off. A final fling before marrying you. I know

141

that it was wrong, I know that I shouldn't have done it and I shouldn't have lied to you, but—'

'There are no buts, Hayley. I know that you've been seeing several men.'

'I should never have gone to that old house. Who told you about it?'

'As I said, a girl I know came to see me. She told me everything.'

'What's her name?'

'Rachael.'

'I don't know anyone called Rachael. All I can think is that someone followed me to that old house and . . .' Hayley paused, her eyes wide as she thought about something. 'My sister,' she finally gasped. 'I'll bet it was my bloody sister. What did she look like?'

'It doesn't matter what she looked like. You were in that house fucking some man and . . . As I said on the phone, our relationship is over. I'll pay the rent to the end of the month and go back to London.'

'OK, if that's what you want,' Hayley sighed. 'My sister . . . Did she come on strong to you?'

'No, of course not.'

'You're lying, Jack. If it was my sister, and I'm sure that it was, she'd have dropped her knickers.'

'No, she—'

'You're as bad as me, Jack. You're a hypocritical . . .'

'Hayley, let's talk,' Jack said, taking her hand. 'OK, so we both made mistakes.'

'You *did* fuck her?'

'Yes, I did.'

'She's a bitch and you're a . . . I suppose we're quits, aren't we?'

'Yes, we are. She told me about you and the other man and I thought . . . We'll put it behind us, OK?'

'OK. Look, I'd better tell you this before my sister does. Men have been calling my home phone number and asking for me. I don't know how they know my name or where they got the number from but . . .'

'What do they say?'

'They want to arrange to meet me. It has something to do with an export business.'

'It's nothing to do with your sister, is it?'

'No, I don't think so.'

'For a quiet little village a hell of a lot goes on here,' Jack said, with a chuckle. 'It's like a soap opera.'

'Even the vicar is dodgy,' Hayley said, shaking her head and grinning. 'He's always looking at young girls. I've seen him chatting to them, cuddling them and . . . He's approached me several times and asked me to meet him in the church.'

'Perhaps he's behind the phone calls?'

'It's possible, I suppose. To be honest, I'll be pleased to get out of this village. The things that go on in that derelict house are . . . I've often seen two girls going into the woods. I reckon that they go to the house. I've seen other people, too.'

'I'll have to take a look at this place.'

'Don't go there, Jack. Keep away from it. Look, I have to go home for a while. I promised mum that I'd help her with the garden. My dad spends all his time in the shed and . . . Why don't you come round later?'

'Really?'

'Yes, come and meet my parents.'

'OK, I will.'

Leaving the bushes and walking back to the pub, Anne knew that Hayley was going to have a right go at her. There again, Hayley *had* screwed Brian. She was as guilty as Jack and she couldn't blame her little sister. Hayley was right about the old house, she reflected as she neared the pub. The things that went on there were amazing: the vicar was a sad pervert, Brian and Alan were old men who leched after young girls ... It was an interesting village, she thought, noticing Brian leaving the pub.

'Where are you off to?' Anne asked him.

'I was looking for you,' he replied, grinning at her. 'Do you want to go to the old house in the woods?'

'Well, I suppose I could ... I was supposed to meet Alan but—'

'I've just been talking to him. He told me about your fantasy and ... I have two friends who are up for it.'

'Really?'

'Alan said that you'd come back to the pub. He's had to go home – he said something about his wife. My friends are on their way to the woods now.'

'That was quick!'

'I thought that as you were coming back to the pub you might be up for it. I told my friends to go to the house and wait for us.'

'Let's go,' Anne trilled, imagining three hard cocks shafting her tight holes.

Brian was fun, she thought as they headed back down the lane. He was an old man but he was good company and damned good at sex. And she was a slut. But she didn't care what she was. As long as she was having fun and earning money, nothing mattered. Following Brian along the narrow path through the trees, she felt her stomach somersault as the house came into view. Three cocks, she thought excitedly as they went in through the front door.

Brian's friends hadn't arrived, so Anne gazed out of the window with expectation reflected in her wide eyes. She'd had two men, she reflected. But to have three using and abusing her naked body would be an

144

amazing experience. She didn't think that the day might come when she'd regret her actions. She wasn't thinking of the future – her thoughts were centred around the excitement and satisfaction of the present. Three men groping her teenage body, three cocks sliding in and out of her holes . . . The future was a million miles away.

'Here they are,' Anne said, watching two old men approach the house.

'Are you ready for this?' Brian asked her.

'Yes, yes – of course I am.' She began to unbutton her top but Brian stopped her. 'What's the matter?' she breathed.

'Let them do that,' he said, smiling at her. 'They'd prefer to strip you naked.' He turned as the men walked into the room. 'This is Anne,' he said. 'Anne, these two are Harry and George.'

'Hello,' the men said in unison, looking her up and down.

'Pleased to meet you,' Anne said as they each passed her some cash. 'Right, well . . . I'm all yours.'

Wasting no time, they ran their hands over her young body, tugging her skirt down, releasing the buttons and slipping her top off her shoulders. Within seconds she was standing completely naked in front of them. One of them had a full head of grey hair and a suntanned face – and he reminded her of her grandfather. But Anne couldn't imagine her grandfather stripping and fucking a teenage girl. Were all old men like this? she wondered as hands ran over the petite mounds of her firm breasts. Would they all fuck teenage girls if they had the chance?

Judging by the crude comments the men made as they knelt before her, she knew that they loved her hairless pussy. As fingers parted her bald pussy lips and massaged the wet flesh within her open sex valley, Anne felt proud of her naked body. She was like a model, she mused dreamily. Old men stripping her naked, admiring her feminine beauty, exploring her mounds and crevices . . . Although they were only using her to satisfy their lust for teenage girls, she felt wanted. This was cold sex, she reminded herself as two fingers drove deep into the tight sheath of her sex-drenched vagina. But she felt wanted.

One of the men moved behind Anne and parted her rounded buttocks, and she felt a quiver run through her contracting womb as he teased the tight ring of her anus with his fingertip. Brian concentrated on her ripe nipples, sucking each in turn, as the other men attended to her sex holes. A wet tongue swept over her anal eye as another drove into the hot sheath of her tight vagina and she let out a rush of breath. Three tongues, she thought happily as Brian licked the elongated teats of her firm breasts. But it was three *cocks* she was really looking forward to.

Anne watched in anticipation as the men rose to their feet and slipped out of their clothes. Finally eyeing their erect cocks, she smiled. They were big, she observed. Brian had also stripped naked. Big, hard, long . . . Following their instructions as one man lay on the floor on his back, she placed her knees either side of his hips and lowered her young body. Holding his cock, she guided him in, gasping as the sheer girth of his organ stretched her young sex duct open to capacity.

The other man knelt behind her, parting her firm buttocks and stabbing at her anal hole with his bulbous knob, and she knew that her fantasy was about to become reality. Brian brought her dream out of the darkness and into daylight by slipping his purple knob into her waiting mouth. Three cocks, she thought happily as her rectal canal opened wide to accommodate the invading penis. The sound of male gasping resounding around the room, her young body rocking as the treble shafting began, Anne breathed slowly and deeply through her nose and closed her eyes.

This was an amazing experience, she thought as the sound of naked flesh meeting flesh echoed in her ears. Her vaginal juices squelching, her firm breasts kneaded by roaming hands, she felt her clitoris swell as never before. Her tight holes shafted, her mouth bloated by a swollen knob, her young body was alive with sex. Hoping that the men had staying power as her young body rocked back and forth, she could feel the two cocks rubbing together through the thin membrane dividing her inflamed vagina and her tight rectum. Gobbling and sucking on Brian's bulbous knob, Anne moaned softly through her nose as hands roamed again over her naked body.

The knob shafting her tight rectum pumped creamy sperm deep into her bowels and her cervix was bathed by spunk from the other throbbing knob. Anne sucked and repeatedly swallowed as Brian's cock flooded her mouth with his male offering. This was it, she thought as her own orgasm neared. Three cocks fucking her hot holes, three throbbing knobs pumping sperm into her young body . . . This was her dream come true.

Her pleasure erupting within the pulsating nub of her solid clitoris, Anne lost herself in her sexual frenzy as her naked body shook uncontrollably in the grip of her ecstasy. This was what her teenage body was for, she thought in her sexual delirium. All three holes shafted by solid cocks, used and abused and filled with spunk . . . and she was earning money in the process. Swinging balls slapping between her parted thighs, her nipples pulled and pinched, her sex ducts inflamed, her dream had come true.

The men finally pulled their deflating cocks out of Anne's quivering body, leaving her panting for breath and awash with sperm. She hoped that they'd be able to shaft her senseless again. Her lust for perverted sex was insatiable, she knew as the burning holes between her young thighs oozed with fresh spunk. Licking the male cream from her chin and lips, she reckoned that the men must be on erection tablets as she gazed at their solid cocks. They were obviously ready for another session already, she mused dreamily as she clambered on top of Brian's naked body. And she was more than ready for another three-way fucking.

Brian's cock entered the inflamed sheath of Anne's spunk-creamed vagina and she opened her mouth as another man offered her his purple knob. She was eagerly awaiting the penetration of her tight rectum but, as the third man knelt behind her and tried to force his knob into her bloated vagina alongside the first cock, she thought that she'd split open. Slipping the knob out of her mouth, she protested.

'You can take it,' the man kneeling behind her said, with a chuckle. 'Just relax and we'll give your little cunt a double fucking.'

'No,' Anne gasped as her vaginal canal stretched painfully to accommodate his huge organ. 'Please, I can't take two cocks.'

Ignoring her, the man managed to drive the full length of his solid cock deep into her inflamed vaginal sheath alongside the other huge penis. The huge knob plunged again into her gasping mouth, completing the triple fucking of her naked body, and she couldn't believe the abuse she was having to endure. Her sex duct stretched to capacity, the two cocks rhythmically shafting her burning vagina, the swollen knobs battering her ripe cervix, she sucked and gobbled on the knob filling her mouth as her clitoris swelled as never before.

This was debased sex beyond belief, Anne thought as her young body rocked with the three-way shafting. Never had she dreamed of taking two cocks into her teenage pussy, but she'd plunged into the seedy world of prostitution and obscene sex and now there was no turning back. This was her life now, she thought as the men gasped and her bloated vagina spasmed. Paid for crude sex, allowing old men to abuse her young body . . . This was her life now.

'She's as tight as hell now,' Brian said.

'I've always dreamed of double-fucking a teenage slut,' the man kneeling behind her gasped. 'Two cocks up one cunt . . . God, this is heaven.'

Anne listened to their vulgar comments as she sucked and licked the knob bloating her pretty mouth. Her vaginal sheath burning like fire, tightening around the two solid cocks, she knew that this was the most debased act she would ever indulge in. There could be nothing more depraved, she thought as the cocks shafting her stretched sex duct swelled. She could sink no lower into the pit of degeneracy.

Someone slapped her naked buttocks hard and Anne's young body jolted. She tried to slip the man's knob out of her mouth and protest again, but he held her head tight. The loud slaps resounded around the room as the gruelling spanking continued and her rounded bottom cheeks stung like hell. She lost control and hot urine spurted from her abused hole and drenched the men's bouncing balls. This really was the bottom of the pit, she was sure as laughter echoed around the room. She was nothing more than a common whore to be used and abused to satisfy the perverted lust of old men.

Her mouth flooding with sperm, Anne repeatedly swallowed hard as her distended vaginal cavern filled with two loads of male orgasmic cream. She'd had enough and needed to rest, but two fingers drove deep into her hot rectal duct and massaged her inner flesh, taking her to hitherto unknown heights of depravity. Her clitoris swelling and pulsating, she moaned through her nose as her orgasm exploded and rocked her young body to the core.

Her mind blown away on clouds of lust, a deluge of hot liquid streaming between her legs as her bladder drained, she thought that her incredible orgasm would never end. Her breasts kneaded by unseen hands, her sensitive nipples pinched and pulled, Anne thought that she was going to pass out as her pleasure heightened. The squelching of sperm, naked wet flesh slapping against flesh, the gulping of spunk . . . The sounds of crude sex resounded around the room until the men slipped their cocks out of her creamed holes and she rolled to one side and lay on the floor quivering in the aftermath of her abuse.

'She's good,' someone said as she panted for breath.

'Well worth the money.'

'We'll fuck the slut regularly.'

'We'll try two cocks up her tight little arsehole next time.'

'And two in her mouth – make her swallow a pint of come.'

'We should bring old Fred with us, he'd like to use the slut's arse.'

Anne listened to the crude conversation as she lay writhing and gasping on the floor with sperm oozing from the burning holes between her wet thighs. They'd finished with her, she was sure, as they talked about going to the pub for a beer. That was it, she thought. The old men had used and abused her, they'd paid for their pleasure, and now they were going to the pub to chat about the dirty little slut they'd fucked and spunked in.

As the men dressed and left, Brian helped Anne up and smiled at her. Her hair dishevelled, sperm dribbling down her chin, streaming down her inner thighs, she was exhausted in the aftermath of her pioneering treble fucking. Brian was nice, she thought as he dressed her. He was a dirty old pervert, but he was also caring. Wondering whether the men would bring Fred with them next time, she imagined four cocks shafting her fleshy holes. Five men, six, seven . . .

'You'd better get home,' Brian said as he finished dressing her.

'I'll stay here for a while,' Anne breathed shakily, plonking herself in the old armchair. 'You go and join the others in the pub.'

'Well, if you're sure?'

'Yes, I'm sure. I'll see you again. OK?'

'Are you up for it again?'

'Definitely. We'll arrange it when I next see you in the pub.'

'You look after yourself. I'll see you tomorrow in the pub.'

As Brian left the house, Anne closed her eyes and reflected on the debauched acts she'd performed with the old men. 'Slut' wasn't strong enough a word to describe her, she thought as she felt her knickers soaking up a deluge of sperm. Slut, whore, tart . . . From a relatively innocent teenage girl, she'd become a wanton prostitute. Looking around the room, she smiled. How many more men would she entertain in the derelict house? How many cocks would she take into her mouth, her young vagina and tight rectum . . . Leaving the chair as she heard someone walk into the hall, she held her breath. Had the men come back for more?

'Hi, Rachael,' Jack said as he appeared in the doorway. 'What are you doing here?'

'I'm . . . I often come here to think,' Anne replied, wondering how he knew about the old house. 'Have you been here before?'

'No, no. Hayley told me about this place. I'm on my way to see her, so I thought I'd take a look.'

'Oh, right. So, are you two back together again?'

'She told me that you're her sister. Why did you come to my place and—'

'Are you angry with me?'

'No, I just wondered why you said all that stuff about her.'

'It's a long story, Jack. My name's Anne, by the way.'

'She's not at all happy with you.'

'I'm sorry, Jack. I knew that there'd be a lot of trouble but . . . You could lie, say that it was some other girl who went to see you. She'd never know, would she?'

'You're right, it might be best. We don't want any problems, especially as I'm going to be your brother-in-law.'

'That means that we can still fuck,' Anne said, giggling as she stared at the bulging crotch of his jeans.

'Anne, I'm going to marry your sister. I don't think that we should—'

'Fuck? Why not? Hayley will never find out.'

'You're a naughty little girl.'

'You're not the first man to say that. We could have some fun, Jack. Imagine you coming to my house and Hayley introducing you to me. She'll never know that we've been fucking. We could fuck on your wedding day – imagine that.'

'I am imagining it, and I can feel trouble brewing.'

'Don't be silly. If there's no danger, there's no excitement.'

'I'd better be going or she'll wonder where I am.'

'Fuck me before you go.'

'Anne, I—'

'Fuck me, Jack. Do my cunt hard, and then go and see my big sister.'

Kneeling in front of him, Anne unbuckled his belt and tugged down his jeans. His cock rising, Jack looked down at her as she licked his rolling balls and ran her wet tongue up and down his veined shaft. He couldn't resist her, she knew as his cock stiffened fully and he began to tremble. She'd just about completed her quest, she reflected. She was with the man whom Hayley intended to marry, seeing him behind her back and using his cock for her own satisfaction. But she was obsessed with sex, with taking her sister's men, and she knew that she wouldn't stop here.

Fully retracting Jack's foreskin and taking his purple knob into her sperm-thirsty mouth, Anne snaked her wet tongue over its silky-smooth surface and savoured the salty taste. Another huge cock and another load of sperm, she thought happily, wanking his solid shaft and cupping his full balls in the palm of her hand. Jack and Hayley would soon be man and wife, and Anne would steal his cock whenever it took her fancy. It would be a nice arrangement, Anne mused wickedly.

Sucking and gobbling on Jack's bulbous middle-aged knob, she knew that her sister was innocent. She wasn't a prostitute and she doubted that she'd screwed Dave in the park. She'd gone to the derelict house and fucked Brian, she reflected. But that had been Anne's idea: she'd put Brian up to it, and Hayley had enjoyed her last fling before marrying Jack. Hayley was completely innocent, but that

153

wasn't going to stop Anne's quest for sexual gratification with Jack or any other man.

Breathing heavily, Jack moaned softly as his sperm gushed into Anne's gobbling mouth and bathed her snaking tongue. She swallowed hard repeatedly, drinking the fresh cream from her soon-to-be brother-in-law's throbbing knob, and she wondered how much sperm she could gulp down in one day. Life was exciting, Anne thought as she wanked Jack's rock-hard shaft and kneaded his heaving balls. Especially as she was sucking Hayley's future husband's cock and drinking the sperm that should have been her sister's.

'You really are a naughty little girl,' Jack breathed as she slipped his deflating knob out of her sperm-bubbling mouth. 'I ought to spank you for the way you've behaved.'

'I wish you would,' Anne replied, with a giggle. 'I could do with a good spanking.'

'Telling me that Hayley has lots of men, and then pulling your knickers down and—'

'Talking of pulling my knickers down,' she cut in, 'I hope you're going to fuck me on your wedding day.'

'I have no doubt that I'll slide my cock into your tight little pussy after the ceremony. The only thing is, if Hayley ever finds out that we've been—'

'Well, I'm not going to tell her. Don't worry, Jack. We won't get caught.'

'God, I hope not. Look, I'd better be going. Are you going home now?'

'No, I'll stay here for a while. Don't forget to tell Hayley that I wasn't the girl who went to your place. Say that it was someone tall with red hair or something.'

'OK, will do. I'll see you soon, I hope.'

'I hope so, too. Be a good boy.'

'Yeah, right.'

As she watched him leave the room, Anne knew that she should go home. It was getting late and dusk was falling, but she didn't feel like ending the day yet. Her knickers were soaked with sperm, she was exhausted, she looked like she'd been dragged through a bush backwards ... She looked like a common slut, she mused, wondering whether to go to the pub for a drink. Leaving the house before it got dark, she walked along the lane and thought about the vicar. Would he be in the church? she wondered. Her young body had had enough sex for one day, but she wanted more.

Nearing the church, Anne noticed that the doors were open and she slipped inside. The tight holes between her slender thighs ached, but the notion of another cock shafting her thrilled her. It had been a good day, she reflected as she neared the altar. The vicar, Brian and his two friends, Jack ... Just one more fuck before going home, she thought, walking across the church to the small office. Hearing the vicar on the phone, she hovered outside the door and listened.

'She's eighteen and she shaves,' he said with a chuckle. 'No, no. Fifty pounds. Oh yes, well worth the money. Yes, that's right. As you know, I've been trying to get hold of one of the local girls for years.'

Grinning, Anne knew that he was talking about her. Was he on the phone to another vicar? she wondered excitedly. Maybe he could get her another client, she thought, imagining several cassocked men with stiff cocks lining up at the altar. The vicar finally finished his phone call so Anne wandered into his office and grinned at him. He looked surprised to see her, but he was soon looking her up and down and licking his narrow lips.

'Have you come back for more?' he asked her.

'If you have another fifty pounds, then yes, I have.'

'I can't afford it twice in one day,' he sighed. 'How about a freebie for a regular customer?'

'It's a shame you haven't got any money. I was going to sell you some photographs of my sister sucking an old man's cock.'

'What?' the priest gasped, frowning at her. 'You mean to say that Hayley—'

'I mean to say that I have photos of Hayley getting mouth-fucked.'

'May I take a look at the photos?'

'I haven't printed them yet, they're still on my camera. You'd like to get inside her knickers, wouldn't you?'

'Yes, very much so.'

'You could use the photos to blackmail her.'

'Now that's a thought. So you'd stand back and watch me blackmail your sister?'

'Yes, why not? She's always been better than me, she's always done well at everything and . . . well, it's time she was brought down a little.'

'How much do you want for the photos?'

'One hundred.'

'You drive a hard bargain, Anne.'

'And you drive a hard cock, vicar. Come on, you can do me over the altar for free.'

Eagerly following her out of the office, the priest closed and locked the church doors before joining Anne by the altar. She didn't intend to sell him the photographs, she thought as she watched him pull his cassock over his head and throw it over a pew. She was just winding him up, teasing him. Following his instructions, she stripped naked and lay on the altar. He was a sad pervert, she mused, looking up at the roof as he stood by the altar and grabbed a huge church candle. But he might bring her more clients, so it was worth playing along with him.

'A sacrifice,' he said, chuckling as he parted her thighs wide and focused on the gaping crack of her hairless pussy. 'I'll offer your naked body to the Devil.'

'You are the Devil,' Anne quipped. 'I wonder what you're going to do with that candle?'

'Stuff it right up your tight little cunt,' the vicar replied unashamedly. 'I'd love to get Hayley on the altar and give her a good candle-fucking.'

'Why?' Anne breathed, gazing at the candle as he pushed the rounded end between the swollen lips of her pussy. 'Do you think that she's better than me?'

'No, it's not that she's better than you. I look upon her as a challenge. I've always got the impression that she's a prude. To get her naked on the altar and give her a damned good candle-fucking would bring her down a peg or two.'

'It would bring her an orgasm or two,' Anne said, grimacing as the huge wax shaft stretched her vaginal canal open wide. 'God,' she gasped. 'It's too big.'

'You wait until I force another candle up your tight little arse,' the priest said, finally pushing the wax phallus fully home.

Anne grimaced again as he worked the candle in and out of her inflamed sex sheath and muttered crude words about tight virgin schoolgirls. Did other girls visit him? she wondered as he leaned over her naked body and sucked her elongated nipple into his hot mouth. He'd said that he didn't see other girls, but she didn't believe him. A sad old pervert like the vicar would forever be chasing after fresh young girls and trying to lure them into the church for sessions of debauched sex.

Taking another candle from the altar, the vicar rolled Anne's naked body over and parted the firm cheeks of her rounded bottom. She squealed as he pushed the end of the candle hard against her tight anal ring but as the shaft slipped past her defeated anal sphincter muscles the sensations drove her into a sexual frenzy. Her sex holes bloated, stretched to the limit, she whimpered and trembled uncontrollably as he twisted the candles within her inflamed sheaths.

This wasn't sex, Anne mused dreamily as the priest sank his teeth into the firm flesh of her naked bottom. This was depraved abuse of a teenage girl's naked body, but she wasn't complaining. Her young womb contracting, her clitoris swelling against the solid shaft of the candle bloating her vaginal duct, she'd never known such heavenly sensations. The candles were far bigger than the cocks she'd taken into her tight sex holes, and she wondered just how far her hot ducts would stretch open.

As the vicar clambered onto the altar and yanked the waxen phallus out of her burning anal sheath, Anne knew that he was going to drive his cock deep into her bowels. His bulbous old knob pressed hard against her inflamed anus and she let out a rush of breath as his penile shaft glided deep into the very core of her quivering body. His huge shaft repeatedly withdrawing and again driving deep into her restricted rectal canal, his swinging balls battering the end of the candle emerging from her inflamed vaginal cavern, he found his rhythm.

'You're so hot and tight,' the priest gasped, his hands resting on the altar either side of her head as he rocked his hips and pummelled her bowels with his swollen knob. 'I'll get Hayley in this position if it's the last thing I do.'

Anne said nothing as he abused her tight rectum, but she did imagine her sister naked on the altar with a candle embedded deep within her tight pussy and the vicar's penis doing her hot rectal tube. Hayley would be with Jack now, she thought. She'd be introducing him to her parents, announcing their wedding plans. Her mother would be pleased and her father would be indifferent, but Anne was delighted to think that she was going to have a sex-crazed brother-in-law who would get his hands inside her knickers at every opportunity.

The vicar's creamy sperm lubricated Anne's burning anal duct as he repeatedly thrust his knob into the dank heat of her bowels with a vengeance. More spunk, Anne mused as her clitoris pulsated against the solid shaft of the candle and erupted in orgasm. She'd never been fucked so much in her life, she thought in her sexual delirium. Jack, Brian and his two friends, and the vicar twice in one day . . . This had to be the last cock until tomorrow, she decided as sperm oozed from her sore anus.

Her orgasm began to fade as the vicar drained his swinging balls and slowed his shafting rhythm. Anne lay convulsing and gasping for breath on the altar. His deflating cock finally slid out of her sperm-bubbling anal sheath and he yanked the candle out of her abused vaginal canal and clambered off the altar. She was completely exhausted, she thought as he rolled her over onto her back and grinned at her. She couldn't take another cock, another orgasm, another load of spunk.

'You look totally fucked,' the priest said, laughing as he helped Anne off the altar.

'I am totally fucked,' she breathed, swaying on her sagging legs. 'God, I need to go home and get into bed.'

'I've only done you twice today. Anyone would think that you'd been fucked a dozen times.'

'I've had five cocks today,' she confessed as she dressed.

'Five? My God, you really *are* a filthy little slut.'

'Some of them, yours included, have fucked me twice. That's why I look totally fucked.'

'I have a friend who might be interested in meeting you,' the vicar said pensively as he walked her to the church doors. 'Would that be OK with you?'

'If he pays me, yes.'

'Good, good. I'll arrange it, then. Er ... here, at the church one evening?'

'Any evening suits me.'

'Right, well ...' Unlocking the doors, the priest slapped Anne's bottom. 'Go on, go home and have a rest.'

Walking home, Anne felt the sperm-soaked knickers sticking to the bald flesh of her inflamed pussy lips. She needed a shower, she knew as she neared her house. What she didn't need was for her mother to see her in this state. Sneaking in through the front door, she crept up the stairs to her room and locked the door. How many more cocks would drive into her young body and fill her with spunk? she wondered as she lay on her bed and closed her eyes. How much more money would she earn?

Eight

Anne had stayed in bed until lunchtime and had finally showered and dressed. She felt confused about her life, which direction she was going in. She still wasn't sure whether Hayley was a prostitute or not. It didn't matter one way or the other, but she was intrigued. Wandering into Hayley's bedroom, she wondered why she'd never really got on with the girl. Why was Hayley always better at everything? Brian had chased after her, Alan wanted her, the vicar was desperate to get his hands inside her knickers and Jack intended to marry her . . . Even Dave had gone to the park with her for a so-called chat.

As she opened the bedside drawer, Anne knew that she shouldn't rummage through her sister's things. But she was intrigued about Hayley's life, where she worked and how she was able to earn so much money. Finding nothing of interest, Anne closed the drawer, wandered over to the desk and switched on the computer. Sitting in the swivel chair, she wished that she could afford a nice desk and a decent computer. But she was earning *some* money at last, and she'd soon have enough to buy whatever she wanted.

Checking Hayley's emails, she noticed one from Dave. 'Hi, sexy,' she read aloud. 'I thought about you again last night. I imagined that we were in the park together, kissing and making love. From the day Anne took me to your house and I first saw you, I haven't been able to get you out of my mind. Meet me in the park this evening at seven. Dave the rave.'

Switching the computer off, Anne shook her head. 'Fucking bitch,' she breathed, wondering how to retaliate. *Meet me in the park this evening at seven.* 'I'll meet you in the bloody park,' she cursed, leaving the chair and looking through Hayley's underwear drawer. Finding several thongs, she decided to steal them. Stockings and suspender belt, she mused, grabbing the items and checking the other drawers. Thinking that Jack might be interested to see a few photographs of Hayley getting fucked by Dave, she slammed the drawers shut before heading back to her own bedroom. She also had the photos of Hayley having anal sex in the derelict house with a man old enough to be her grandfather, she thought. Jack would undoubtedly be interested to see those.

Slipping a suspender belt on, Anne rolled a pair of stockings up her long legs and gazed at her reflection in the mirror. The black suspender belt framed the puffy lips of her hairless pussy. She grinned. No man could resist her young body, she though happily. Thinking again that Hayley was a bitch, she decided not to wear any knickers. This was war, she thought. Bounding down the stairs as the phone rang, she decided that she'd go all out to ruin every relationship her sister had.

'Hello,' she breathed, pressing the receiver to her ear.

'Is that Hayley?' a man asked her.

'Yes, speaking.'

'My name's Don. I'm phoning about your export business.'

'OK, Don. My consultation fee is two hundred pounds. That's for one hour.'

'Yes, that's fine. Where and when?'

'I'm available tomorrow morning. I'm in Hazelgrove Village, just outside Cranmoore.'

'Yes, I know the place.'

'You can pick me up at ten, if that's all right with you?'

'Yes, that's perfect.'

'Good. I'll be waiting outside the church.'

'Thanks, Hayley, I'll see you tomorrow.'

Another client, Anne thought happily, downloading her photographs to her computer before leaving the house and heading for the park. Another cock, more spunk, more money . . . Clutching her camera, she knew that she was an hour early but it was a lovely evening and she decided to sit on the bench and enjoy the sun. Her eyes closed, she tried to relax. But she couldn't stop thinking about Hayley meeting Dave in the park and sneaking into the woods for a session of crude sex. Her sister was a real bitch, Anne thought angrily.

Hearing someone approaching, she half-opened her eyes and saw a middle-aged man walking towards her. Watching him through her lowered eyelashes, she parted her thighs slightly and displayed the puffy lips of her hairless pussy. She pretended to be sleeping as he stopped a few yards away and gazed at the most private part of her young body. Never before had she exposed herself like this, and she realised the excitement she'd been missing as her clitoris stirred and called for attention and her young womb contracted.

The man stood there for several minutes, and Anne reckoned that his cock was stiffening and his full balls rolling. It wasn't every day that he'd find a teenage girl in the park with her hairless pussy blatantly on display, she thought as she parted her slender thighs a little further. It was his luck day and, if he had any money with him, he might be even luckier. Finally stirring, stretching her arms above her head and opening her eyes, she looked up at him.

'Oh, er . . .' she gasped, pressing her naked thighs together. 'I must have fallen asleep.'

'You looked so serene,' the man said, sitting beside her. 'I'm Geoff, by the way.'

'I'm Anne – pleased to meet you.'

'I usually walk through the park after dinner. I haven't seen you here before – are you local?'

'Yes, I live up the road.'

'What's the camera for?'

'Oh, just in case I see anything of interest. You'd be surprised at some of the things I see.'

'There are some lovely sights in the park,' Geoff said, gazing at Anne's naked thighs. 'I noticed that you're wearing stockings. I thought they were old-fashioned, not something a teenage girl would wear these days.'

'I like stockings,' she said, looking down at her long legs. 'I don't wear tights because they're so restricting.'

'In what way?'

'Well, all sorts of ways. I'd never wear tights, especially in the summer when it's hot.'

'I suppose it's better to have some cool air between your legs.'

'This is a funny conversation,' Anne said, with a giggle. 'I don't know you, and we're talking about my stockings and—'

'Does it worry you?'

'No, not at all.'

'My wife wears stockings and she doesn't wear panties during the summer months. She likes a cool breeze wafting up her skirt, which is understandable.'

'I must admit that I don't wear any knickers when it's hot like this.'

'As we're on the subject, I might as well tell you that she shaves. She reckons that it's far better than—'

'That's a coincidence,' Anne cut in. 'I use cream to get rid of the hair.'

'Really? Well, I never thought I'd be talking to a young girl who doesn't wear panties and has no pubic hair. And stockings are . . . I just love stockings.'

'It sounds like you and your wife get on really well together.'

'We used to,' Geoff sighed. 'Sadly, we don't have a sex life any more.'

'Oh, I thought . . . What with shaving and no knickers and stockings . . .'

'She looks great, but she lost her sex drive a long time ago. Do you have a boyfriend?'

'No, not at the moment.'

'I wish I was younger,' Geoff said, grinning at her. 'When I was your age . . .'

As he talked about his teenage years and the girls he'd known, Anne thought about allowing him a little pleasure. He was undoubtedly lying about his wife, but that didn't bother her. Although she felt sorry for him, she also wanted his money. What would he pay to slip his tongue between the wet lips of her hairless pussy? Did he have any money with him? This was a new day, she hadn't had sex yet, and she was desperate for sperm. Checking her watch, she reckoned that she could spare him twenty minutes.

'You must miss going with young girls,' she said.

'Yes, I do. Still, that's all part of getting old. All I have now are memories of teenage girls and, to be honest, they're fading fast.'

'Maybe I could revive your memories.'

'How do you mean?'

'Follow me.'

Leaving the bench, Anne walked across the grass to the woods and followed the narrow path into the trees. Geoff was right behind her, like an obedient dog, and she wondered again whether he had any money. She stopped in a small clearing amongst some bushes, placed her camera on the ground and turned to face him. He brushed his greying hair back, his face beaming as he looked her up and down. He must have known what she had in mind as she lifted her short skirt up over her stomach and exposed her tight crack, the hairless pinken lips of her teenage pussy.

'Beautiful,' he murmured, dropping to his knees and gazing longingly at Anne's feminine intimacy. 'Please may I touch?'

'Only if you beg,' she giggled.

'Oh, please, please let me touch,' he begged.

'You're a dirty old pervert,' Anne said to him, enjoying the power her teenage body had over this man who was old enough to be her grandad.

'I know I am,' Geoff said, staring hungrily at her moist young sex lips.

'OK then,' she said, her pretty face smiling down at him. 'Go on, revive some of those distant memories.'

Saying nothing, Geoff ran his hand up Anne's stockinged thighs and traced the fleshy swell of her bald sex lips with his fingertip. She breathed deeply as he opened her tight crack and exposed her pinken inner folds. Should she allow him to sink his hard cock deep into her tight vagina and spunk her? Or should she take his purple knob into her wet mouth and suck out his orgasmic cream?

Moving forward, Geoff licked the pink funnel of wet flesh surrounding the entrance to Anne's hot vagina. Lapping up her flowing milk, he clutched her naked buttocks, moved up her open sex valley and sucked her erect clitoris into his hot mouth. Her excitement rising, she trembled, her breathing fast and shallow as he repeatedly swept his tongue over the sensitive tip of her clitoris. This was heavenly, she thought as her young womb contracted and her sex cream flowed freely from her open vaginal hole. But it wouldn't be long before Hayley and Dave needed the woods for their illicit fucking.

'Would you like to fuck me?' she asked him.

Geoff looked up at Anne's pretty face and smiled. 'There's nothing I'd like more,' he said.

'Do me really hard,' she ordered him. She got down on all fours and jutted out her sweet rounded buttocks. 'Give me a good seeing-to, you old pervert, and then go home to your wife.'

Wasting no time, Geoff slipped his trousers down and knelt behind her addictive young body. Anne grinned as she felt his swollen knob slip between the bald lips of her sweet pussy. Yet another hard cock, she mused happily as her tight duct stretched open to accommodate the sheer girth of his veined shaft. His heavy balls pressing against the gentle rise of her mons, he withdrew slowly until the wet wings of her inner lips hugged his purple globe. He was big, she thought as he propelled his knob deep into her contracting vagina and then withdrew. Grabbing her shapely hips, he began his fucking motions, rocking her trembling body with every thrust of his solid organ.

Anne listened to the squelching of her creamy pussy milk and the slapping of his lower stomach against her rounded bottom as her quivering womb contracted. She wouldn't mention money because she needed hard sex as much as he did. There was no

167

need to charge every man who shafted her tight pussy, she reflected. Besides, she'd felt rather sorry for this man. He'd obviously lied about not having sex with his wife and she reckoned that he deserved to have his memories of teenage girls revived.

Geoff came quickly, shooting his spunk deep into Anne's rhythmically contracting vaginal duct as he repeatedly rammed his knob hard against her creamy-wet cervix. She'd hoped that he'd have lasted longer but this was probably the first time in decades that he'd screwed a teenage girl. His sperm oozed from her bloated vaginal hole and streamed down the smooth flesh of her inner thighs in rivers of milk as he finally slowed his shafting rhythm.

'I needed that,' he breathed shakily. 'I can't thank you enough for allowing me to—'

'Any time,' Anne cut in as he slipped his deflating penis out of her tight sheath. 'You might find me sitting on the bench the next time you walk through the park.'

'I'll be looking out for you every day,' Geoff said, standing and tugging his trousers up. 'You're beautiful.'

'No, I'm not,' Anne said with a giggle as she clambered to her feet. 'I'm just an ordinary girl.'

'Well, I think you're beautiful. I might see you tomorrow, if I'm lucky.'

'I'm sure your luck will be in.' Checking her watch, she realised that Dave and Hayley would be arriving at any minute. 'Go now,' she said, kissing Geoff's cheek. 'I'll see you again, OK?'

'I certainly hope so. Thanks – thanks so much.'

Watching Geoff walk away, Anne grabbed her camera and crept through the bushes to a spot where she could survey the park. Her knickers filled with sperm as she squatted behind a bush and she looked out across the park. She noticed Dave walking towards her. Her timing was perfect, she thought, watching as he sat on the bench only yards from her hide. Within minutes she saw Hayley approaching. Hayley was wearing a red miniskirt, knee-length leather boots and a loose-fitting blouse. Her long blonde hair cascaded over her shoulders and she looked stunning. But she was a cheating slut, Anne reminded herself.

Hayley joined Dave on the bench and began chatting to him, but Anne got the impression that she wasn't happy. She looked grumpy, shaking her head negatively as she listened to Dave. Anne couldn't hear what was being said, which annoyed her, but she couldn't get any closer without being seen. Dave was doing most of the talking and Anne wondered why they hadn't gone into the woods for sex. She also wondered why Hayley had bothered with make-up. She looked as though she was ready to go out for a meal rather than roll about in the woods getting fucked.

Hayley and Dave finally left the bench and walked into the woods, and Anne followed at a distance. This was it, she thought as they entered the small clearing. Squatting behind a bush, hoping that they wouldn't spot her, she checked her camera and waited for the inevitable fucking to commence. Perhaps they weren't going to have sex, she mused as Hayley whispered something to Dave. He gazed at the ground with his hands in his pockets, not looking at all happy, and Anne wondered what was going on. Had they argued? Had Hayley dumped him for another man?

'You don't want me to send you any more emails, then?' Dave said.

'I've told you, Dave,' Hayley sighed. 'I'm getting married soon. Besides, you're supposed to be going out with Anne.'

'Anne and I have split up. I don't know what she wants, but it's certainly not me.'

'I really like you, Dave. I know how you feel and ... You'll find another girl, I'm sure of it.'

'It's you I want, Hayley. Anne's too young for me. You and me, we're the same age, perfectly suited.'

'The man I'm marrying is in his forties,' Hayley said, biting her lip. 'Mum and dad aren't happy about it, but—'

'He's old enough to be your father. It's no wonder that your parents aren't happy. Why are you marrying him?'

'Because I—'

'And why did you screw Alan if you're marrying another man?'

'Who told you about that?' Hayley asked. 'Has Alan been blabbing in the pub?'

'It's a village, Hayley. Everyone knows what's going on.'

'God, I don't want the whole village knowing that I . . . It was a one-off, a last fling before I—'

'That's all I'm asking for,' Dave cut in, smiling at her. 'Just one time with you, Hayley. That's all I ask.'

It was obvious that they hadn't been seeing each other all along and Anne realised that she'd been very wrong about her sister. It seemed that she'd got everything wrong about Hayley, she reflected. She wasn't a prostitute, she wasn't seeing the vicar, she hadn't been fucking Dave ... Recalling the email, she also realised that Dave had been chasing Hayley, pestering her for sex, not the other way round. Apart from Hayley's last fling with Alan, which Anne couldn't understand, the girl had been totally innocent.

'May I ask you something?' Dave said. 'How come you have so much money?'

'I wish I had,' she sighed dolefully. 'The truth is that I'm in debt.'

'What? But you have a new car and . . . I thought that you had a great job and you were loaded?'

'No way. I do have a good job but . . . The car isn't paid for, I owe a fortune on my credit card . . . Jack, the man I'm marrying, thinks I'm on a good salary. He's been talking about us buying a house together. My credit rating is dreadful and I'll never get a mortgage, but I don't know how to tell him. That's why I've been dithering about marrying him. He thought that I'd been wavering because of our age difference.'

'You'll have to say something to him, Hayley.'

'Yes, I know. But it's worse than that. I'm on the verge of bankruptcy. That's why I went off the rails with Alan. I just didn't know what to do so . . . It was crazy, but I went mad and fucked like never before. I did things that I've never dreamed of doing, Dave.'

'Did you enjoy it?'

'Yes, that's the problem. I've never had such varied and . . . and crude sex. The things we did were disgusting, but I loved every minute of it.'

'And, you want more?'

'Yes, yes, I do. But I can't . . .'

'Hayley, have a last fling with me,' Dave persisted.

Anne watched with bated breath as Hayley unbuttoned her blouse and slipped the garment off her shoulders. Unhooking her bra and tossing her clothes over a bush, she displayed her ample breasts, her ripe milk teats, to Dave's wide eyes. This was an amazing revelation, Anne reflected as her sister tugged her miniskirt down and kicked it aside along with her shoes. Hayley wasn't a whore, she was just confused . . . and heavily in debt. Anne felt sorry for the girl as she watched Dave kneel in front of her and pull her knickers down to her ankles. Bankruptcy? she mused, wondering how the hell her sister was going to get out of this mess.

Dave parted Hayley's full sex lips and ran his tongue over the pinken inner folds nestling within her open valley, and Anne again felt sorry for the girl. Hayley was only doing this to find some escape from her terrible problems, she thought. Finding some solace in sex, she'd committed crude sexual acts with Alan and was now about to screw Dave. Hayley was going to have to tell Jack, Anne thought as Dave moved behind the girl and parted the firm cheeks of her naked bottom. She couldn't marry Jack and then reveal the shocking truth about her finances.

'I like that,' Hayley breathed as Dave pushed his tongue into her tight bottom-hole. 'Dave, I want you to . . . When I was with Alan, he spanked me.'

'You want me to spank you?'

'Yes.'

'OK, bend over.'

Grinning, Anne took several photographs as her sister bent over and touched her toes. Dave stood behind her and repeatedly spanked the firm flesh of her tensed buttocks, and Anne reckoned that Hayley was hooked on crude sex. Two dirty sisters, she mused, taking more photos. Hayley wasn't Little Miss Perfect after all, she thought as the loud slaps resounded around the trees. Heavily in debt, on the verge of bankruptcy, turning to debauched sex with men . . . Unable to believe what she was hearing as the girl asked Dave to thrash her with a branch from a bush, Anne held her hand to her mouth.

This was incredible, she thought as Dave snapped a branch off a nearby bush and stood behind Hayley. The branch swished through the air, the rough leaves landed squarely across the girl's naked buttocks, and she yelped like a dog. Again and again the branch flailed her rounded buttocks to leave thin weals in its wake, and Hayley cried out. Grimacing, Anne watched the gruelling thrashing, taking a photograph now and then as Hayley's screams echoed in her ears. The girl's naked buttocks glowing a fire-red, she finally asked Dave to stop.

'Now do my arse,' she breathed shakily, kneeling and leaning over a log. 'Fuck my arse like you've never fucked before.'

'If Anne could see you now,' Dave said with a chuckle as he slipped his trousers off. 'She always said that you were a prude.'

'I was,' Hayley replied. 'But I'm in such a mess now that . . . I'm beyond caring.'

Watching as Dave yanked her sister's crimsoned buttocks wide apart and pressed his purple knob hard against the tight ring of her anus, Anne wondered what the vicar would think if he discovered the shocking truth about Hayley. He'd ram a church candle up her arse, she reckoned. He'd certainly pay well for the photographs . . . But Anne knew that she dared not show the evidence of her sister's debauched behaviour to anyone. The girl had already had more than enough problems. The last thing she needed was the vicar blackmailing her into crude sex over the altar. Anne knew that her quest to destroy her sister had to end. If anything, she should try to help the girl. But how? There was nothing Anne could do, she knew as Dave's veined shaft sank into the girl's rectal duct.

Holding Hayley's hips, Dave withdrew his solid cock until her anal ring hugged the rim of his knob, and then rammed into her again. Anne watched her sister's body jolting with each thrust of Dave's cock, her own clitoris swelling and her sex milk flowing into the crotch of her tight knickers as the sight sent her arousal soaring. Why hadn't Dave fucked her like that? she wondered dolefully. If he had taken Anne to the woods and fucked her arse and . . . It was no good looking back, Anne thought, taking several more photographs. Her ex-boyfriend was fucking her sister, so there was no point in looking back.

'Dirty slut,' Dave gasped. 'I've dreamed of this, of fucking your tight little arse and . . .'

'Harder,' Hayley breathed. 'Fuck my arse really hard.'

'You bet I will. I'll fuck your arse and fill you with spunk.'

'God, yes. Give me more, I want more.'

It was difficult to believe that this was Hayley, Anne mused as she slipped her hand down the front of her wet knickers and massaged her erect clitoris. Hayley the prude, Little Miss Perfect, was having her arse fucked in the woods. Wishing again that Dave had fucked her properly, Anne placed her camera on the ground and massaged her erect clitoris faster. She was desperate for an orgasm, but she knew that she'd have to stifle her whimpers of pleasure. Running her fingers up and down her wet sex valley, massaging her creamy juices into the sensitive tip of her clitoris, she lay back on the ground and parted her legs wide.

As Dave announced that he was coming, Hayley cried out and Anne held her breath as her own climax erupted and rocked her young body to the core. She could hear her sister's whimpers of pleasure, Dave's moans of satisfaction, as she massaged her clitoris faster and thrust two fingers deep into her contracting vagina. Her orgasm peaking, she writhed and whimpered on the ground, praying that she wouldn't be heard as cries of sexual gratification resounded around the trees.

Slowing her clitoral massaging as her climax finally began to fade, Anne hoped that Hayley would soon go home and leave Dave alone in the woods. She'd get him to fuck her arse, she thought in her wickedness. Would he like to have two sisters one after the other? Fuck one sister's arse and then drive his cock into the other girl's tight little bottom-hole? Alan would be up for it, she reflected as she slipped her wet fingers out of her inflamed vaginal sheath. So would Brian and Rick and . . .

'You were amazing,' Hayley gasped. She rolled off the log and sprawled her naked body out on the ground. 'I really needed that.'

'So did I,' Dave replied with a chuckle. 'I wish that Anne had been more like you.'

'I'm glad she's not, Dave. I wouldn't want Anne to get into this sort of thing. We've never really got on together but . . . She's got a good future ahead of her. I'd hate to see her ending up like me.'

It was the other way round, Anne thought guiltily. Hayley had ended up like Anne. She was screwing around, committing crude sexual acts and . . . The difference was that Hayley had dreadful financial worries. Turning her thought to her parents, Anne wondered what they'd say if they discovered that their daughters had grown up to be common sluts. They were so proud of Hayley and had high hopes for Anne. To find out that their girls had turned into dirty whores would destroy them.

'Are you coming to the pub for a drink?' Dave asked Hayley as they dressed.

'No,' the girl sighed. 'I think I'll stay here for a while. I need some time alone to think.'

'Come on, Hayley. It'll do you good to—'

'No, Dave. I'm behind with the payments on my car and they're taking it away in a couple of days. I'm in no mood to sit in the pub.'

'You're going to lose you new car?'

'Yes, I'm afraid so. You go to the pub, I'll be all right here.'

'OK, well . . . Thanks, it was great.'

As Dave left the clearing, Anne decided to talk to Hayley. She couldn't just wander into the clearing because Hayley would guess that she'd been hiding in the bushes, so she walked through the trees to the park and sat on the bench. Hayley would emerge from the woods at some stage, she reckoned as the evening sun warmed her young body. Still reeling from the dreadful news about her sister's financial situation, Anne wondered what the girl would do without her car. The railway station was miles away, but she had to get the train to London every day to go to work. Anne couldn't see a way out of the mess, but she thought that it might help if Hayley had someone to talk to.

'What are you doing here?' Hayley asked her accusingly as she emerged from the woods.

'We need to talk,' Anne said, smiling at her sister.

'Talk about what?' She joined Anne on the bench and sighed. 'About you going off with my boyfriends?'

'No, no . . . Hayley, I know about your situation.'

'What are you talking about?'

'Your financial situation.'

'Who . . . How do you . . .'

'It doesn't matter how. Let's put this feud behind us. I want to help you, if I can.'

Hayley hung her head. 'No one can help me,' she said. 'I've brought this on myself and . . . well, there's no way out.'

'Hayley, I know about Alan and Dave.'

'What do you know about them?'

'The things you did with them.'

'Anne, please stop talking in riddles.'

'You fucked Alan in that derelict house in the woods and you've just been with Dave . . .'

'You've been spying on me. You little bitch.'

'Let's not argue – I'm trying to help.'

'Were you watching me?'

'Yes,' Anne confessed. 'I was spying on you. And I know how I can help you.'

'I'm going home,' the other girl snapped, leaping up from the bench. 'To think that you've been spying on me—'

'For fuck's sake, Hayley,' Anne bellowed. 'I know how you can get out of this mess.'

'How?'

'The things you did with Alan and Dave . . . I do the same things with men.'

'So? How is that going to help me?'

'Men pay me for sex,' Ann said softly.

Hayley stared open-mouthed at her little sister, obviously in shock as she held her hand to her head. Anne didn't feel guilty or embarrassed about her confession. She was beyond such emotions, she thought as Hayley again sat beside her on the bench. Her quest wasn't to destroy her sister now, it was to save her from ruin, and she knew how to help her. Hayley had had anal sex with Alan, she'd been thrashed with a branch by Dave . . . The vicar would pay well to spend some time with the girl.

'You're a prostitute?' Hayley finally breathed.

'Yes.'

'I don't believe it. You're my little sister, you can't be a . . .'

'I take money from men in return for sex, Hayley. And you can do the same.'

'What?' the girl gasped, holding her hand to her mouth. 'I'm not going to—'

'All you have to do is what you did with Alan and Dave. The difference is that you'll get paid for it.'

'But . . . Anne, I owe a hell of a lot of money.'

'And you can earn a hell of a lot of money.'

'I'm going to need time to think about this. It's come as a shock to discover that you're a prostitute. It's going to take time to come to terms with that, let alone working as a prostitute myself. How did you start? I mean, how did you get into it?'

'That's a long story. Hayley, the vicar will pay—'

'The vicar? You mean, he pays you for . . .'

'Yes, he does. So does Brian, Alan's friend. Oh, and there's a man who comes down from London. The people who have been phoning the house and asking for you . . . They believe that you're a prostitute.'

'Yes, I know,' Hayley sighed. 'I know where the mix-up came from. There was a call yesterday and I asked the man a few questions. There's a girl calling herself Hayley and our phone numbers are very similar.'

'I took another call earlier from a man who wants sex. He asked for you and . . . well, I told him that my name's Hayley and I'm meeting him tomorrow morning.'

'Anne, how can you do this? To sell your body for sex is . . . It's awful.'

'It's profitable,' Anne retorted. 'He's going to pay two hundred pounds for an hour.'

'Really? God, that's a lot of money.'

'It's cheap, Hayley. I'll be putting my prices up soon. So, do you want to join me? We'll go into business together and—'

'No, no, I can't,' Hayley cut in. 'I know that I'm in debt, but I can't turn to prostitution.'

'How much are the payments on your car?'

'Five hundred a month.'

'That's easy – you can earn that in one week. Why don't you keep your job, for the time being, and work with me in the evenings? You can keep your car and you'll soon pay your credit card off.'

'Anne, I can't do it. It's tempting but . . . I just can't do it.'

'I saw what you did with Dave just now. The only difference is that—'

'I'll get paid for it, I know. But . . . sex with the vicar? God, I could never do that.'

'Come to the church with me now. If he's there, we'll—'

'Anne, no.'

'It's that or bankruptcy. The choice is yours, Hayley.'

'All right, but I'm only going to talk to him. I'm not going to give him a hand job for a few pounds, if that's what you're thinking.'

'Come on, we'll see whether he's there or not.'

As she led her sister across the park, Anne reckoned that they could do well in business together. Men would pay a small fortune to have two sisters attend their most intimate needs, she knew as they neared the church. And the vicar had been asking about Hayley, so she was sure that he'd be up for it. The trouble was that Hayley wasn't at all keen on the idea. If the vicar looked her up and down and suggested anal sex over the altar, she'd run a mile. Anne knew that she was going to have to work on Hayley to get her to agree.

Entering the church, she grinned as she noticed a light coming from the office. Ordering Hayley to hide, she said that she'd talk to the vicar and find out how much he'd pay for two sisters. Hayley wasn't happy and said that she didn't want to go through with it, but she finally agreed to at least talk to the man and waited in a dark corner outside the office door. Ann walked boldly into the office and grinned at the man of God.

'How would you like to have my sister and me?' she asked him.

He rose to his feet and stared at her 'You mean . . . I can have Hayley over the altar?'

'For a price, yes.'

'Well, er . . . I'd love to. How much?'

'Two hundred,' Anne said, knowing that Hayley was listening.

'Two hundred? But—'

'There are no buts, vicar. Take it or leave it.'

'I'm not rich, Anne.'

'OK, let's forget it.'

'No, no. I have my savings so . . . yes, I'll pay once a week.'

Hayley wandered into the office and smiled at the vicar. 'Cash up front,' she said, much to Anne's surprise.

The vicar looked her up and down. 'Of course,' he said quietly. 'I don't have that sort of money here but . . .'

'How much have you got?' Hayley asked him.

He opened the desk drawer. 'Fifty,' he said.

Snatching the cash, Hayley pulled her knickers down her long legs and slipped them off her feet. 'For fifty pounds, you may lick me,' she said, lifting her short skirt up over her stomach. 'Think of this as an introductory offer. Anne will give you a wank while you lick me.'

Sitting on the edge of the desk and lying back, Hayley parted her thighs wide as the vicar gazed in awe at her sparse blonde pubes. Anne stared in disbelief as her sister parted the fleshy lips of her pussy and exposed her inner folds. They were in business, she thought happily as the vicar knelt on the floor and licked the other girl's wet sex crack. Slurping between her parted sex lips, lapping up her flowing milk, he lifted his cassock and displayed his solid cock. Anne wasted no time, kneeling and grabbing his hard shaft as he licked and slurped between Hayley's slender thighs.

Hayley breathed heavily, her young body trembling, as Anne wanked the vicar. This was perfect, Anne thought, imagining the money they could earn. They'd build up a list of clients, pay off Hayley's debts, and then get a flat together. Wondering about renting the cottage that Jack was staying in, she knew that she'd have to put a stop to the marriage. The last thing she needed was Hayley getting married and ruining their new-found business.

The vicar's cock twitching, his full balls heaving, Anne wanked his rock-hard shaft faster as Hayley neared her orgasm. The girl was gasping, her beautiful body shaking uncontrollably, as the vicar sucked her erect clitoris into his hot mouth. Easy money, Anne thought, watching her sister's eyes rolling. Hayley was beautiful, she mused. The lips of her pussy were puffy and succulent, her breasts were large . . . Two sisters in business, she thought excitedly.

Hayley cried out as her pleasure exploded. Her head lolled from side to side and she stretched the fleshy lips of her pussy open wide as the vicar worked on her pulsating clitoris. The man of God was nearing his orgasm, Anne knew as his cock swelled in her hand. She though about sucking his purple knob into her mouth and sucking out his spunk, but he'd only paid fifty pounds. All he'd get was a wank, she decided.

'I want to fuck her,' the priest gasped, rising to his feet and pressing his swollen knob between Hayley's pussy lips.

'No,' Anne said, grabbing his cock. 'You can spunk over her pussy, but you're not fucking her.'

Rubbing the vicar's purple globe hard against her sister's pulsating clitoris, Anne grinned as the girl cried out in the grip of her climax. The priest's sperm gushed from his throbbing knob, splattering Hayley's smooth stomach and running down her open sex valley to her gaping vaginal hole. He threw his head back and let out a low moan of pleasure. He was desperate to push his cock into Hayley's tight vagina, but Anne wouldn't allow it. The introductory offer didn't include a fuck, she thought as his sperm-flow finally stemmed.

'Naughty boy,' she murmured as his cock began to deflate in her hand.

'She's beautiful,' the vicar gasped, gazing at Hayley's sperm-dripping sex crack. 'I'll get the money and . . . Come here tomorrow evening and I'll fuck both of you.'

'I think this is going to be a good arrangement,' Hayley said shakily as she propped herself up on her elbows.

'It is,' Anne agreed. 'And the vicar has a friend who will pay us.'

'Yes, yes, I have several friends,' he said, lowering his cassock as Hayley clambered off the desk. 'We'll arrange evenings and—'

'How many friends?' Anne cut in.

'I know of at least three who will pay you.'

'OK, contact them and arrange separate evenings for each of them.'

'Yes, yes, I will. May I just look at your tits, Hayley?'

'No,' the girl replied firmly. 'You don't have enough money. Next time you can have all of me.'

'Let's go,' Anne said, moving to the door. 'We'll be in touch, vicar. Contact your friends, and let me know the arrangement tomorrow.'

'Thank you, girls,' the man of God breathed, his face beaming as they left his office.

Once they were outside the church, Anne turned to Hayley and grinned. 'Well,' she said. 'You did surprise me. I thought that you were going to run off.'

'I need the money,' Hayley sighed. 'I don't like doing this but—'

'You had a massive orgasm,' Anne cut in, with a giggle. 'You're not trying to tell me that you didn't enjoy it?'

'No, but ... he's our local vicar, Anne. We've known him since we were kids, for God's sake.'

'I don't see what that has to do with it. We've got cunts, he's got cash . . .'

'Don't put it that way, it sounds awful. Anyway, I suppose we're in business.'

'We certainly are,' Anne trilled as they walked home. 'We'll soon have your debts cleared. You keep all the money we earn until you're straight, and then we'll go halves.'

'It will take a long time, I'm afraid.'

'Don't worry about that – we'll sort it out.'

'I feel that I'm getting to know you,' Hayley said, placing her arm around Anne's shoulders as they neared their house. 'We'll go up to my room and make our plans, OK?'

'Our plans for earning a fortune,' Anne said, hoping she could dissuade Hayley from marrying Jack.

Nine

Anne and Hayley had chatted for several hours before finally going to bed. The outcome had been good, apart from one thing Hayley had said that had shocked Anne. Hayley wasn't going to marry Jack, which was good news, but she had confessed to being in love with Dave. She'd said that she'd never screwed him behind Anne's back, but she'd wanted him from the day that Anne had taken him to the house and introduced him to her family. Anne hadn't said anything in response to her sister's revelation, but she knew that she was going to have to get Dave out of the way.

'I'm ready when you are,' Hayley said, wandering into Anne's bedroom. 'I shouldn't have taken the day off work, but—'

'Don't worry about that,' Anne cut in. 'I just hope that this man is willing to pay both of us.' Following Hayley down the stairs, she decided to say something about Dave. 'If you end up with Dave,' she said as they left the house, 'I mean, will you still work with me?'

'Let's take this one step at a time,' Hayley sighed. 'I have enough on my plate as it is without worrying about a future with Dave. Of course, it really depends on him. I haven't told him how I feel, so let's wait and see what happens.'

As she walked to the church with her sister, Anne knew that Dave was going to be a problem. He'd wanted Hayley all along, and he'd be over the moon if she declared her love for him. But there was no way that he'd agree to her working as a prostitute with her little sister. He could become a real problem, and one that would have to be dealt with. But how? Sitting on the low wall outside the church with Hayley, Anne decided to see Dave later that day and deal with him.

'You look great,' she said, eyeing Hayley's short skirt, her naked thighs. 'But you look great whatever you wear.'

'So do you, Anne. I don't know why you've never had any confidence.'

'I suppose it's because you've always done so well. You have lovely blonde hair and . . .'

'Your hair is great. Auburn hair is lovely, but you need to grow it.'

'Your tits are bigger than mine,' Anne said, giggling as she jutted her breasts out.

'Not all men like big tits, I can assure you. You're eighteen and lovely, Anne. Stop worrying about your looks.'

Hayley was right, Anne thought, checking her watch and looking up and down the lane. She hoped that the man would turn up and was pleased to be working with her sister. After years of squabbling, they were becoming friends. Their parents would think it strange that they didn't argue any more, but they'd never discover why. Gazing at Hayley, her blue eyes and full red lips, Anne recalled the lesbians in the derelict house. She never did go back for more lesbian sex, she reflected. Maybe she'd go to the house one lunchtime and see the girls, lick the girls.

'Hayley?' a man asked as he pulled up in his car.

'Yes,' Hayley replied.

'Who's your friend?' the man asked.

Anne leaned through the open passenger window. 'We're sisters,' she said. 'Would you like to screw two sisters?'

'How much?'

'Three hundred. You get one for half-price.'

'OK, get in.'

Sitting in the car's back seat with Hayley, Anne ordered the man to turn the car round and drive to the woods. He was in his fifties with greying hair and a suntanned face, and not at all bad-looking. He was wearing a white shirt and tie and was obviously a businessman. And, by the look of his car, he had money. Did he have a wife? Anne wondered. Did all married men go to prostitutes? This was going to work out well, she thought as he pulled up on the grass verge by the woods. Hayley looked rather anxious, but Anne knew that she'd be all right. Once she had her knickers off and the man was licking her pussy, she'd relax.

As she led the man to the old house, Anne thought how nice it would be to own the place. If they earned enough money that might be possible, she mused as she entered the house. It would need a hell of a lot of work done to it to make it habitable, but it would make a lovely home. As the man followed her into the front room, Anne realised that this wasn't the ideal place to work from. But it was all they had. Besides, was it comfort he wanted or two dirty young sisters to entertain him? Frowning at Anne, he asked her whether she owned the house.

'Yes, we do,' she lied. 'We haven't moved in yet because we're going to have it rebuilt. There's a mattress in one of the upstairs rooms, if you prefer?'

'No, no, this is fine.' Passing her the cash, he grinned at Hayley. 'Shall we start with you stripping naked?' he asked her.

186

'We'll both strip,' Anne said.

'How about a lesbian show?'

'Er . . . no,' Hayley replied. 'We're sisters, so—'

'Even better,' he cut in, with a chuckle. 'Still, not to worry.'

The girls undressed slowly, teasing him as he watched with bated breath. His cock would be as hard as rock, Anne thought as she displayed the firm mounds of her petite breasts. Dropping her skirt and tugging her knickers down, she realised that Hayley had never seen her naked. And she had no idea that she'd shaved her pussy. Wondering what her sister was thinking as she gazed at her bald sex lips, Anne felt a little embarrassed. It was one thing stripping in front of men, but not in front of her sister.

Hayley looked Anne up and down, her pretty face smiling as she winked at her little sister. Everything was going to work out, Anne was sure as the man stood in front of Hayley and kneaded the firm mounds of her ample breasts. His free hand slipped between Anne's slender thighs: he stroked the bald lips of her teenage pussy and ran his fingertip up and down her wetting sex crack. Sucking Hayley's ripe nipple into his mouth, he drove a finger deep into Anne's contracting vagina and massaged her wet inner flesh.

Moving his other hand between Hayley's thighs and driving a finger deep into her tight vagina, he slipped Hayley's nipple out of his mouth and sucked on one of Anne's elongated milk teats. He was obviously pleased with his purchase, Anne thought as she grinned at her sister. Wondering which girl he'd choose to screw first as he yanked his fingers out of their wet pussies and unbuckled his belt, Anne reckoned that he'd take Hayley.

Holding the root of his solid cock and ordering the sisters to kneel on the floor on all fours, the man knelt behind Anne as she took her position and parted her naked buttocks. She could feel his swollen knob running up and down her milk-dripping vaginal slit as she turned her head and gazed at her sister. Hayley smiled at her, and Anne reckoned that she was happy with the situation. They were a team, she thought cheerfully as the man's cock drove deep into her tightening sex sheath. They were going to work well together, and they'd earn a small fortune. The man slapped Hayley's naked buttocks and commented on the thin red weals fanning out across her naked flesh.

'Are you into spanking?' he asked the girl.

'Yes,' Hayley breathed. 'I'm into anything and everything.'

'It looks as though you've had the whip.'

'It was a branch of a bush,' she told him. 'I had my arse thrashed and then fucked.'

'I'll be seeing you two on a regular basis,' the man said, much to Anne's pleasure. 'I've been looking for a couple of high-class sluts, and you two are perfect.'

Anne wondered whether she should have charged him more as he slipped his rock-hard cock out of her contracting vagina and moved behind Hayley's naked body. High-class sluts? she mused happily as he thrust his pussy-wet organ into Hayley's tight vagina. He was right, she thought as he drove his cock fully home and Hayley let out a rush of breath. They weren't common whores, they were high-class sluts. Common prostitutes charged a few pounds for a blow job, she reflected. High-class girls could demand a fortune for their services.

As the man began his fucking motions, Anne listened to the squelching of her sister's vaginal juices, the slapping of his lower stomach against her naked bottom cheeks. Then he moved behind Anne, driving his solid cock deep into her spasming vaginal duct, and she wondered which girl would be lucky enough to take his spunk. Her naked body rocking with the illicit fucking, she gasped and trembled as her clitoris swelled against the man's pussy-slimed shaft. She needed an orgasm, she knew as she felt her vaginal milk streaming down the smooth flesh of her inner thighs. Would he be able to manage a second erection? she wondered as he yanked his cock out of her yearning pussy and once more drove the entire length of his shaft deep into Hayley's sex-drenched vagina.

Sure that Hayley was going to have his spunk pumped into her pussy, Anne wondered what the man was doing as he withdrew his juice-dripping cock and parted the rounded cheeks of her crimsoned buttocks. Grinning as she watched him run his tongue up and down Hayley's anal crease, she wondered whether her sister was enjoying his crude attention. The girl gasped and trembled, answering Anne's question as the man slipped his tongue into her rectal canal. Sucking and slurping, tonguing her anal duct, he finally left her and settled behind Anne's naked body, parting her firm bottom cheeks wide.

Anne trembled as the tip of his wet tongue now teased her anal hole. Would he fuck her there? she wondered dreamily, imagining his cock forcing its way deep into her rectal sheath and his fresh spunk jetting from his throbbing knob. Again moving his oral attention to Hayley's tight bottom-hole, the man licked and slurped, letting out low moans of pleasure as he savoured the taste of her most private duct. Anne thought about licking her sister's pussy as she listened to the man's slurping. She'd enjoyed her time with the teenage lesbians, she reflected. But to lick her sister's clitoris and suck out her vaginal milk . . . .

'I want one girl squatting over my face,' the man

said, settling on the floor on his back. 'And the other girl squatting over my cock.'

'You choose,' Anne said, eyeing his erect organ.

'I'll fuck you,' he said. 'Your sister can rub her cunt into my face.'

Facing each other and taking their positions, the girls smiled at each other. They really did work well together, Anne thought as she guided the man's cock deep into her sex-drenched vaginal sheath. Watching his tongue lapping at her sister's sex hole, she felt her own clitoris swell. Never had she thought that she'd get on with Hayley, let alone work with her as a prostitute and share a client. Hayley closed her eyes as the man sucked and licked her clitoris, and Anne began to breathe heavily as she bounced up and down on his huge cock. They were a great team, she thought again as Hayley began to gasp.

The man's sperm jetted from his throbbing knob and bathed Anne's cervix. Hayley cried out as her orgasm erupted. Anne threw her head back, whimpering as her climax exploded within the bulb of her solid clitoris. The gasping sounds of crude sex resounded around the derelict house as Anne lowered her head and focused on her sister's writhing body, an expression of pure sexual ecstasy depicted on her face. She should have charged the man a lot more money, she thought as his spunk spewed from her rhythmically contracting vagina.

Her orgasm began to wane and she slowed her bouncing rhythm as Hayley rocked her hips and ground her wet inner flesh into the man's gasping mouth. Was the man using them for sex, or were they using him? Anne wondered as her clitoris began to deflate and she shuddered her last orgasmic shudder. Watching as he sucked out Hayley's pussy milk, gulping down her female cream, she wondered whether the sex was over. Hayley hadn't been fucked and spunked, she reflected, hoping that it was her turn next.

Ordering the girls to kneel either side of him, the man looked at their flushed faces as they took their positions. He was more than happy with his purchase, Anne was sure as he gazed at each pair of firm breasts in turn and licked his lips. His cock was flaccid, wet with spunk and girl-juices, and she wondered whether he'd manage to fuck Hayley. It would be a shame if she didn't get her fair share of fresh spunk, Anne thought. But, as he instructed her to suck and lick him until he was hard again, she reckoned that her sister would have her share after all.

Anne leaned over and licked the man's wet shaft as Hayley lapped up the spilled sperm from his rolling balls. Their tongues slurping, their stares meeting, they smiled as his cock stiffened and stood to attention. Hayley retracted his foreskin and sucked his purple knob into her pretty mouth as Anne ran her tongue up and down his veined shaft, and his cock twitched and his balls heaved as he moaned softly. Hayley then licked his solid shaft and Anne sucked on his bulbous knob until he ordered them to take their positions as before, but to swap places.

Hayley knelt astride the man's hips and eased the full length of his erect cock deep into her wet vaginal sheath as Anne lowered her naked body and pressed the bald lips of her teenage pussy against his open mouth. Sounds of sex resounded around the room again as Hayley bounced up and down on his huge cock. Anne watched her sister being fucked as the man's tongue entered her own gaping vaginal hole and worked its way deep into her cream-drenched sex duct. This was real sex, she mused dreamily as he sucked out her pussy milk and drank from her teenage body. This was also a great way to earn a lot of money.

Hayley would soon be out of debt, Anne felt sure as the trembling girl bounced up and down faster. Watching Hayley's outer lips rolling back and forth along the huge cock, Anne noticed her sister's solid clitoris protruding between them. Hayley had a beautiful body, she thought, but she reckoned that she should shave her pubic hairs. Smooth, bald lips, her tight sex crack clearly visible . . . Men would like that. Men would pay dearly for two sisters with hairless pussies.

As the man's teeth sank gently into Anne's vaginal flesh, sending her arousal rocketing, she again pondered on the future. She'd waited years for Hayley to move out of the house but now she wanted to find a place to share with her sister. They'd invite clients back to their flat, give them sex in return for cash and . . . The village was too small, she decided as Hayley shafted herself on the man's cock and began to gasp. Word would soon get round, and it wouldn't be long before the locals discovered what the sisters were up to.

Hayley cried out as her orgasm erupted. The man's sperm flooding her contracting vagina, her clitoris pulsating wildly, she threw her head back and bounced up and down faster on his solid cock as Anne's own clitoris exploded in orgasm. The sight of Hayley's gaping vaginal lips heightened Anne's own pleasure and she again imagined spending some time with the young lesbians in the room upstairs. Was she bisexual? she wondered as images of a girl's tongue licking between her swollen sex lips filled her mind. What would her sister say if she were to discover that she'd had sex with two teenage girls?

'No more,' the man gasped through a mouthful of Anne's wet vaginal flesh as Hayley rode his cock. 'I'm worn out.'

'You were good,' Anne praised him as her climax faded. 'One of the best clients we've got.'

'And you two were amazing. We'll definitely meet again.'

'Let us know if you have any friends who might be interested in meeting us,' Hayley whispered shakily, sliding the man's cock out of her sperm-dripping vagina and clambering to her feet.

'Will I get a discount?' he said, chuckling as Anne stood up. 'Ten per cent off for every friend I introduce to you?'

'No,' Anne replied. 'You're doing well as it is.'

He smiled at her as he swayed on his trembling legs. 'I want a permanent arrangement with you,' he said softly as he dressed. 'I've been with dozens of girls, but I've never had such a good time.'

'We'll always be here for you,' Anne assured him, imagining the money they were going to earn. 'I'll give you my mobile number – ring any time.'

Anne wasn't sure that the derelict house was a good place as she thought she heard someone outside the window. Dressing, she imagined Alan or Brian lurking beneath the window, watching the sex show. Her thoughts turning to Dave as Hayley chatted to the man, she decided to meet him. If he discovered that Hayley was in love with him, he'd chase after her and the future would be in ruins. The photos of Hayley's debauchery might shock him and send him running, she reckoned. But if Hayley found out . . . It wasn't worth the risk, she concluded, writing her phone number down for the man.

'I'll call you next week,' he said. 'Probably on Monday.'

'OK,' Anne said, returning his smile. 'We'll be ready for you.' Watching the man leave the house, she turned to Hayley. 'That went very well, don't you think?' she asked her.

'All that money,' the girl gasped. 'I can't believe that we've earned all that money.'

'And there's a lot more where that came from. So are you happy with our new business?'

'Yes, yes, I am. But . . . the thing is . . . I can't stop thinking about Dave. If he found out that I'm working as a . . . as a prostitute, he wouldn't want to know me.'

'Forget about him,' Anne said firmly. 'You're trying to get out of debt and avoid bankruptcy. You go chasing after Dave, telling him that you're in love with him, and you'll end up—'

'I know, I know,' Hayley sighed. 'But I can't help the way I feel about him. I never went behind your back, Anne. When you were seeing Dave, I never tried to steal him away.'

'I know that. To be honest, I found him boring. All he ever wanted to do was sit in the pub talking football with his mates.'

'I'm going to arrange to see him,' Hayley said as they left the house. 'I might see him this evening and have a chat.'

'About football?' Anne quipped, trying not to show her displeasure. 'Because that's all he'll want to chat about.'

'I have to talk to him, Anne. I have to tell him how I feel about him. Anyway, he certainly wasn't boring when I was last with him. I'd never had such a good time.'

'I was hoping that we could go to the church this evening and see the vicar. Still, if you'd rather see Dave than earn a few hundred . . .'

'I'll see Dave, and then we'll see the vicar.'

Anne knew that she had to get to Dave before Hayley went blabbing her mouth off to him about love. Walking along the narrow path through the trees, she reckoned that he wouldn't be around until the evening. He'd probably go to the pub at five o'clock, by which time Hayley would be there waiting for him. Alan would be in the pub too and Brian might be there and ... Coming up with an idea as they reached their house, she went up to the bathroom.

'The vicar just called,' she said, leaving the bathroom and finding Hayley in her bedroom. 'He wants us there at six this evening.'

'Can't we go later?' the girl sighed. 'I wanted to talk to Dave first.'

'I can see that Dave is going to ruin our business plans,' Anne said. 'What do I do, tell the vicar that we can't make it?'

'Tell him that we'll be there at seven. That'll give me an hour with Dave.'

'He wants us there at six, Hayley. Look, maybe we should call the whole thing off. I'll go alone to see the vicar and you ... you go and talk love with Dave.'

'No, I—'

'If you want to stay in debt, that's your problem. I'm only trying to help you, and I can't do that with Dave on the scene.'

'I only want an hour with him.'

'All right, meet Dave at seven o'clock. That'll give us an hour with the vicar, which should be long enough.'

'OK, I'll be at the church at six.'

Anne had no ulterior motive – she genuinely wanted to help her sister. She could have worked alone and made a fortune, but she didn't want to see Hayley go bankrupt. She spent the day resting in her room and finally left at five-thirty and walked to Dave's house. She had no idea what her plan was, but she hoped to at least keep him away from the pub until she came up with something. She waited a few yards from his house – she knew that he always went to the pub at five so it would be easy enough to waylay him and lure him to the park. Hayley wouldn't be in the pub until seven, she thought, checking her watch. Where the hell was Dave? she wondered as the time passed. Five-fifteen, five-twenty . . .

'Hi,' she called as he finally walked towards her.

'Oh, hi,' he said, smiling at her. 'Where are you off to?'

'I was just passing. Are you going to the pub?'

'Yes, I've had a hectic day and I need to relax. How's Hayley?'

'I don't know, I haven't seen her today. Dave, would you like to go to the park with me?'

'No, I need a drink. Maybe some other time.'

'Dave, we need to talk.'

'What about? Can't we talk in the pub?'

'We could, but people will be around.'

'I'm going to ask Hayley to come to the pub,' Dave persisted. 'I need to talk to her about . . .'

'Hayley is in London,' Anne lied. 'She's arranging her marriage.'

'I don't think that she wants to get married. She was talking to me yesterday about it, and I don't think . . . I reckon that she wants to be with me.'

'You've got it all wrong, Dave.'

'No, I haven't. She's in a bad situation at the moment. She hasn't told anyone else about it, but we had a long chat yesterday and she told *me* all about it. I know that I can help her.'

'I know about her situation, Dave, and there's nothing you can do to help her.'

'I have some money saved and I'm soon to be promoted. I'll get a flat and Hayley can come to live with me and—'

'So you want to look after the baby?'

'What?' Dave gasped, frowning at her.

'The baby, Dave. That's why she's getting married.'

'But I thought . . . God, I didn't know about that.'

'Look, come to the park for a while and we'll talk.'

'OK,' he finally conceded.

Heading for the park, Anne wondered why she was bothering to help Hayley get out of debt. She also wondered why she'd spun such a massive lie to Dave. He was bound to tell Hayley and all hell would be let loose. Reaching the park, she led Dave into the woods and sat on the grass in the clearing. He hovered, shuffling his feet and looking anxious as she rested her chin on her knees and displayed the bulging crotch of her tight knickers. This wasn't the time for sex, she mused as he paced up and down.

'I suppose that changes things,' he finally said. 'I didn't realise that she was getting married because . . . I wish that she'd told me the truth.'

'She hasn't told anyone, Dave. And she won't be at all pleased if you tell her that you know the truth. The best thing is to leave her alone, let her get on with her life.'

'Yes, you're right. Actually, there is another girl who's been chasing after me. You don't want me and neither does Hayley, so I might as well see her.'

'What's her name? Is she local?'

'Yes, she goes to the college. Her name's Dee.'

'Oh, er . . .' Anne stammered, recalling licking the girl's wet pussy. 'Yes, I think I know her. Where did you meet her?'

'At the old house in the woods, of all places. I got talking to her and she said that she was waiting for a friend so I thought it wouldn't go any further. She kept chatting me up, coming on strong and, as it turned out, her friend was another girl. I've seen her around the village a few times and ... well, I might as well go out with her.'

'Yes, that's a good idea,' Anne said. 'Did you meet her friend?'

'No, I didn't. Apparently, they go to the house to do some ghost-hunting.'

'I've seen a lot of things there but never ghosts. Anyway, I think that you'd be far better off with her than with Hayley.'

'Yes, you're right. Well, I'm off to the pub. Are you coming with me?'

'No, I'll ... If you see Hayley, don't mention anything.'

'Don't worry, I won't tell her about our chat. Are you sure you don't want a drink?'

'No, I'm fine. I'll just sit here for a while and chill out.'

'OK – see you around.'

That was a relief, Anne thought as Dave left the clearing. Now she was free to run the business with her sister – and earn some real money. Leaving the clearing, she walked to the church and sat on the low wall. The next problem would be Hayley turning up at six o'clock, she thought, looking up and down the lane. She'd have to tell her that the vicar couldn't make it and had arranged another evening. This was becoming complicated, she knew as Hayley walked towards her.

'You look great,' she said, admiring Hayley's red miniskirt and leather boots.

'Mum said that I was dressed like a tart,' the girl

muttered. 'If only she knew how right she was. Shall we go into the church?'

'Er, hang on,' Anne said, following the girl up the path. 'I was going to—'

'Why are churches always so cold?' Hayley cut in, walking down the aisle to the altar.

'I suppose they're old buildings. Hayley, I was going to say that—'

'Good evening, girls,' the vicar called, his face beaming as he emerged from his office.

'Hi,' Anne said. 'Are you . . . are you ready for us?'

'I'm always ready for two horny little sisters. I have plenty of money in the office, my cock is hard and . . . I'll go and lock the doors and I'll be right with you.'

Breathing a sigh of relief, Anne smiled at Hayley. Things couldn't have worked out better, she reflected as the vicar walked towards them, wearing a huge grin. Hayley was up for it, the vicar had cash, and Dave wouldn't present a problem now. Watching the vicar slip out of his cassock, Anne focused on his erect penis and grinned. Hayley also gazed at his cock, her blue eyes wide as his huge balls rolled. Passing each girl a leather strap, he clambered onto the altar and instructed them to whip his cock.

'What?' Hayley breathed, frowning at Anne.

'Whip my cock,' he repeated as he lay on his back with his member pointing to the church roof. 'Give it a good whipping until it shoots spunk.'

'If you say so,' Anne murmured, raising the leather strap above her head.

'Take it in turns,' the vicar said. 'First one, and then the other.'

Bringing the strap down across his solid cock, Anne giggled as his naked body jolted. Hayley then brought her strap down, the leather cracking loudly against the priest's twitching shaft. His full balls

199

rolling, his cock twitching, the girls took turns to lash his cock as he writhed in his illicit ecstasy on the altar. Anne didn't think that he'd reach an orgasm by having his cock whipped, but she was more than happy to play the game. The loud cracks echoing around the church, his cock glowing a fire-red, he begged for more as the girls each lashed his swollen organ.

Anne stood back as Hayley seemed to lose control and whipped the vicar's cock with a vengeance. Anne had never dreamed that her sister was like this, she reflected as the vicar gasped in the grip of his peculiar pleasure. Then again, working as a prostitute was the last thing on earth that Anne would have thought she'd do, let alone her sister. All this had started when she'd thought that Hayley had chased after Dave, she reflected as the vicar announced that he was about to spunk. What would have happened if she'd never suspected that her boyfriend was seeing her sister?

Hayley giggled as the vicar's spunk jetted from his burning cock. Repeatedly bringing the leather strap down across his abused organ, she lashed his prick harder until he rolled onto his stomach and begged her to stop. Eyeing his naked buttocks, she repeatedly brought the strap down across his tensed flesh again and again, giggling as he writhed on the altar. Anne realised that Hayley was going too far and grabbed her arm, halting the gruelling thrashing as the vicar begged for mercy.

'My God,' the vicar cried, rolling onto his back. 'That was a *real* thrashing.'

'You can have more if you want,' Hayley said, raising the leather strap high above her head.

'No, no,' he gasped. 'Please, no more.'

'What next?' Anne asked him, gazing at his sperm-drenched cock and balls. 'By the look of your cock, I don't think you're in a fit state to fuck us.'

'I want Hayley,' the priest gasped. 'I want Hayley's cunt in my mouth.'

Hayley stripped naked, exposing her hairless crack to her sister's wide-eyed gaze as she clambered onto the altar and knelt astride the vicar's face. Anne couldn't believe that the other girl had shaved, but she was pleased to think that she was obviously settling in well to her new job. Watching as the vicar pushed his tongue into Hayley's gaping sex hole, Anne was surprised by the puffiness of her sister's sex lips. She was beautiful in every way, she mused as the vicar slurped and sucked. But she was also stone-broke.

Wondering how Hayley had got herself into her terrible financial position, Anne wandered into the vicar's office and opened the desk drawer. The vicar would be too busy enjoying himself to notice that she'd gone, she was sure as she rummaged through the drawer. Grabbing a wad of cash, she found a brown envelope and opened it. Pulling out several photographs of the teenage lesbians writhing in ecstasy on the mattress in the derelict house, Anne wondered what other photos the priest had hidden away. He must have been hiding in the house, she thought, hoping that he hadn't taken photos of *her* with the girls.

Hanging onto the cash and the photos, Anne went back to the altar to find Hayley in the middle of a massive orgasm. The vicar was drinking her sex milk, his cock as hard as rock as he gulped down her orgasmic offering. He was a dark horse, Anne thought, stuffing the cash and photos into her hand-bag. What else had he been up to? she wondered as Hayley leaned forward and sucked his ripe plum into her sperm-thirsty mouth. Slipping back to the office, Anne rummaged through the other drawers and discovered a half-written letter to the young lesbians.

'Blackmail,' she breathed as she read: '*Unless you share your young bodies with me, I'll show the photographs to your parents and I'll be going to your college and . . .*' The vicar was a dangerous man, she thought angrily as she headed back to the altar. And dangerous men had to be dealt with. Watching her sister gulping down the priest's spunk, Anne grabbed her camera from her handbag and took several photographs. Two can play at blackmail, she reflected, imagining the vicar's bishop gazing at the lewd pictures.

Thinking again that the derelict house wasn't a good place to take her clients, Anne grabbed a leather strap from the floor and gazed at the vicar's flaccid cock as Hayley sat upright on his face. She was going to have to find somewhere else to entertain her clients, she thought as she brought the strap down across the limp shaft of his spent prick. The priest cried out through a mouthful of Hayley's vaginal flesh as Anne repeatedly lashed his crimsoned cock. Begging for mercy, he tried to cover his genitalia with his hands, but Hayley grabbed his wrists and pinned him down.

'Blackmail,' Anne said, lashing his spunk-dripping cock. 'You're blackmailing two friends of mine.'

'No, no,' the man of God managed to gasp.

'Dee and Angela?'

'Oh, I . . . I was only . . .'

'What's this about?' Hayley asked her sister.

'The vicar has photographs of my lesbian friends and he's threatened to tell their parents about them unless they have sex with him.'

'Lesbian friends?' Hayley echoed. 'Er . . . anyone I know?'

'I don't think so. Why, are you interested?'

'No, no,' Hayley breathed, obviously lying. 'I just wondered who they were.'

'Please . . .' the vicar cried as the strap once more lashed the swelling shaft of his fire-red cock.

'What's the matter, vicar?' Anne asked him. 'Don't you like it?'

'No, I . . .'

'Let him go,' Anne told Hayley. 'I want him to do something for us.'

Freeing the man of God, Hayley grabbed her knickers and pulled them up her long legs as he almost fell off the altar and staggered on his trembling legs. Anne pulled a photograph from her handbag and held it up before the naked vicar. His stare darted between the picture and Anne – he obviously knew that he was in trouble. He stammered something incoherent as Hayley took the photo and gazed at the young girls' bodies entwined in lesbian lust.

'They're beautiful,' Hayley said softly.

'They're also being blackmailed,' Anne murmured. 'They're just young girls, learning and experimenting with sex, and you come along with your sordid mind and—'

'They're sluts,' the priest retorted. 'Sluts need a good fucking. I've already told them that I have the pictures and—'

'They must be as worried as hell,' Hayley said. 'How could you do that?'

'I want you to give me five thousand pounds,' Anne said, glaring at the vicar.

'What?' he gasped. 'If you think that I'm going to—'

'OK, I'll send the photos to your bishop.'

Hayley grabbed the man as he tried to snatch the photograph. 'I don't like blackmail,' she said. 'You'd better do as Anne says, or you'll not only be out of a job but featured in the national newspapers.'

'We'll wait here while you get the money,' Anne said, sitting on the edge of the altar.

'I don't have that sort of cash lying around. And even if I did . . .'

'Those poor young girls must be having sleepless nights,' Hayley murmured. 'How on earth could you do such a thing to them?'

'We'll be here tomorrow morning,' Anne said. 'You'd better have the cash, or else. Come on, Hayley, let's go home.'

As she left the church Anne knew that the vicar would pay up. She didn't like threatening him, but he'd threatened the young lesbians and had to pay for his crime. Besides, five thousand would go a long way to getting her sister out of debt. Holding Hayley's hand as they walked along the lane, she recalled the girl's comments when she'd looked at the photo of the young lesbians. Was Hayley into other girls? she wondered as they reached their house.

'How about going on to the pub?' Anne suggested. 'I could do with a drink.'

'Good idea,' Hayley replied. 'Anne, I . . . I don't think that we should take the vicar's money. I mean, five thousand pounds is a hell of a lot cash.'

'And you *need* a hell of a lot of cash,' Anne returned.

'You know the lesbians, then?'

'Yes, they're friends of mine.'

As she walked into the pub and ordered the drinks, Anne knew that Hayley was interested in the teenage girls. She took the drinks to a table and passed the photos to her, watching her face for her reaction. Hayley studied them, her blue eyes lighting up as she looked through the pictures several times. Had she indulged in lesbian sex? Anne wondered as she finally slipped the photos back into her bag. Was there even more to her big sister than met the eye?

Ten

Hayley had had her breakfast and gone to work by eight o'clock. She hadn't wanted to take another day off and possibly lose her job, and Anne had quipped about her not giving up her day job until 'the business' was bringing in decent money. Anne was happy to think that she was getting on so well with Hayley. They'd come a long way in a few days, she thought, recalling the arguments they'd had in the past. Those days were over, she reflected as she left the house and headed for the church. They were not only in business together, but they'd become good friends.

'Hi,' Dave called as he hurried along the lane and approached Anne. 'Sorry I didn't join you and Hayley in the pub last night. I thought I'd better leave you both alone to chat.'

'Thanks,' Anne said. 'We did have some things to sort out.'

'So where are you off to?'

'I have to go and see the vicar.'

Dave frowned. 'The vicar?' he echoed.

'I have to talk to him about something. Don't worry, I'm not getting married.'

'Thank God for that. By the way, I saw Dee last night on my way home from the pub. We're seeing each other this evening.'

'That's great, Dave. She's a . . . she's a nice girl. I hope things work out for you both.'

'So do I, but . . . she seems to be well in with another girl – Angela, I think that's her name. They're always together and I'm just wondering whether she'll be able to drag herself away to see me.'

'I'm sure she will, Dave. Where are you meeting her?'

'In the pub.'

'Don't go talking about football to your mates and ignore her.'

'No, I won't. I miss you, Anne. I thought that we were going to be long-term together but . . . Not to worry.'

'Perhaps we should meet in the park now and then. If you want to, that is?'

'Yes, in the woods where we were last night. I'd like that.'

'I thought you would. OK, I must go. I'll see you soon.'

'Maybe this evening?'

'Yes, maybe.'

Dave wasn't so bad, Anne thought as she neared the church. But she wasn't sure how long he'd last with Dee, especially if Angela was always hanging around. Wondering whether the girls would be at the old house at lunchtime, she decided to go and take a look. Her lesbian experience had played on her mind, and she needed to discover her true feelings. Was she bisexual? she wondered as she walked into the church. Grinning as she imagined having sex with Dave's new girlfriend, she imagined sucking his spunk out of her young pussy. Her arousal rising, she pushed all thoughts of sex from her mind as she walked down the aisle.

Nearing the office, Anne heard the vicar on the phone and waited silently outside the door. 'Five

207

grand,' he said. 'Yes, of course I have the money. But that's not the point.' Anne wondered who he was talking to as she peered round the door and spied on him. 'If she finds out about the other photos I've taken . . . What about the other girls? If she finds out about them, especially Dawn, then I'm in real trouble. No, I'm going to give her the money and hope that it ends there. Yes, yes, I will.'

Creeping back to the church doors, Anne stepped outside and waited for a few minutes. The vicar obviously had several dark secrets, she reflected, wondering who Dawn was. It would be best not to ask him about the other girls until he'd paid up, she decided. But if he was blackmailing young girls into having sex with him, she'd have to put a stop to it. Finally wandering back into the church and noticing the priest standing by the altar, she walked slowly towards him. He was an evil man, she mused. There again, he was only trying to have sex with beautiful young girls, she reminded herself. But it was the way he was going about it that annoyed her.

'Anne,' he said, turning and facing her. 'Look, this is crazy. I took a few photos and . . .'

'And now you're blackmailing my two friends.'

The vicar chuckled. 'It's not real blackmail,' he said, shaking his head. 'I just wanted to screw the girls. I mean, I would never force them.'

'You've threatened to tell their parents. That's forcing them, isn't it?'

'I wouldn't have said anything to their parents. If they didn't want sex, then I'd have left it at that. And do remember that they're sluts. It's not as if they're young virgins or anything.'

'Have you got the money?'

'Yes, in the office,' the priest sighed.

Following him, Anne wondered again who Dawn

was. 'I can't stay because I'm meeting a friend,' she said. 'She's worried about something and she needs someone to talk to.'

'Anyone I know?' the vicar asked, opening the desk drawer.

'Her name's Dawn.'

His face turned pale as he stared at her. 'Dawn Sudbury?' he gasped. 'The girl from Craven Farm?'

'Yes, that's her.'

'Anne, we need to talk,' the priest murmured, sitting down at the desk.

Anne sat opposite him and frowned. 'Talk about what?'

'I'm not a bad person,' he began. 'Like any other man, I'm into young girls, teenage girls. Being a vicar, I'm in contact with many girls. As you know, I run the summer fêtes, do the Christmas stuff and . . . and I know just about everyone in the village. Some of the villagers' daughters come to me with their problems and—'

'And you blackmail them?'

'No, not exactly.'

'You either do or you don't.'

'It's not blackmail, Anne. I wish you'd stop using that word.'

'I know about the other girls,' Anne blurted.

'What? You mean . . .'

'I know about Dawn and the others.'

'Oh, I see.'

'My friends, the lesbians, are really worried. They think that you're going to go to their parents and the college and—'

'I'd never do that. They started taunting me, that's how all this began. They'd come here wearing short skirts and flashing their knickers and . . . They were teasing me, so I thought I'd get something on them and retaliate. When I followed them to that old house in the woods and I saw what they got up to, I was stunned. And Dawn did the same thing. She came here showing off her knickers and making sure that I could see her tits down the front of her T-shirt and—'

'Who was the man you were talking to on the phone?'

'I might have guessed that you were hovering somewhere listening to me. His name is Brian.'

'Not the Brian that I know from the pub?'

'Yes, that's the one. This village is full of teenage girls, and we just want some of the action. I'll tell you a few things about this village. Anita, the young girl who lives in the old school house, screws older men behind the pub. Jenny, the girl from the corner shop, is screwing Mrs Barker's husband, the man who owns the garage. Caroline, the prim and proper girl from the big house up the lane, is screwing Jake, the farm hand. I just want some of the action, and so does Brian.'

'Yes, but ... Blackmail is dreadful.'

'It's not blackmail. Anyway, look at Hayley.'

'What about Hayley?'

'Hayley's so-called photographic business. Surely you know about it?'

'No, I ...'

'You don't know anything, Anne. You've started selling yourself for sex and ... You know nothing about this village or the people in it.'

'Tell me about Hayley.'

'She's had financial problems because she lent some money to a photographer friend of hers in London. She's trying to get the money back by taking photographs of girls and selling them on the Internet.'

'But ... what girls?'

'Any girls who will strip naked for her, and there

are quite a few in this village. She pays them twenty pounds to strip and pose for the camera.'

'I don't know what to say,' Anne murmured. 'I'd always been so envious of Hayley and . . . I just don't know what to say.'

'Don't say anything.' Passing her the cash, the priest smiled. 'Take the money and don't say anything to Hayley or anyone else about the things I've told you. And don't tell Hayley that you know about her photo business.'

'No, no I won't. But, why are you giving me the money?'

'I know that you want it to help Hayley out and . . . well, I can easily afford it. I'll want sex over the altar in return, though,' he added with a chuckle.

'Yes, yes, of course. But I still don't understand why you're giving me five thousand pounds?'

'As I said, it's to help Hayley out. And, I have to be honest, it's to stop you causing trouble. After all, you are blackmailing me.'

'No, I wasn't really going to . . . This has been quite enlightening. I'd never thought that . . . I don't know what I thought. How do you know about Hayley's photo business?'

'She told me during one of our Friday-evening chats.'

'But you said that she didn't come here?'

'I thought you knew about her visits, that's why I mentioned Friday evenings. When I realised that you knew nothing about it, I said that I'd been lying. She doesn't come here for sex, we only chat. And she sells me a few photographs.'

'The pictures of the lesbians in the old house – did she take them?'

'There's no fooling you, is there? Yes, she took them. The girls posed for her and—'

'So she paid the girls to pose, sold the photos to you, and you were using them to blackmail the girls into having sex with you?'

'Anne, Hayley and I have been working together on this. She takes the photos and sells them on the Internet. She also sells them to me and I ask the girls for sex.'

'So she knows that you blackmail them?'

'It's not blackmail but, yes, she knows about it.'

Stunned by the vicar's revelation, Anne held her hand to her mouth. Was he lying about Hayley? she wondered. He hadn't been honest in the past, and she knew that he'd do pretty much anything to get his hands up young girls' skirts. But surely Hayley wasn't involved in his scam? This changed everything, she thought angrily, wondering whether Hayley really had gone to work. Perhaps she was lurking in the derelict house with her camera? Perhaps she was—

'Are you all right?' the vicar asked Anne, breaking her reverie.

'No, not really,' she sighed. 'Having just discovered that my sister is not only into this blackmail business with you but that she's also selling dirty photos on the Internet, I'm far from all right. I've been trying to help her to get out of debt, and she's been lying to me.'

'She hasn't lied to you, Anne. It's just that she hasn't mentioned her little business venture to you.'

'That's lying, as far as I'm concerned. What else have you got to hide?'

'Nothing, nothing at all.'

'You wouldn't give me five grand unless you had something else to hide. Remember that I have photos of you with Hayley on the altar. The bishop would be very interested to see—'

'Now, that *is* blackmail,' the priest cut in. 'Hayley was horrified when you took those photographs of us. And when you demanded five thousand pounds . . .'

'I wondered why she wasn't keen on the idea. But I still think that you're hiding something from me.'

'I've confided in you, Anne. I've told you everything, so let's leave it at that.'

'I want to know more about Hayley,' Anne persisted. 'I don't even know where she works. If she works at all, that is.'

'I don't know everything about your sister,' he sighed. 'We have our regular chats, but I don't know everything. Just leave it, Anne. The money I gave you is to—'

'Stop me from interfering?'

'It's to stop you talking to Hayley. Hayley is a grown woman of twenty-two. What she does is her business, so don't go blabbing to her or asking her questions.'

'Why has she set up in business with me? She seems to be doing well enough with you and her photos, so why bother with me?'

'Because you were poking around the derelict house, you started charging men for sex, you took her phone calls and arranged to meet men . . .'

'So she's been a prostitute all along?'

'Yes, she has. It's a shame that you poked your nose in.'

'I didn't poke my nose in. I thought that she was screwing my boyfriend and . . . It doesn't matter now. I'm going home.'

'All right, but don't go saying anything.'

'No, I won't.'

'Give Hayley the money and—'

'Give Hayley the money? After the way she's . . . I'll see you around.'

As she left the church Anne thought what a fool she'd been. Hayley had taken her for a ride, she reflected angrily. And she was sure that the vicar was hiding something. Hayley was doing more than paying teenage girls twenty pounds to strip in front of the camera, and she was determined to find out what it was. There were a lot of teenage girls in the village, she thought. Girls also came from surrounding villages to go to the college, so Hayley wouldn't be short of victims. Pondering on the scam that Hayley was running with the vicar, Anne thought it was quite clever. Hayley took the photos, the vicar bought them and then threatened to expose the girls unless they had sex with him. It was *very* clever, she reflected.

On reaching her house she bounded up the stairs and went into Hayley's bedroom. She sat at the desk and switched the computer on, reckoning that Hayley's photos would be in a hidden folder. The problem would be trying to find them. 'Shit,' she breathed when the computer asked her for a password to access a folder. Tapping her fingers on the desk, she tried several words that she thought might be relevant to her sister, but none of them worked. 'Date of birth,' she breathed. 'OK, let's try "Hayley". Shit . . . How about "vicar"? No, no, no. What about, the pet rabbit she used to have? "Boxer".'

The screen flashed and up came a list of photographs. Anne clicked on the first one and found herself staring at a naked teenage girl. She realised that the photo had been taken in the derelict house, but she had no idea who the girl was. The second picture showed a naked girl with a solid cock in her mouth and sperm running down her chin. Who was the man? Anne wondered, unable to see his face in the shot. These weren't just pictures of naked teenage girls, she thought as she looked at the third picture of a girl with a huge cock embedded deep in her bottom-hole. This was porn.

Wondering whether Hayley had a website as she copied the photos to a CD, Anne finally switched the computer off and went to her own bedroom. Lifting a corner of the carpet and hiding the cash beneath a loose floorboard, she wondered again why the vicar had parted with so much money. If he'd wanted to help Hayley out, he'd have given *her* the money. So why give it to Anne? Reckoning that he was hoping that she'd stop her snooping, she decided to go to the derelict house and take a closer look at the rooms. As she left the house, Anne reckoned that Hayley must have a website if she was selling photos on the Internet. She'd look into that later, she thought as she walked down the lane to the woods.

The house seemed quiet, but Anne reckoned that the smell of sex hung heavy in the air. How many times had Hayley been there with her camera? she wondered as she climbed the stairs. Wandering into the room where she'd had lesbian sex, she gazed at the mattress on the floor and recalled the girls licking her vaginal hole and sucking on her erect clitoris. Would they turn up at lunchtime? Or would Hayley turn up, hoping to photograph naked teenage girls?

Wandering into another room, Anne didn't expect to find anything as she opened an old wardrobe. Hayley, or anyone else, would hardly leave any evidence of sex in the house. How come the place was used as a sex den? If it was that well known among teenage girls and dirty old men, no one would have any privacy there. She went down the stairs and walked into the front room where she gazed at the old armchair and recalled the first spanking she'd had there. Her life had been turned upside down in such a short time, she reflected as she gazed through the broken window. From an ordinary teenage girl, she'd been transformed into a nymphomaniacal, bisexual prostitute.

Sensing someone approaching, Anne dashed through the hall and hid in what had once been the kitchen. She hadn't been able to see who the girl was but she thought it best to keep out of sight. Hearing footsteps in the hall, she peered round the door and stifled a gasp as she saw Hayley walking into the front room. What the hell was she doing there? Had she come to meet someone? She was carrying a leather bag, and Anne reckoned that she had her camera with her. If that was the case, then she would be expecting to use the camera. But who did she plan to photograph? Anne only had to wait a few minutes to find out.

'Hello,' a girl called as she walked into the hall.

'In here,' Hayley replied.

Anne didn't recognise the teenage girl, but thought how attractive she was with her long blonde hair and with her petite breasts clearly defined by her tight T-shirt. Anne could hear what they were saying but she thought it was too risky to venture into the hall right then. If Hayley saw her . . . Still, she finally crept into the hall, knowing that Hayley couldn't say anything – Anne was allowed to be in the house as much as anyone else, and there was nothing that Hayley could do about it.

'There's the money,' Hayley said as Anne spied through the crack in the door.

'I'm still not sure that I want to do this,' the girl muttered anxiously.

'I hope you're not going to back out,' Hayley replied with a hint of anger. 'If you want to get into modelling and earn some real money, this is the place to start.'

'It's just that . . . I mean, who will see the photos?'

'We've been through all this, Katie. I'll send the photos to my agent and if he likes the look of you he'll sign you up as a model.'

216

'So no one else will see the photos?'

'He might send them to other agents. If you want to be a model, you'll have to accept that people will see the photographs. How can you get into modelling if you don't want anyone to see your photos?'

'OK,' the girl sighed, pulling her T-shirt over her head.

Reaching into her bag, Hayley pulled out a folder. 'Sign this, and then we can get started,' she said, passing the girl a pen.

'What is it?'

'It's just a document saying that you agree to have the photos taken. Don't worry, it's just standard procedure.'

'It says here that the copyright won't be mine. What does that mean?'

'All it means is that you won't actually own the photographs. Just sign it and we can get started.'

Anne realised that the girl was naïve and had no idea what she was signing. Watching as she passed the document back to Hayley and then unhooked her bra, Anne focused on the small mounds of her teenage breasts. The girl had a good body, Anne thought as the would-be model stepped out of her skirt and pulled her knickers down. Her blonde pubes did little to conceal her tight sex crack and she looked anxious as she stood in front of Hayley with her arms folded across her firm breasts. This was a con, Anne thought, knowing that Hayley would sell the photos to the vicar.

Hayley ordered the girl to place one foot on the arm of the chair as Anne watched with bated breath. Katie was beautiful, Anne thought, eyeing the opening crack of her young pussy as she took her position. And the vicar would soon be threatening to show the photographs to her parents unless she allowed him to fuck her. Anne knew that the priest would never force the girl into having sex with him, and it would be partly her fault for allowing the photographs to be taken, but it was still a con. Hayley was a bitch, she thought as the camera clicked. This had nothing to do with modelling and there was no agent. It was just a huge con.

'Very good,' Hayley said, kneeling on the floor and focusing on the girl's young pussy. 'Now, I want you to open your lips really wide.'

'But I thought . . . I mean . . .' Katie stammered.

'Katie, this is all part of the procedure. You have to prove to my agent that you're not shy or going to back out if he signs you up. You're *not* shy, are you?'

'No, it's just that . . . I thought that you wanted ordinary photos.'

'I don't think you're the right girl for this,' Hayley sighed. 'It's a shame because my agent is looking for a girl just like you. He was saying the other day that he needs a teenage girl with natural blonde hair and . . . oh well, I'll just have to find someone else.'

'No, it's OK,' the girl breathed, parting the fleshy lips of her pussy and exposing her pinken inner folds. 'I really want to get into modelling, so I'll do anything you say.'

'Good girl. You won't regret this, especially when you start earning real money.'

Anne thought of walking into the room and putting a stop to the scam, but her arousal heightened as she gazed at the young girl's open vaginal hole, the nub of her exposed clitoris. Hayley took several photographs and then ordered Katie to push two fingers into her vagina. Anne thought again that this was porn and had nothing to do with modelling. The girl complied, managing to push two fingers deep into her vaginal sheath as Hayley took several photographs. But she didn't look very happy.

Wondering where Hayley found the girls, how she broached the subject of modelling, Anne still couldn't believe that her sister was working the scam with the vicar. The whole thing was incredible, she thought as the girl followed Hayley's instructions and bent over with her feet wide apart. Gazing longingly at the puffy flesh of Katie's sex lips bulging between her slender thighs, Anne felt her clitoris call for attention, her juices of arousal seep into the tight crotch of her knickers. Twenty pounds wasn't a great deal of money, she thought. But the girl was obviously doing this as a way into modelling. It was a complete and utter con, Anne thought, wondering why her sister had no scruples.

Kneeling behind the girl, Hayley placed her camera on the floor and parted the firm orbs of her naked buttocks as Anne looked on with bated breath. Moving closer, Hayley licked Katie's tight anal ring, grabbing her shapely hips and holding her firmly as she tried to break free. This was amazing, Anne thought as her sister moved down and licked between the teenager's puffy vaginal lips. It was beyond belief that Hayley was behaving like this.

'I want to get dressed now,' the girl gasped, trying again to break free.

'And I want to lick you,' Hayley returned.

'Please . . . this has nothing to do with modelling. I want to go now.'

'Katie, this has *everything* to do with modelling. Do you know how much you could earn from lesbian photos?'

'No, no, I don't.'

'You'll get around five hundred pounds for a few shots of a girl licking your pussy. That's about ten minutes' work, Katie. You'd only have to work for ten minutes a day, and you'll have more money than—'

'Just ten minutes a day?' the girl asked.

'Yes, just ten minutes of your time. If you'd rather not do it, just say so. There are plenty of other girls who would jump at the chance of earning that sort of money.'

'I know, but . . .'

'All I'm trying to do is help you. You don't find it unpleasant, so you?'

'No, I suppose not.'

'Once you're used to being licked, you'll earn a fortune. I'm only trying to help you.'

'All right,' she finally conceded. 'I'll do it.'

Anne watched as Hayley parted the girl's outer sex lips and ran her tongue up and down her open valley. Hayley was obviously bisexual, she mused, wondering whether it ran in the family. Katie was naïve beyond belief, and Hayley was a devious little cow. Licking and sucking between Katie's sex lips, Anne wondered whether she'd reach an orgasm as she listened to the slurping sounds of lesbian sex. Her own clitoris calling again for her intimate attention, Anne slipped her hand down the front of her knickers and massaged the solid protrusion.

Although the scam was despicable, Anne began to wonder whether she should join her sister and the vicar in their illicit business venture. Her clitoris responded to her intimate caress, her juices of lust flowing from her neglected vaginal hole, and she imagined licking the young girl's open pussy and sucking out her teenage milk. There was something that she'd often thought about but never done, she thought as she massaged the sensitive tip of her erect clitoris. She'd never licked the shaft of a solid cock as it glided in and out of a wet pussy. Picturing a huge cock fucking the young girl's tight vagina, she imagined running her tongue along the veined shaft, sucking the girl's clitoris and then sucking the spunk out of her sex sheath.

There was so much that she had to experience sexually, Anne thought happily as her sister licked and sucked on Katie's clitoris and the girl cried out in the grip of her lesbian-induced climax. Anne's own orgasm erupted within the pulsating bulb of her solid clitoris and she held her breath, trying to stifle her gasps of pleasure as she watched her sister commit the illicit lesbian act. But she was only eighteen years old, and she had all the time in the world to experiment and learn the fine art of crude sexual acts with both men and girls.

'You're a dirty little girl,' Hayley breathed as she lapped up the last of Katie's sex milk as it flowed from her gaping vaginal entrance. 'You're also beautiful.'

'That was heavenly,' the girl breathed shakily. 'I've . . . I've never been licked before.'

'You and I are going to do well, Katie. We'll work well together and you'll earn a lot of money. By the way, do you have any friends who would like to get into modelling?'

Standing up, Katie smiled at Hayley. 'There is one girl who might . . .' she began. 'She . . . she likes other girls, if you know what I mean.'

'I know exactly what you mean. You have my mobile phone number so give it to her and ask her to ring me.'

'Yes, yes, I will. May I dress now?'

'OK, get dressed and we'll carry on tomorrow.'

'What, more photos?'

'Yes, but . . . but I want you to learn how to lick me.'

Slipping away as the girl dressed, Anne left the house and settled on the soft grass behind a bush. She could see the house from her hide, and she wondered whether Hayley would go and see the vicar once she'd said goodbye to Katie. She might go straight to the church and sell him the photographs, she thought, wondering how much he'd pay her. She'd also give him the girl's address so that he could blackmail her. Anne watched as Hayley left the house with Katie in tow and kept her distance as she followed them through the trees to the lane. Hayley turned right at the lane and headed towards the church, so Anne followed Katie in the other direction.

She reckoned that the girl had come from the neighbouring village and she wondered whether to catch up with her and introduce herself. She knew that she should talk to her, warn her about the vicar and his scam, but she wasn't sure how to put it. Walking faster and nearing the girl, Anne eyed her swaying hips, her rounded bottom. She was a real beauty, she mused, recalling her firm young breasts, her open vaginal slit. Finally walking by her side, she turned and smiled at her.

'I'm Anne,' she said. 'Looks like we're heading in the same direction.'

'Oh, er . . . hi, I'm Katie. I'm on my way home.'

'I was looking for a friend but I must have missed her. She goes to that old house in the woods.'

'Do you mean Hayley?' Katie asked her.

'Yes – have you seen her?'

'I was . . . I'm a friend of hers, we were at the house just now.'

'Damn, I must have missed her by minutes. Still, not to worry.'

'I think she's gone home.'

'Oh, right. Are you one of her models?'

'Well, yes, I am.'

'So am I.'

'Really?' Katie said, grinning at Anne.

'You must be the girl I'll be working with.'

'Working with?'

'Hayley said that she wants me to do some lesbian shots with a girl she was seeing this morning. That must be you.'

'Yes, I suppose so. '

'Shall we go and sit down somewhere? How about finding a spot in the woods where we can chat?'

'OK,' the girl murmured, turning off the lane and heading through the trees. 'Actually, I do need to talk to someone about this modelling business.'

'Well, I'm your girl.'

Anne had intended to warn Katie about the vicar. But her clitoris was swelling and her vaginal milk was flowing into her tight knickers, and she couldn't stop thinking about Katie's young body. She'd wanted to experiment with lesbian sex with Dee and Angela, but Katie was young and fresh and ... and available? Sitting down next to Katie in a small clearing, Anne gazed at her T-shirt faithfully following the contours of her small breasts and outlining the protrusions of her ripe nipples, and she knew that she had to have her teenage body.

'It's nice here,' Anne said, moving closer to the girl. 'An ideal place for outdoor lesbian photos.'

'Yes, I suppose so,' Katie breathed. 'Don't you mind doing lesbian stuff?'

'I love it,' Anne replied. 'I mean, I have a boyfriend but ... I also love being with another girl. How about you?'

'I haven't done much,' Katie said softly. 'Hayley licked me and tomorrow she wants me to lick her. I'm not sure that I want to do it, though.'

'Would you like me to help you?'

'Help me? But how?'

'Lie back and relax and I'll show you.'

Anne couldn't help herself as Katie lay back on the grass with her young thighs parted slightly. She was beautiful, Anne mused, running her fingertip up and down her inner thighs. So young and fresh and innocent ... Was she a virgin? she wondered as she slipped her hand up her short skirt and pressed her fingers into the warm swell of her tight knickers. Had she had a cock driving deep into her hot vagina and splattering her ripe cervix with fresh spunk?

Pulling the girl's knickers down her slender legs and slipping them off her feet, Anne lifted Katie's skirt high up over the smooth plateau of her stomach and gazed longingly at the swollen lips of her teenage pussy. Katie's sex crack was tightly closed, Anne observed, her stomach somersaulting at the prospect of lesbian sex as she leaned over and kissed the gentle rise of the other girl's. Breathing in Katie's girl-scent, she pushed her tongue out and licked between the fleshy cushions of her outer lips and tasted her there.

'You're beautiful,' Anne murmured and parted the girl's legs wider to gain better access to the most private part of her body. 'I'm going to teach you how to love another girl.'

'Yes,' Katie sighed as Anne's tongue delved into her wetting crack and swept over the tip of her sensitive clitoris. 'Yes, I'd like that.'

Easing a finger deep into Katie's vaginal duct, Anne sucked and licked her erect clitoris. She tasted wonderful, she thought dreamily as she massaged the hot inner flesh of the girl's tightening sex sheath. It was a shame that the vicar was going to threaten her and, more than likely, violate her unsullied young body. He'd force his huge cock deep into her teenage love hole. He'd fuck her mouth and shoot his creamy spunk down her throat, she reflected. He'd drive his

224

solid penis deep into her hot rectal tube and flood her bowels with his unholy seed. Maybe Anne could save her from the man of God.

'Do you masturbate?' Anne asked her as she slipped a second finger into her creamy-wet vaginal sheath.

'Yes,' Katie confessed.

'Are you a virgin?'

'Yes, I . . . I am.'

'We're going to do sixty-nine,' Anne said, retrieving her fingers from the girl's young love duct. She slipped her own panties off. 'Are you going to be OK with this?' she said, kneeling astride Katie's head.

'Yes, I'd like to try it.'

'Good.'

Lowering her body and pressing the swollen lips of her bald pussy against Katie's mouth, Anne leaned forward and ran her tongue up and down the girl's yawning vaginal crevice. She could feel Katie's tongue delving into her vaginal entrance, exploring her hot inner flesh. Katie was savouring her first taste of girl-milk, and Anne wondered what her thoughts were. She seemed to be enjoying the experience, she thought as the girl mouthed and sucked between the fleshy pads of her hairless sex lips. Reciprocating, Anne pushed her tongue deep into the young girl's vaginal hole. Savouring her flowing love-milk, she slurped and sucked, drinking from Katie's trembling body. It would be nice to reach their orgasms together, she mused dreamily as the girl parted her slender thighs wide.

This was only Anne's second lesbian experience, and she pondered on her own thoughts and feelings. The taste of a teenage girl's pussy was heavenly, she mused. The gentleness, the softness . . . She'd been licked and sucked to orgasm many times, but the feel of a girl's wet tongue between her love lips was completely different. Katie was beautiful, she thought as she sucked the girl's erect clitoris into her hot mouth. Lesbian sex was beautiful.

Katie's clitoris erupted in orgasm as Anne reached her lesbian-induced climax, and the girls' entwined bodies writhed on the grass beneath the trees as they sucked and licked. Anne imagined a cock sliding in and out of the girl's hot vaginal duct as she recalled her latest fantasy. She'd lick the wet shaft, tongue the swollen knob each time it emerged and she'd suck the girl's solid clitoris. To drink fresh spunk from a girl's vaginal sheath must be heavenly, she mused in the grip of her powerful orgasm.

Katie's slender body convulsed and bucked as she rode the crest of her orgasm. Her thighs twitching, she breathed heavily through her nose as she sucked on Anne's pulsating clitoris and sustained her massive orgasm. Anne knew that this was her chance to introduce the girl to the fine art of sex as she parted the firm cheeks of her naked buttocks. Pushing her finger deep into Katie's rectal duct and massaging her hot inner flesh, Anne grinned as her lesbian lover let out a wail of pleasure. She was hooked, she knew as Katie reciprocated and drove a finger deep into the dank heat of Anne's tight rectal tube.

Finally coming down from their sexual heaven, the girls writhed and gasped for breath, their young bodies shaking uncontrollably in the aftermath of their lesbian loving. Anne thought of the perverted vicar as she lay on her back looking up at the trees. He was going to threaten Katie, use the photographs to blackmail her into having crude sex with him. Hayley was as bad if not worse than the vicar, she reflected. How many other young girls had she lured to the derelict house for her so-called photographic sessions?

'I must go home,' Katie said, grabbing her knickers and rising to her feet. 'But . . . I mean . . . I'd like to see you again, if that's OK?'

'Of course it's OK,' Anne replied, smiling at her. 'I don't think we should meet at the old house, though. Perhaps we'll make this our secret place. It's nice and secluded here.'

'Yes, I'd like that.'

'Say, ten o'clock?'

'Yes, I'll be here. Thanks for . . . I'll see you tomorrow.'

As Katie left the clearing Anne wondered what to do. She wanted to watch the vicar force his huge cock deep into Katie's virgin pussy and fuck her senseless. But she also wanted to protect the girl from the evil man. And what the hell was she going to say to Hayley? she wondered as she left the clearing and headed home. Should she confront her sister, or say nothing? Passing the pub, she wondered why she hadn't seen anything of Rick or Jack. Brian and Alan had been ominously quiet, she reflected. Were they hoping to strip Katie and fuck her virgin pussy? Anne knew that she should save the girl, but the thought of watching her take an old man's cock into her tight pussy sent her arousal soaring.

Eleven

'Did you get the money from the vicar?' Hayley asked Anne over breakfast.

'No,' Anne replied. 'He doesn't have that sort of cash so . . . well, that's that.'

'But he told me that . . . I mean, I thought that he had the money?'

'I didn't like the idea of blackmailing him any more than you did, so I let it go. Are you working today?'

'Yes, I'd better get going or I'll be late. Do you have any clients lined up for this evening?'

Anne wasn't sure what to say as she sipped her coffee. 'Yes,' she finally replied. 'I'll see you this evening and tell you about it.'

'Great. OK, see you later, little sister.'

Anne went straight up to Hayley's bedroom as the girl left the house. Hayley obviously knew that Anne had the five thousand pounds, but she couldn't say that she'd been talking to the vicar about it. Fortunately, Anne's mother was out shopping so she had plenty of time to search Hayley's computer. Sitting at the desk, she began browsing the folders. She wasn't sure what she was looking for, but she reckoned that she'd find something of interest.

There were folders within folders, making it a time-consuming job, but she finally discovered something of great interest. 'The girls' names, addresses and phone numbers,' she breathed, printing out the list of victims before deleting the folder. Hayley would know that her little sister had been at her computer, and Anne wondered how to wreck the drive and make it look as though it had just gone wrong. Looking through system files, she deleted everything she could find. Ignoring the warning notices flashing up on the screen, she finally switched the machine off and then turned it on again.

'Good,' she breathed as a notice flashed up stating that there had been a fatal error. 'That's the end of that.' Taking the list of girls to her bedroom, she wasn't sure what her plan was as she sat on the end of her bed. She had taken the girl's names from Hayley's computer, and she had a CD packed with photographs, but what was she going to do with the evidence? Switching her own computer on, Anne gazed at the photos she'd taken of Hayley in the derelict house. Spanking, anal sex, cock-sucking . . . She had enough evidence of the girl's debauched life but what could she do with it?

She thought about visiting the vicar and checked the time. Eight-thirty. She had to meet Katie in the woods at ten, she reflected. Should she wander into the church with Katie and watch the vicar for his reaction? Hayley would have sold him the photographs by now so he'd recognise the girl and wonder what was going on. Coming up with an idea as she gazed at the list of girls' names and phone numbers, Anne went down to the lounge and rang the first number.

Alison listened intently as Anne explained the situation to her. Having heard the business proposition, she was very keen to meet Anne at the church, and so was the next girl on the list. Several of the girls were out, but Anne managed to round up half a dozen. Grabbing her camera and leaving the house, she went to the church to see whether the vicar was around. It was probably too early in the morning, she mused as she crept through the open doors and stole down the aisle. Hearing voices coming from the office, she waited outside the partially open door and listened.

'I hope that you haven't told her about our little business deal?' Hayley said. 'And what about the money?'

'Of course I haven't told her,' the vicar replied. 'She'll probably give you the cash later, so don't worry.'

'I *am* worried. We've worked hard for that money – you should never have given it to her. In fact, you should never have got involved with her in the first place.'

'Don't worry, Hayley. I had a long chat with her and she's fine. I didn't say anything about our business, and I'm sure that we'll get the money back later. Now, let's move on to the little beauty in these photographs. What was her name?'

'Katie, and she's a virgin.'

'Mmm, just what I'm looking for. So you've made the arrangements?'

'Yes, I got Dave to ring her earlier. He made out that he was my agent and told her to be outside the church at nine.'

'And I'll do my usual,' the priest said, with a chuckle. 'I'll go outside and chat to her and—'

'You'll show her the photographs, bring her in here, and have your wicked way with her.'

As she slipped out of the church and hid behind some bushes, Anne couldn't believe that Dave was involved in the scam. This was getting worse by the minute, she thought, wondering what to do as she saw Hayley leave the church. Within minutes Katie arrived and sat on the low wall. The plan was good, Anne thought. But what was the vicar going to say to the girl? He couldn't simply produce the photographs because Katie would realise that Hayley had given them to him.

She watched the vicar leave the church and walk towards Katie but Anne couldn't hear what he was saying to her. Whatever he'd said had worked, she thought as the girl followed him into the church. Katie was wearing a skimpy crop-top and a short skirt, and she looked extremely sexy. Recalling her time in the woods with the girl, Anne slipped into the church and waited outside the office door. There was no way the perverted vicar was going to violate Katie's young body, she thought as she listened to their conversation.

'I don't know what this is all about,' the vicar said. 'I was outside and I saw a chap waiting by the wall. The he went off and left this envelope behind.' He opened the envelope and pulled out several photographs. 'And then you turned up and . . . I recognised you immediately.'

'Oh,' Katie gasped, holding her hand to her pretty mouth as the priest showed her the photographs. 'I . . . I don't know where they came from.'

'It's obviously you in the pictures. You must know about them.'

'Well, yes . . . I mean . . . May I have them back, please?'

'These photos are disgusting, Katie. Do your parents know what you get up to?'

'No, no, they don't. You see, the man is an agent and he wants me to . . . If I could just have them back . . .'

'An agent? I think I'd better have a word with your parents, Katie.'

'No, please don't.'

'You've obviously gone off the rails and it's my duty to help you. As a vicar, I can't just ignore this. I can't stand by and—'

'Please, I'll burn them—'

'Burning them won't change anything. It won't change the fact that you've behaved like a ...' Perching on the edge of his desk, the vicar rubbed his chin. 'Maybe I can help you,' he murmured pensively.

'How?' Katie asked him anxiously, brushing her long blonde hair away from her flushed face.

'I should show these to your parents, but ... Why don't you pose for me? You can show me how you posed for the photos.'

'What? You mean ...'

'Take your clothes off and show me how you posed for the camera.'

'But you're a vicar and ... I can't take my clothes off.'

'Then I'll just have to show these to your parents.'

'Why do you want me to pose?'

'Because it will be your punishment, Katie. Either your parents punish you, or I do.'

'But ... you won't touch me or anything?'

'I simply want to humiliate you as a way of punishing you. Having stripped naked in front of me, I doubt that you'll ever do anything like this again. It will teach you a lesson, Katie.'

'Well, I'm not sure.'

'Or would you rather that your parents should punish you?'

'No, no ... all right, I'll do it,' Katie finally conceded.

Anne watched as the girl slipped her crop-top off and displayed the firm mounds of her braless breasts to the perverted vicar. Her nipples rose proud from the dark discs of her areolae in the relatively cool air of the church and she hung her head in shame as the priest gazed at them. Anne was in two minds as to whether to put a stop to the vicar's scam or watch the girl take her first hard cock into her virgin pussy. She also wondered if she should join in and lick the man of God's pussy-wet cock as he fucked the innocent teenager.

'And now your skirt,' the vicar ordered the girl.

'You'll give me the photos if I do it?' Katie asked him in her naïvety.

'Yes, and that will be the end of the matter.'

Lowering her skirt, Katie stepped out of the garment and stood in front of the man in her shoes and tight knickers. He gazed at the tight material running between her slender thighs and licked his lips, and Anne knew exactly what he was thinking. Ordering Katie to remove her knickers, the priest watched as she slipped her thumbs in between the tight elastic and her slender hips. Katie had no choice, Anne knew as the girl hesitated. Either she exposed the most private part of her young body to the perverted man, or she'd have to face her parents.

Would the vicar carry out his threat if she didn't do as he'd asked? Anne wondered as Katie slipped her knickers down an inch or two. Her sparse blonde pubes came into view and Anne could clearly see the top of her tight crack. If the vicar went to the girl's parents with the photos, he'd have to explain how he'd got hold of them, she reflected. He wouldn't gain anything by getting the girl into trouble, and she doubted that he'd bother if she didn't comply with his humiliating demands.

'You're a pretty little thing,' the priest said as Katie tugged her knickers down to her knees. 'Take your panties off and stand with your feet wide apart.'

'There,' she said, complying with his instructions. 'May I get dressed now?'

'Not yet, Katie. Turn around and bend over. Bend over and touch your toes.'

'I've done all you've asked,' the girl whimpered, turning and bending over. 'May I have the photos now?'

Eyeing the fleshy swell of her vaginal lips nestling between her slender thighs, the vicar grinned. 'You're a *very* pretty little thing,' he breathed, running his fingertips over the unblemished flesh of her firm buttocks.

'I have to go now,' Katie said, standing and facing him.

'What would your parents say if I were to tell them that you came here and stripped naked? If I said that you gave me the photographs and you asked me for sex, I'm sure—'

'No,' she breathed shakily. 'Please, I've done everything . . .'

'Get onto the desk,' the vicar ordered her. 'Lie on your back on the desk and I'll examine you.'

'But—'

'Just do it, Katie.'

Taking her position, the girl gazed wide-eyed at the priest as he stood beside her and ran his fingertips over the small mounds of her teenage breasts. Clutching her camera, Anne wanted to take some photographs so that she could blackmail the vicar, but she thought that he might hear the shutter clicking. All she could do was watch as the man ran his fingers down over the girl's smooth stomach to the gentle rise of her mons. Spinning round as she heard a woman calling for the vicar, Anne squatted behind a pew as the man left the office and closed the door. Once he was in conversation with the woman, she slipped into the office.

'Are you all right, Katie?' she whispered.

'Anne . . . what are you doing here?'

'I've come to save you.'

'No, he's going to tell my parents about the photos and—'

'No, he won't. Come on, get dressed and we'll get out of here.'

'Anne, I can't. He has the photographs of me and—'

'Oh, we have a guest,' the vicar said, standing in the doorway. 'What a nice surprise.'

'We're leaving,' Anne stated firmly.

'Leaving? But the fun hasn't even started. Why don't you lick Katie's little cunt and make it nice and wet in readiness for my cock?'

'She's a virgin – you're not going to do anything to her.'

'Anne, I told you that you know nothing about this village or the people in it. Unless you want to get yourself into serious trouble you'll keep your nose out of my business.'

'I'm afraid that my nose is well and truly stuck in your business, vicar.'

'In that case, I'll visit your parents and show them the photographs that I have of you. The choice is yours: you either lick her cunt or—'

'I'm not a virgin,' Katie confessed. 'If the vicar pays me, he can do what he likes to me.'

'What?' Anne gasped. 'But you told me that—'

'I lied.'

'You want money in return for . . . I can't believe this, Katie.'

'I don't pay girls for sex,' the vicar said.

'From now on you do,' Anne returned. 'Hayley is no longer in charge of the girls. I have names, addresses, phone numbers . . . I'm in charge now, vicar.'

'Don't make me laugh,' he said, with a chuckle.

'Ah, you must be Alison,' Anne said as a teenage girl appeared in the doorway.

'Yes, I am. The other girls are here, too.'

'What's going on?' the priest asked, frowning at Alison. 'I told you that I'd show the photographs to your parents unless you—'

'Ignore him,' Anne cut in, gazing at the flock of young girls standing behind Alison. 'I'm in charge now. Money, please, vicar.'

'What?'

'One hundred, please. If you want Katie, that is.'

'And if I don't?'

'Then you'll never enjoy a teenage girl again. I have all Hayley's photographs, and I'll take yours before I leave. The game is over, vicar.'

Alison lifted her short skirt and pulled down the front of her tight knickers. 'Don't you want this, vicar?' she said with a giggle as he gazed at the hairless lips of her tempting young pussy.

'Yes, but—'

'One hundred is cheap, vicar,' Anne cut in. 'Think yourself lucky.'

'You do realise that Hayley will go mad when she finds out about this? She's been running the business for two years and . . .'

'And now I'm running it.'

'Brian won't be at all happy.'

'Brian will have to pay for sex, just like the rest of the clients.'

Turning to Katie, Anne smiled. 'You don't have to work for me,' she said. 'You can leave, if you want to.'

'I'll stay,' the girl replied, parting her slender thighs.

'Good girl. OK, are the rest of you happy about working for me?'

'We're all happy,' Alison said. 'We've talked about your idea, and we're all happy.'

Turning to the vicar, Anne waved her hand over Katie's naked body. 'She's all yours,' she said. 'I want to use you as a guinea pig, so I won't charge you this time.'

'That's very good of you,' the priest murmured sarcastically.

'In future, you'll pay the same as the other clients.'

The girls crowded round as the vicar slipped his cassock off and displayed his erect penis to their wide eyes. Anne gazed at the girls and smiled as the vicar slipped his purple knob between the firm lips of Katie's pussy. The young women were fresh and extremely attractive, she mused happily. The girls she hadn't been able to contact would no doubt be pleased to join her in her new business venture, she was sure as she watched the vicar's solid cock drive deep into Katie's tight vagina.

Taking the photographs of Katie from the desk drawer, Anne tore them into small pieces and dropped them into the waste-paper basket. Things were working out well, she thought as the vicar repeatedly drove his solid knob deep into Katie's teenage pussy. But she still had Hayley to contend with. Her thoughts turned to Dave and she wondered what his involvement was. How long had he been working with Hayley?

Deciding to teach the girls a thing or two about sex, Anne ordered the vicar to slow his thrusting rhythm. Smiling as his cock glided slowly in and out of Katie's tight vagina, she leaned over and licked his pussy-wet shaft. Katie's milk tasted wonderful, she thought as the girls watched her. Stretching the girl's swollen love lips wide apart and sweeping her tongue over the sensitive tip of her erect clitoris, she knew that she wasn't far away from her climax.

'OK, watch and learn,' Anne said to her eager audience. Resting her head on Katie's smooth stomach with her pretty mouth just above the girl's sex crack, she looked up at the vicar. 'I know that some of you will have experience, but watch me anyway.'

'What's going on?' the vicar asked her, stilling his solid cock deep within the girl's wet sex sheath.

'One thrust into her pussy and then one into my mouth,' Anne told him. 'Pussy, mouth, pussy, mouth . . . Got it?'

'No problem,' he replied.'

Opening her mouth wide, Anne tasted Katie's sex milk each time the vicar slipped his cock out of her pussy and drove his purple knob into Anne's waiting mouth. The girls moved closer and watched the alternate thrusting: mouth, pussy, mouth, pussy. Finally standing upright, Anne ordered a pretty little blonde to take her place. The vicar was doing well for the money, she thought as the girl opened her mouth and repeatedly sucked on the man's vagina-wet knob. The other girls jostled each other, desperate for their turn as the vicar gasped.

'Have you all tasted spunk?' Anne asked them.

'I haven't,' a dark-haired beauty said.

'OK, you go last and the vicar will come in your mouth.'

As each girl took her turn to suck Katie's sex juices from the man's bulbous knob, Anne reckoned that she was going to earn a lot of money from her employees. She'd have to teach them the fine art of lesbian sex, she thought as the vicar neared his orgasm. There'd be clients who would pay to watch two teenage girls licking each other's clitorises to orgasm. She'd have to buy school uniforms, nurses' outfits, leather and latex gear . . . She'd need handcuffs and whips for her fetish clients, she thought, ordering the last girl to take her position as the vicar said that he could hold back no longer.

Watching the vicar's huge cock slip out of Katie's tight vagina and drive into the dark-haired girl's mouth, Anne grinned as he reached his orgasm and his spunk jetted from his swollen knob. Between each vaginal and oral thrust, his jism rained over the girl's hair and splattered her pretty face. She could hear the girl swallowing every time the vicar's knob left Katie's vagina and drove into her mouth. She was leaning how to please a man, Anne reflected. All the girls were learning, and they'd soon be well practised in the art of committing crude sexual acts.

The vicar staggered back as his cock deflated, leaving spunk oozing from Katie's inflamed sex sheath and dribbling down the other girl's cheek. Time for a lesson in lesbian sex, Anne decided, ordering one of the girls to lap up the spunk flowing from Katie's hot pussy. Again, the girls lined up, eagerly awaiting their turn to suck the vicar's spunk from Katie's vaginal duct. Anne gazed at the priest as the first girl knelt on the floor and pressed her pretty mouth into Katie's open sex valley. His cock stiffened and she hoped that he'd be able to penetrate each girl before the lesson was over.

Anne dashed out of the office and closed the door behind her as she heard someone in the church. She stared at her sister as the girl walked down the aisle. This was it, she thought anxiously. The confrontation was about to take place. Hayley didn't look at all happy as Anne stood in front of her and smiled. She'd have discovered that her computer had been wrecked, and . . .

'What the hell is going on?' Hayley breathed, glaring at Anne. 'Who's in the office with the vicar?'

'My girls,' Anne replied.

'*Your* girls? What the hell are you talking about?'

'The girls on your list of victims are now working for me. There'll be no more threats, no blackmail . . .'

'Now you listen to me, young lady,' Hayley hissed. 'Or, I should say, young slut. I've worked hard over the past two years to build up—'

'It's over, Hayley,' Anne cut in. 'The things you've done are despicable. Conning those young girls into thinking that they'll be models, taking photos of them and selling them to the vicar so that he can blackmail them into having sex with him . . .'

'You *have* been doing your homework, haven't you?'

'I know everything, Hayley. You conned me, used me and—'

'You're an interfering little bitch. The first thing you're going to do is give me the five thousand pounds. Then you're going to give me the list of names and addresses you stole from me, and the photographs. Now get yourself home and I'll deal with the girls.'

'I'm not going anywhere.'

'OK, on your head be it.'

Watching as Hayley marched into the office and yelled at the girls, Anne couldn't believe that this was her sister. She'd turned out to be a right little bitch. But without the photographs to blackmail the girls with, there was little that she or the vicar could do. Hayley had always been stubborn, she reflected. She'd never give in, Anne knew as someone walked into the church. Turning, she stared as Brian and Alan walked down the aisle.

'What are you two doing here?' she asked them as they stood in front of her.

'Hayley called us,' Alan said. 'Apparently she needs some help.'

'Oh, I get it,' Anne sighed. 'You're all in on this. You, Brian, Dave . . .'

'You should never have interfered, Anne,' Brian said, shaking his head. 'Things were fine until you—'

'Get her over the altar,' Hayley bellowed as she left the office with the girls in tow. 'Strip her, and tie her over the altar. You're going to give me the photographs, Anne,' she hissed. 'And the money.'

Anne could do nothing to save herself as the men almost tore her clothes off. The vicar emerged from the office with several lengths of rope, and Anne knew that she was going to be subjected to a terrible sexual ordeal as he gazed longingly at her naked body. As Hayley grabbed a leather whip from beneath the altar and ordered one of the girls to lock the church doors, Anne wondered whether she should give the money and photographs back. Hayley had always won, she reflected dolefully as the vicar tied her hands behind her back. It had been futile to believe that she could beat her sister. Pushed over the altar, her feet parted wide, Anne grimaced as fingers ran over the firm flesh of her naked buttocks.

'I've been training the girls,' Hayley said. 'I've been training them to work for me as prostitutes, and you've tried to push me aside and take my place.'

'Go to hell,' Anne spat.

'Alan, don't stroke her arse,' Hayley shouted, passing the man the leather whip. 'Thrash her until she promises to give me the money and the photographs.'

Yelping like a dog as the first lash of the whip jolted her naked body, Anne was determined not to give in to her sister's demands. Again, the leather tails flailed her tensed buttocks, leaving thin weals fanning out across her pale flesh. She'd enjoyed being spanked and thrashed in the past, but this was a gruelling,

241

merciless thrashing, and she wasn't sure that she could endure it. The leather tails swiping again the crimsoned flesh of her naked buttocks, she cried out as the pain permeated her young bottom.

Anne's young buttocks stung like hell and she was about to concede defeat when the thrashing stopped. She dared not turn her head to see what was going on as she heard movements behind her. Hayley ordered Alan to continue with the thrashing, but he did nothing. There was obviously some sort of altercation going on, Anne thought as Hayley again ordered Alan to thrash her sister. Finally lifting her head off the altar, Anne frowned as she saw Brian holding Hayley's arms behind her back while Alan tore her skirt and blouse away from her trembling body.

'You'll pay for this,' Hayley hissed as the vicar tied her hands behind her back.

'You've gone too far,' Brian said, forcing her naked body over the altar as Anne moved aside. 'You've cheated us out of money, you've threatened to show my wife the photos of me and—'

'Unless you let me go, I'll . . .' Hayley began futilely.

'You'll what?' Anne asked her as one of the girls untied her hands. 'The girls want to work for *me*. You're finished.'

'Is that right?' Alan asked the flock of girls.

'Yes,' the blonde replied. 'We all want to work for Anne.'

'You little bitches will pay for this,' Hayley screamed. 'I'll tell your parents and—'

The first lash of the leather tails cut Hayley's words short and she struggled to break free but the vicar pinned her down over the altar. This was revenge, Anne thought happily as Alan again lashed the unblemished flesh of her sister's naked buttocks. Grabbing her clothes and dressing, she couldn't believe that, after all these years, she'd finally beaten Hayley. But what would happen once they were at home together? Would Hayley submit and allow Anne to run the business? Grabbing a huge candle from the altar and passing it to the vicar, Anne knew that the girls were on her side as they giggled.

'Do you submit?' she asked Hayley as Alan halted the gruelling thrashing.

'Never,' Hayley spat.

'The candle, vicar. Force it right up her arse and we'll see whether she changes her mind.'

'My pleasure,' the vicar replied with a wicked chuckle.

Two of the girls held Hayley's fire-red buttocks wide apart as the vicar knelt on the floor behind her. Pushing the rounded end of the candle hard against the tight anal ring, he ignored Hayley's threats as he managed to force the wax phallus into her hot rectal duct. The girls gasped as the candle drove deeper into her trembling body until no more than an inch protruded from her stretched anal hole. That's teaching the bitch, Anne thought, ordering Brian to ram his cock into her pussy and fuck her.

Hayley's threats echoed around the church as Alan's cock forced its way deep into the restricted sheath of her vagina. Again and again she screamed her threats, until Brian clambered onto the altar and pushed his swollen knob into her pretty mouth. The church fell quiet, apart from the squelching sounds of sex and naked flesh slapping naked flesh, and Anne knew that the girl was going to submit before long. Without the men on her side, without the flock of teenage girls, Hayley would be alone. And there'd be nothing that she could do about the situation.

The girls were learning fast, Anne thought as the dark-haired beauty settled between Hayley's parted feet and licked Alan's thrusting cock shaft. A girl worked the huge candle in and out of Hayley's tight bottom-hole and another held her head up, forcing her to take Brian's bulbous knob deep into her throat. The vicar then joined Brian on the altar and forced his prick into Hayley's bloated mouth alongside Alan's, and Anne took several photographs of her sister's wanton whoredom.

Brian gasped as his spunk gushed from his throbbing cock and flooded Hayley's gobbling mouth, and Alan let out a low moan of pleasure as he filled the girl's tight vagina with orgasmic milk. Well and truly fucked, Anne thought happily as her sister writhed on the altar. In more ways than one. This was the girl's come-uppance, but Anne was still worried about her sister's reaction once they were at home together. There again, what could she do?

Alan finally pulled his deflating cock out of Hayley's spunked vagina and the vicar took his place. Ramming his rock-hard member deep into the girl's inflamed vaginal sheath, he grabbed her hips and began his fucking motions as Brian slipped his knob out of her sperm-bubbling mouth. The girls giggled as Hayley struggled and moaned through her nose, but Anne was more interested in the knocking that was sounding on the church doors. She walked up the aisle and opened the doors an inch or so to find herself gazing at Dave. What the hell was he doing there? she wondered. Was he looking for Hayley?

'What are you doing here?' he asked her.

'Dealing with a monster,' Anne returned. 'What do you want?'

'I came to see the vicar.'

'Yes, and I know why. You're working with him and Hayley, aren't you?'

'I'm not working with anyone. I just wanted to—'

'Pretend to be Hayley's agent and con young girls?'

'What's that got to do with anything? That was a joke.'

'Some joke, Dave.'

'Hayley was playing a joke on a girl and I helped her. Are you going to open the doors or not?'

'No.'

'Anne, all I want to do is talk to the vicar about marrying Hayley.'

'You want to *marry* her?'

'I asked her and she said yes. You lied to me about her being pregnant and—'

'I was trying to save you, Dave. I was trying to . . .'

'Trying to split us up, more like. That was a terrible thing to do, Anne.'

'You'd better come and see what your future wife gets up to behind your back,' Anne said, opening the doors wide. 'You won't like it, but you have to know.'

Locking the door behind her and following Dave down the aisle, Anne grinned as he stared in disbelief at Hayley. The vicar was sliding his solid cock in and out of the girl's sperm-flooded vagina and Alan's cock was pushed into her mouth. Dave stood motionless and gazed at the lewd spectacle. That was the end of his marriage plans, Anne was sure as one of the girls worked the huge candle in and out of Hayley's tight bottom-hole. Hoping that Dave would want to retaliate by whipping Hayley's crimsoned buttocks, Anne took his hand and walked him closer to the altar. He turned and gazed at her, his expression conveying his anger as he forced a smile.

'That's what Hayley is like,' Anne said. 'She's a common whore.'

'She said that she'd marry me,' Dave sighed. 'She told me that she was in love with me and—'

'She doesn't know what love is,' Anne cut in.

'I came here to talk to the vicar about marriage and ... I should have listened to Jack.'

'You know Jack?'

'Yes.'

'What did he say?'

'He wanted to marry Hayley but he caught her screwing around. He's moving out of his rented cottage and going back to London. I thought that Hayley and I would rent the place but ... well, that's off now.'

'Are you really sad?' Anne asked him as the men pumped their spunk into Hayley's writhing body.

'It was you I wanted all along,' Dave said, watching the vicar repeatedly ram his orgasming knob deep into Hayley's tight vagina. 'Dee is fun but she prefers to be with Angela and ...'

'You mean that you wanted me more than you did Hayley?'

'Yes. You're more fun, you're more attractive ... I wanted you more than anyone else.'

'You've made my day,' Anne trilled as the vicar pulled his deflating cock out of her sister's sperm-bubbling vaginal duct.

'Hayley cheated on Rick, she treated Robin despicably, she's conned me ...'

'Give her a good fucking,' Anne suggested eagerly as the vicar moved aside. 'Go on, Dave, fuck her rotten.'

Unzipping his trousers, Dave moved behind the girl and ran his purple knob up and down her sperm-dripping sex slit. The girls cheered as he drove the entire length of his solid cock deep into her vaginal sheath, impaling her completely on his huge

246

weapon. Hayley turned her head and stared at Dave as Alan yanked his spent cock out of her mouth. She looked stunned, and extremely guilty, as their stares met. Anne grinned triumphantly at Hayley as Dave fucked her. She'd beaten her sister at long last, she thought.

'Dave,' Hayley began. 'I . . . They forced me.'

'Of course they did,' he replied.

'It's true. Tell him, Anne. Tell him—'

'I've no need to tell Dave anything,' Anne cut in. 'He knows what you are. We all know what you are.'

'You're a tight-cunted little whore,' Dave gasped, fucking her with a vengeance.

'I'm going to be your wife, Dave,' she said futilely. 'We'll get married and . . .'

'We'll get married, and you'll fuck every man you can get your hands on? Yeah, right.'

'Dave, listen to me . . .'

Brian clambered onto the altar and pushed his swollen knob into Hayley's mouth, silencing her as Dave repeatedly battered her spermed cervix with his bulbous knob. Anne felt a little sorry for her sister as Dave reached his orgasm and pumped his orgasmic milk into Hayley's already spunk-brimming vagina. But her sister deserved this, Anne thought. The whipping, the candle, the double-ended fucking . . . she deserved this for the way she'd treated the young girls.

The vicar wouldn't get away with his treatment of the young girls, Anne vowed. He'd have his comeuppance before long, she'd make sure of that. Walking up the aisle and leaving the church, she headed for the derelict house. Life was strange, she mused as she followed the narrow path through the trees. She'd never dreamed that the tables would turn and that she'd beat her sister. Hayley never did have a well-paid job, Anne thought as she wandered into the old house. Her sister's life had been one of lies and deceit.

She sat in the old armchair and looked around the room. This was where it had all started, she reflected, recalling Alan spanking her naked bottom. Had she not suspected that Hayley was screwing Dave, had she not left the pub and gone to the derelict house with Alan ... Leaving the chair and gazing through the broken window as she heard someone outside, Anne saw an old man walking towards the house. She was about to hide somewhere but he walked straight into the front room and stared at her.

'Who are you?' he asked her.

'I'm Anne,' she replied. 'Who are *you*?'

'My name's Johnson. I own this house.'

'Oh, er ... I see.'

'You shouldn't be here – you're trespassing.'

'Yes, I know ... I'm sorry.'

He smiled at her. 'It doesn't matter,' he breathed. 'I'm selling the place, so—'

'How much?' Anne cut in.

'More than you could afford, young lady. I'm selling the entire estate.'

'Oh, right.'

'I'm fifty-five and I live alone, so I'm moving abroad. What would you want this old house for?'

'I used to play here when I was a kid. I've always dreamed of living here.'

'I have a buyer for the estate, but he doesn't want this place. I suppose I could sell it separately.'

'I only have five thousand,' Anne sighed. 'That wouldn't be enough to buy one room.'

The man looked her up and down and grinned. 'You're a pretty little thing,' he said. 'Perhaps we can come to some arrangement or other?'

'I'm sure we can,' Anne said. 'But five thousand won't be enough to—'

'Let's talk about it,' he cut in, stroking her cheek. 'I'm going to be left with this dump unless I can get rid of it. No one wants the place so ... I hear that you're a businesswoman?'

'Well, sort of. Who told you that?'

The man chuckled. 'I keep my eyes and ears open, Anne. So, shall we talk business?'

'Come upstairs,' she said softly, taking his hand. 'There's a mattress on the floor in one of the rooms. We'll be more comfortable there.'

Following her up the stairs, the man eyed her rounded bottom, her naked thighs. 'I'm sure that this old house will be yours soon,' he said. 'As long as you put it to good use.'

'Oh, I will,' Anne murmured, leading him into the room and settling herself on the mattress. 'Now, let's get down to business.'

nexus

The leading publisher of fetish and adult fiction

TELL US WHAT YOU THINK!

Readers' ideas and opinions matter to us so please take a few minutes to fill in the questionnaire below.

1. Sex: Are you male ☐ female ☐ a couple ☐?

2. Age: Under 21 ☐ 21–30 ☐ 31–40 ☐ 41–50 ☐ 51–60 ☐ over 60 ☐

3. Where do you buy your Nexus books from?
☐ A chain book shop. If so, which one(s)?

_____

☐ An independent book shop. If so, which one(s)?

_____

☐ A used book shop/charity shop
☐ Online book store. If so, which one(s)?

_____

4. How did you find out about Nexus books?
☐ Browsing in a book shop
☐ A review in a magazine
☐ Online
☐ Recommendation
☐ Other _____

5. In terms of settings, which do you prefer? (Tick as many as you like.)
☐ Down to earth and as realistic as possible
☐ Historical settings. If so, which period do you prefer?

_____

☐ Fantasy settings – barbarian worlds
☐ Completely escapist/surreal fantasy
☐ Institutional or secret academy

☐ Futuristic/sci fi
☐ Escapist but still believable
☐ Any settings you dislike?

_____

☐ Where would you like to see an adult novel set?

_____

6. In terms of storylines, would you prefer:

☐ Simple stories that concentrate on adult interests?
☐ More plot and character-driven stories with less explicit adult activity?
☐ We value your ideas, so give us your opinion of this book:

_____

_____

_____

7. In terms of your adult interests, what do you like to read about? (Tick as many as you like.)

☐ Traditional corporal punishment (CP)
☐ Modern corporal punishment
☐ Spanking
☐ Restraint/bondage
☐ Rope bondage
☐ Latex/rubber
☐ Leather
☐ Female domination and male submission
☐ Female domination and female submission
☐ Male domination and female submission
☐ Willing captivity
☐ Uniforms
☐ Lingerie/underwear/hosiery/footwear (boots and high heels)
☐ Sex rituals
☐ Vanilla sex
☐ Swinging
☐ Cross-dressing/TV
☐ Enforced feminisation

☐ Others – tell us what you don't see enough of in adult fiction:

_____

_____

_____

8. Would you prefer books with a more specialised approach to your interests, i.e. a novel specifically about uniforms? If so, which subject(s) would you like to read a Nexus novel about?

_____

_____

_____

9. Would you like to read true stories in Nexus books? For instance, the true story of a submissive woman, or a male slave? Tell us which true revelations you would most like to read about:

_____

_____

_____

10. What do you like best about Nexus books?

_____

_____

11. What do you like least about Nexus books?

_____

_____

12. Which are your favourite titles?

_____

_____

13. Who are your favourite authors?

_____

_____

14. Which covers do you prefer? Those featuring:
(Tick as many as you like.)

- ☐ Fetish outfits
- ☐ More nudity
- ☐ Two models
- ☐ Unusual models or settings
- ☐ Classic erotic photography
- ☐ More contemporary images and poses
- ☐ A blank/non-erotic cover
- ☐ What would your ideal cover look like?

_____

15. Describe your ideal Nexus novel in the space provided:

_____

_____

_____

_____

16. Which celebrity would feature in one of your Nexus-style fantasies? We'll post the best suggestions on our website – anonymously!

_____

THANKS FOR YOUR TIME

Now simply write the title of this book in the space below and cut out the questionnaire pages. Post to: Nexus, Marketing Dept., Virgin Books, Random House, 20 Vauxhall Bridge Road, London SW1V 2SA

Book title: _____

NEXUS NEW BOOKS

To be published in February 2009

NEXUS CONFESSIONS: VOLUME 6
Various

Swinging, dogging, group sex, cross-dressing, spanking, female domination, corporal punishment, and extreme fetishes . . . *Nexus Confessions* explores the length and breadth of erotic obsession, real experience and sexual fantasy. This is an encyclopaedic collection of the bizarre, the extreme, the utterly inappropriate, the daring and the shocking experiences of ordinary men and women driven by their extraordinary desires. Collected by the world's leading publisher of fetish fiction, these are true stories and shameful confessions, never-before-told or published.

£7.99   ISBN 978 0 352 34509 7

To be published in April 2009

ON THE BARE
Fiona Locke

Fiona Locke's *Over the Knee* has become a cult classic and is considered a definitive work of corporal punishment and fetish fiction. This anthology of short stories is even stronger, portraying the bratty, the spoilt and the wilful as they each get their stinging just-deserts from masterly purveyors of discipline. Full of the authentic and exquisite details her fans adore, these stories are spanking masterpieces for true connoisseurs.

£7.99   ISBN 9780352345158

If you would like more information about Nexus titles, please visit our website at www.nexus-books.co.uk, or send a large stamped addressed envelope to:

Nexus
Virgin Books
Random House
20 Vauxhall Bridge Road
London SW1V 2SA

NEXUS BOOKLIST

Information is correct at time of printing. To avoid disappointment, check availability before ordering. Go to www.nexus-books.co.uk.

All books are priced at £6.99 unless another price is given.

NEXUS

☐ ABANDONED ALICE	Adriana Arden	ISBN 978 0 352 33969 0
☐ ALICE IN CHAINS	Adriana Arden	ISBN 978 0 352 33908 9
☐ AMERICAN BLUE	Penny Birch	ISBN 978 0 352 34169 3
☐ AQUA DOMINATION	William Doughty	ISBN 978 0 352 34020 7
☐ THE ART OF CORRECTION	Tara Black	ISBN 978 0 352 33895 2
☐ THE ART OF SURRENDER	Madeline Bastinado	ISBN 978 0 352 34013 9
☐ BEASTLY BEHAVIOUR	Aishling Morgan	ISBN 978 0 352 34095 5
☐ BEING A GIRL	Chloë Thurlow	ISBN 978 0 352 34139 6
☐ BELINDA BARES UP	Yolanda Celbridge	ISBN 978 0 352 33926 3
☐ BIDDING TO SIN	Rosita Varón	ISBN 978 0 352 34063 4
☐ BLUSHING AT BOTH ENDS	Philip Kemp	ISBN 978 0 352 34107 5
☐ THE BOOK OF PUNISHMENT	Cat Scarlett	ISBN 978 0 352 33975 1
☐ BRUSH STROKES	Penny Birch	ISBN 978 0 352 34072 6
☐ BUTTER WOULDN'T MELT	Penny Birch	ISBN 978 0 352 34120 4
☐ CALLED TO THE WILD	Angel Blake	ISBN 978 0 352 34067 2
☐ CAPTIVES OF CHEYNER CLOSE	Adriana Arden	ISBN 978 0 352 34028 3
☐ CARNAL POSSESSION	Yvonne Strickland	ISBN 978 0 352 34062 7
☐ CITY MAID	Amelia Evangeline	ISBN 978 0 352 34096 2
☐ COLLEGE GIRLS	Cat Scarlett	ISBN 978 0 352 33942 3
☐ COMPANY OF SLAVES	Christina Shelly	ISBN 978 0 352 33887 7
☐ CONCEIT AND CONSEQUENCE	Aishling Morgan	ISBN 978 0 352 33965 2
☐ CORRECTIVE THERAPY	Jacqueline Masterson	ISBN 978 0 352 33917 1

NEXUS CLASSIC

NEXUS CONFESSIONS

NEXUS ENTHUSIAST

NEXUS NON FICTION

-------- ✂ -------------------------

Please send me the books I have ticked above.

Name ....

Address ....

....

....

.... Post code ....

Send to: **Virgin Books Cash Sales, Direct Mail Dept., the Book Service Ltd, Colchester Road, Frating, Colchester CO7 7DW. Tel: +44 (0) 1206 255800, Fax: +44 (0) 1206 255930, Email: cashsales@tbs-ltd.co.uk**

US customers: for prices and details of how to order books for delivery by mail, call 888-330-8477.

Please enclose a cheque or postal order, made payable to **Nexus Books Ltd**, to the value of the books you have ordered plus postage and packing costs as follows:

UK and BFPO – £1.00 for the first book, 50p for each subsequent book.

Overseas (including Republic of Ireland) – £2.00 for the first book, £1.00 for each subsequent book.

If you would prefer to pay by VISA, ACCESS/MASTERCARD, AMEX, DINERS CLUB or SWITCH, please write your card number and expiry date here:

....

Please allow up to 28 days for delivery.

Signature ....

Our privacy policy

We will not disclose information you supply us to any other parties. We will not disclose any information which identifies you personally to any person without your express consent.

From time to time we may send out information about Nexus books and special offers. Please tick here if you do *not* wish to receive Nexus information.   ☐

-------- ✂ -------------------------